D1524944

CROSSING THE LINES

When Cops Turn Corrupt, The Rot Reaches Deep

Michal Regunberg

AR PRESS

Crossing the Lines: When Cops Turn Corrupt, The Rot Reaches Deep

First printing October 2023

Library of Congress Cataloging-in-Publication Data

Regunberg, Michal
crossing the lines: when cops turn corrupt, the rot reaches deep / by michal regunberg

Paperback ISBN: 9798865941170
Hardcover ISBN: 9798865941347

Published by AR PRESS, an American Real Publishing Company
Roger L. Brooks, Publisher
roger@incubatemedia.us
americanrealpublishing.com

Edited by Abby Crane
Interior Design by Eva Myrick

Printed in the U.S.A.

ACKNOWLEDGEMENTS

It certainly does take a village to write a novel, especially a first novel. I have deep gratitude for a number of people and organizations without whom I could not have finished this journey. At the top of the list is author and journalist Hank Phillippi Ryan, who has been a mentor and guide throughout the process of writing, editing, and proofreading the book.

Grub Street and its course on "Jumpstarting Your Novel" was an invaluable tool in beginning of the writing process, and Ellen Sussman and the Sonoma Writer's Camp also spurred me onward and provided useful feedback.

Thank you to Dana Isaacson, Karen Bellovich and Michele Lowe for all their editing, proofing and feedback. I also want to thank those friends who read the novel and provided their thoughts and suggestions, including Walter Robinson, Michael Fernandez, and Julie Brown. I'd also like to thank my dear friend Lisa Sheprow, who early on helped me develop the story line.

Thank you! I truly could not have gotten here without each and every one of you.

Some of this stuff is true.

WHEN COPS TURN CORRUPT, THE ROT REACHES DEEP

Table of Contents

PROLOGUE: BOSTON 1979

Hank James, the head of the Boston Police Drug Control Unit, had been carefully planning this drug raid in Dorchester for more than a month. Then, just as the unit was ready, an informant had tipped them off about a large stash of cocaine he'd spotted hidden in the drug dealer's house; it was go-time.

A detail-oriented kind of guy, James had studied the location of the raid in Dorchester carefully, driving by the house both on his way to and from his office at police headquarters in downtown Boston for several weeks. He already knew that his best vantage point for the raid on this starless October night would be from the front seat of the black Ford Crown Victoria—"Crown Vic"— which was now parked in front of a yellow, three-story house on the top of Pope's Hill on Neponset Avenue. James had come equipped with a cup of Dunkin' Donuts coffee—black, no sugar— and a walkie talkie to communicate with his men. His number two, Sergeant Hawley, was behind the wheel so Hank could focus on what was about to happen.

There was a stillness in the air and very little traffic on the street. The dealer's house sat on a corner, with not much yard either in the front or the back.

The suspect—Rob Gold—and his wife and daughter occupied the first two floors of the house. Hank and his men knew Gold wasn't in the house. Their informant had told them that Gold had driven off earlier with another man in a grey Cadillac.

They had rehearsed the raid several times—both on paper and in a dry run—like it was a football game and everyone had to know their moves. Hank was confident that each of his men was ready to carry out the mission. He had the plan laid out across his lap...but still, there was always the chance that things could go wrong and people—both cops and civilians—could get hurt. Sure, danger and death were part of the job, but it was still tough knowing that people's lives and safety were at stake.

From his seat, Hank saw ten detectives from the DCU arrive at the house in three separate unmarked cars around ten o'clock, parking along the street on both sides of Gold's house. The detectives turned off their engines and headlights.

On his walkie-talkie, James, known as a "steady Eddie" kind of guy, gave the go-ahead. With guns drawn, the cops bolted from their vehicles: five rushing to the back of the house while the other five approached the front door. Hank had a perfect view of what was about to go down.

After his men knocked on the door, Hank could see a woman, whom he assumed was the dealer's wife, dressed in blue jeans and a dark blue sweater open the door. The woman quickly moved out of the way as five guys, with guns pointed straight ahead, barged into the apartment.

Hank watched while also listening closely to the chatter. He had assigned Detective Dalton Cross as the leader of this raid. It was Dalton's informant who had been to the house earlier that night and let them know about the hidden cocaine.

Hank heard Cross yell at someone in the house: "Get in the kitchen and stay there." He also heard Cross let in the detectives from the back of the house, and then Cross essentially narrated the raid: "We are searching the closets downstairs and—whadda we got here? We just found a huge stash of coke!"

Hank instantly felt better about the raid; the cocaine was there, just as the informant had promised. Hank let himself breathe, as he realized he had been holding it in.

"Stay the fuck in the kitchen," Cross yelled at someone.

Everything was going according to plan. Once Cross let him know they had found the hidden cocaine, Hank got out of the car and entered the house. As soon as he went through the front door, Hank saw two women standing in a tight embrace, with one woman crying: "Stop! Stop!" Nearby in the living room, several other detectives turned over couch cushions while, in the kitchen, others rifled through kitchen drawers, looking for cocaine or other contraband.

Cross was directing the search in the living room. Wearing a black leather jacket and Red Sox baseball cap, Cross watched as a detective placed the bags of cocaine in a plastic trash bag and handed it to him.

"Mark that bag and turn it into headquarters," Hank said, then he looked at the two women.

"Which one of you is Rob Gold's wife?"

"That would be me," said the woman with the brown, shoulder-length hair and wearing jeans and a sweater.

"Please tell me your name."

"Eileen Gold," the woman said as tears ran down her face.

"And who are you?" Hank asked the other woman.

"I'm Kate Maloney, Eileen's sister."

Ever the gentleman, Hank said: "I am sorry that we had to disrupt your evening this way, but we have a job to do. Is there anyone else in the house?"

"Yes, my nine-year-old daughter," Eileen said.

"And where is she?" Hank asked.

"Upstairs in bed," Eileen said. "Please don't disturb her," she said, with a pleading urgency to her voice. "She was very upset to witness what just happened, and I sent her up to bed," Eileen added.

"She was downstairs when the men arrived?" Hank asked.

"Yes, briefly," said Gold's wife. "But I told her to go up to her room, and my sister went upstairs with her."

At some point, Hank would need to talk to the girl and find out what she saw. Looking around now, Hank clapped his hands and said: "Men, I think that our work here is finished; you can all leave."

As the DCU officers readied to leave, Hank looked at the women and said to Gold's wife: "Where is your husband?"

Eileen shook her head.

"I don't know. He left some time ago with a friend and said he would be gone for a few hours. That's all I know."

"We will definitely want to interview both of you down at the station. That can wait until tomorrow. I will call you to set that up."

With that, Hank turned toward the door and started to walk out to his car.

"Before you go, I need to tell you what my niece and I saw," Kate said.

"Yes, please," Hank said.

"We saw that officer," Kate said, pointing to Cross. "He took money from behind a shadowbox in the living room." She pointed to the shadowbox, and James followed her hand and saw the shadowbox and the fake flowers that were in the drawer in the front.

Kind of tacky, Hank thought to himself.

"I am more than a little surprised and shocked to hear that," James said.

"Detective Cross, I will want a full report on this and will need to talk to you about it," Hank said with a sternness in his voice. Then, he said to the rest of the unit on his walkie-talkie: "I think we got what we came for. Good job! And good night."

CHAPTER ONE

Carly Howell was skimming the stack of newspapers on her desk; she did that religiously...every morning...like clockwork. Carly brought in her cup of coffee with cream and a little sugar, waved to folks in the newsroom, climbed the stairs at the television station—Channel 8 'BRN—to the investigative unit on the second floor, hung up her coat, said hello to her boss Jim Cordry—who was in the office next door—and started to peruse the headlines of *The Boston Globe* and *The Boston Herald*. She would always start with the Boston papers before she would tackle *The New York Times* and *Wall Street Journal*.

Carly even turned to the sports pages. It was hard not to be a little excited about the Boston Celtics and their first season with Larry Bird, who had helped turn the team from a losing one the previous season to a winning one that all of Boston was focused on. She wasn't a native Bostonian and didn't go to basketball games often, but the couple of times she had been to the Boston Garden—or the "Gahden," as Bostonians called it—and watched a game, it was really fun to be part of the crowd, and she found herself cheering. She had even bought a Celtics t-shirt.

The phone rang and threw Carly off a bit; she wasn't expecting a call.

"Good morning, this is Carly Howell," Carly said as she answered the phone.

"Good morning back at 'ya," a man's voice on the other end said.

"How can I help you?" Carly asked.

"Well, that depends. I am pretty sure I have a story for you, one that you are not going to want to miss or let someone else do," the voice said in a kind of tease.

"Okay, y ou've got my attention. What's your name, and what is the story?"

"My name is Rob Gold, and the story is about bad cops stealing from me during a raid on my house."

"Whoa? Really?" That information did take Carly by surprise. "Please, tell me more."

"I will, but I'd rather meet in person. I think it would be far better if you met me and heard the story. Are you game for that?"

Carly was willing to do almost anything for a good story. Also, meeting someone in person was always preferable; it was a much better way to get a true sense of someone.

"Okay. When and where?"

"How about the New Town Diner in Watertown at two this morning?"

"Two in the morning? Really? That is a weird hour, isn't it?"

"Some of us keep weird hours," Gold said and laughed.

"Let's make it eleven instead. I want to make sure I'm awake and alert," Carly said, then added: "This had better be a damn good story!"

"Oh, it is. Trust me."

Trust me, Carly thought. She didn't know this Rob Gold guy from Adam, and now he was asking to meet her in the middle of the night. The whole situation was outside of Carly's comfort zone. *But sometimes*, she thought, *you need to stretch the limits.*

Carly got off the phone and poked her head into Jim's office to tell him what just happened and what she was about to do.

"Be careful," Jim said.

"I'll do my best."

Carly left the station at the end of the day and drove to her apartment on Commonwealth Avenue in the Back Bay to relax, have dinner, and watch a little television. She thought she might take a nap, but she quickly realized that she was too nervous and intrigued to do so. At ten thirty, with a little flurry of nerves turning inside her stomach, Carly got into her red Honda Accord and drove to the diner in Watertown about fifteen minutes away. She had a habit of always being early, and tonight was no exception. After she arrived at the diner, Carly parked her car, turned off the motor, and sat in her car until it was time.

At eleven, she got out of her car and stepped over the threshold of the diner; it was a cool fall night. As she walked into the diner, Carly had a feeling that she just might be crossing a line she'd never crossed before. She could feel the queasiness in her stomach, and she hugged her body to take the chill out as she got a 360 degree view of the dimly lit diner. A tart whiff of freshly brewed coffee, mixed with the lingering aroma of bacon fat, stung Carly's nostrils. She had no doubt that, when she got back to her apartment, the diner's smell on her clothing would be a reminder of this moment.

The diner was a go-to hangout for those who kept odd hours: a combination of truck drivers and kids dressed in their disco best who'd find their way there after clubbing and drinking. Most of the red faux leather stools at the counter were taken by men with their Red Sox caps and sweatshirts and young, long-haired guys flirting with their disco diva dates, who wore platform shoes and short, sequined dresses and miniskirts.

Carly looked around and spotted a guy sitting alone at a booth facing the door. The man saw her right away and stood, motioning to her. Carly knew that men were drawn to her and used that to her advantage. Her blonde, shoulder-length hair bobbed gently as she walked over, and her crystal blue eyes sparkled, even in the darkness. At twenty-nine, Carly fit right in with the crowd, and she'd decided a pair of black bell-bottom pants and a tight-fitting red sweater were the right outfit for the moment. She also donned a pair of dangly pearl earrings and a gold bracelet.

Carly gave the guy, who had given his name as Rob Gold, the once-over as she approached the booth. He definitely stood out from the crowd in his tight, neatly-pressed grey wool slacks and bright blue shirt. The shirt's collar was open, with enough buttons unbuttoned to bare his chest. Gold chains dangled from around the man's neck. Closer up, Carly noticed that, even in low light, his face looked like a rock that had been through a gravelly stream; a little beat-up and pockmarked. The man had a bit of a Boston's Italian North End mafia look to him, which Carly thought was, somehow, fitting. Carly mustered her confidence and reached out her hand.

"Hi. Carly Howell," she forthrightly introduced herself. "I assume you're Rob."

"Yes. Thanks for meeting me. I know it's probably late for you, but it's my normal schedule. I work all day and then get back out on the street at night." Rob smiled.

Carly smiled back politely as Rob extended his arm as an invitation to sit down. She thought Rob was a bit cavalier about his afterhours "work," but she wanted to hear his story nonetheless.

"Would you like anything to drink or eat?" Rob asked.

"I guess I'll have a cup of decaf."

"Sure." Rob motioned to the waitress, and she rushed to the table, smiling at Rob, and took the order. Carly could tell by the waitress's reaction that he was a regular here.

On a mission, Carly wasted no time.

"What's the story?"

"No small talk for you, I see." Rob smiled and looked Carly in the eyes.

"It's late, and I came here to see what the story is—if there even is a story."

"It's about cops stealing."

"From whom?"

"From yours truly, from the public, and all Bostonians."

"Why call me?"

"I've seen you a few times on TV and was impressed. You and your boss have taken on corruption—like when you did the story about no-bid contracts that the mayor handed out in Boston. That's what this is. I think you've got the guts to take on a story like this."

The flattery had worked.

"Thanks. Now tell me what happened." Carly reached into her bag and took out the lined notepad: a reporter's best friend. In that moment, she felt her stomach calm down and her adrenaline kick in. "But first, what do you do for a living?"

"I have a deli and sandwich shop downtown in the Financial District; it's called 'The Hen.'"

"Thanks! Go on with the story."

"One night, about two months ago, a friend came over to my house. We were doing a little 'business,' if you get my drift. So, we get in his Caddy and drive, maybe a mile. We're cruising down a quiet street in Dorchester to meet up with another guy when I see the blue lights and hear the siren. The cop car pulls us over. We can see their guns, even in the dark, and the street itself was deserted. They had us all to themselves. They barked out the usual shit: 'Hands up! Walk to that building. Spread your legs and arms out.' We did as we were told."

"Then, while we're facing the wall, the cops search my friend's car and come back waving a heavy wad of cash in our faces."

"How much?"

"It was about five grand. They claimed they found it hidden in the seats. They cuffed us and took us down to the Area C station on Gibson Street, which is just a few blocks from my house."

While scribbling notes, Carly asked, "What were the charges?"

"Larceny. They were waiting for us."

"What do you mean waiting?"

"It was a total setup. They wanted to get me out of my house so they could plant the drugs there. See, while I was at the police station—and I know this was no coincidence—members of the Drug Control Unit raided my apartment," Rob said.

As Carly listened to Rob, she thought that there might be a bigger story to Rob's situation.

"So, that's the real story, right? Not your getting pulled over, but the drug raid on your house?"

"Exactly! My wife Eileen and her sister Kate and my nine-year-old daughter Jill were at home the whole time. My sister-in-law said she watched this one detective—who we later learned was Detective Dalton Cross—take money that I'd hidden in a shadowbox—you know, a kind of 3D frame—hanging on the wall in my living room. Kate watched from the doorway as Cross shoved a wad of my money into his pocket. When he saw her looking at him, he got all hot under the collar, telling her to 'get the fuck out of there.' When the raid was over, the cops said they'd seized about fourteen ounces of cocaine. I don't know where they got the drugs or how they got them into my house. They were planted."

Wow, Carly thought to herself. If this were true, it was a clear case of police stealing, even if Gold was, in fact, a drug dealer. Carly had to admit that she was intrigued, but then she wondered if she could really believe Rob.

"Anything else taken?" Carly asked.

"Sure. Six tickets to *Man of La Mancha*, gold jewelry, and a key."

"A key to what?"

Rob deflected the question.

"That's a story for another day, but I was really looking forward to that musical."

Carly couldn't help smiling; she always appreciated a sense of humor.

Rob continued, anxious to tell his story to a new audience.

"So, I waited two days before my wife Eileen and me went down to police headquarters, trying to get the money and the tickets and jewelry back. I knew it was gone, but I wanted the cops to know that I knew what they were up to."

Writing furiously, Carly tried to get everything down, but she wasn't about to let Rob's story go too far without challenging it.

"How much was in the shadowbox, and why put it in a shadowbox if you weren't hiding something?"

Carly took a sip of coffee and glanced around to see if anyone was looking their way; they weren't. They were too busy snuggling with each other and dancing to the music that was playing on the jukebox—Kool & the Gang.

"Good questions," Rob said as he took a quick sip of coffee.

Carly noticed Rob's carefully manicured nails as he picked up the cup and brought it to his lips. She thought that there was something kind of sexy and smooth about this guy.

"I knew I picked the right reporter. There was $8,000. Truth is, I'm not the most trusting person in the world, and a friend of mine—a guy named Brian—lent me the money to cover some IRS debt. I didn't want Eileen to know about that, so I figured it was better to hide it."

"And what did you do after confronting the cops?"

"I didn't want this cop to get away with stealing, so I got an attorney and filed larceny charges against Cross."

"That was pretty ballsy of you."

"Yeah, my lawyer told me that it was the first time in, like, twenty years or so that a lawsuit like this had been filed against a cop in the city of Boston."

That statement made Carly sit up straight. She thought that this story could, in fact, be a big deal.

"Why should cops be allowed to get away with stealing and dealing?" Rob asked.

"Good point, but isn't it risky coming to see me? Any article I write will publicly expose your 'extralegal' activities, which, for the record, you are not denying...are you?"

Rob didn't answer the question directly, but he looked her straight in the eyes with a sternness she noticed.

"This story is bigger than me. It is about a police department that is corrupt through and through. They don't even try to hide it. That needs to be called out, don't you agree?"

"Of course. But, given your criminal record, you've got to admit you might not make the best witness against them."

Carly stared across the table at Rob, and he glanced away. He was going to have to give her much more to work with.

"And just to be clear, you are not denying that there was cocaine in the house, right?"

Rob dodged the question, leading Carly to believe that drugs were in the house at the time of the raid and not planted by the cops as he was alleging.

"I've never done the things these guys have done," Rob said. "And, for sure, the cops will do everything they can to put roadblocks in your way, as well as try to convince you that I'm a bad guy and shouldn't be believed. But that doesn't change the fact that what I am telling you is the truth. And I know of other cases where cops have stolen from their targets. It may be the law of the streets, but that doesn't make it right. There should be justice for all—if you get my drift."

"I should also mention that it wasn't just my wife and sister-in-law who saw the cop take the money; my daughter did, too."

That statement made Carly sit up.

"How old is she?"

"She's nine," Rob said. Carly knew she would have to find a way to talk to the sisters and the daughter. For now, though, she thought she had heard enough. She closed her notebook somewhat abruptly, grabbed her coat, and got up from the table.

"Okay. Thanks, and goodnight. I'll call you soon."

"Well, okay." Rob looked a little surprised to see that Carly was leaving so soon. "I will be waiting. I won't let this go, so if you won't do the story, I am sure I can find someone else who will." That statement was a not-so-subtle threat.

Driving home to her apartment, Carly went over what she had just heard. Rob's story definitely intrigued her, but could she really believe this guy? And how bad a guy was he really? She parked the car in her parking spot in the alley behind the building, climbed the two   flights of stairs to her apartment, opened the multiple locks, walked in, hung up her coat, decided to take a couple of tokes from a joint to relax, threw off her shoes, and flopped down on her brown velvet sofa.

"Holy shit."

CHAPTER TWO

After a night of tossing and turning, Carly decided that her first stop the next day should be *The Boston Globe* archives. She wanted to look closer at Rob's record and determine if he had any sort of hidden agenda. Carly thought going through news archives might be easier than trying to go through police records. She also had a friend at the paper she was pretty sure could help her.

She headed to the *Globe* building just off the expressway on Morrissey Boulevard in Dorchester. As soon as she entered the large and expansive lobby, with the sun streaming in through the wall of windows, Carly was struck by the distinct smell of newsprint and ink; it was both acrid and sweet. *The Boston Globe* printed the paper on the same premises as the newsroom, and the aroma permeated the place, reminding Carly of her days as a City Hall reporter for the *Springfield Union* in Springfield, MA. After signing in, Carly picked up the phone at the front desk and called her pal, reporter Mary Lou Lyons. The two women had worked together for the *Springfield Union* and remained in touch now that they were both in Boston.

Mary Lou met Carly in the lobby.

"What's going on, Carly? How can I help you?"

"You're not going to believe this. Actually, I'm not sure *I* believe it. I had a guy tell me about cops stealing money from him during a drug raid, and I need to find out as much as I can about him before I delve any deeper into the story."

"Of course! I'd love to know more, but I get that you probably can't tell me anything."

"Sorry, but I don't know that I know much more yet. I'm in the discovery mode. I'll fill you in when I can, promise."

Mary Lou escorted Carly to the *Globe*'s records library in the bowels of the building. The records library was a room set aside from the day-to-day newsroom upstairs, and it was filled with stacks of yellowing papers, as well as a couple of microfiche readers along the back of a wall. Amidst it all, there was a woman sitting at a desk. After greeting her, Mary Lou said to the librarian: "We're looking for any articles or files that feature a local guy named Robert Gold. Can you help?"

"Sure thing," the librarian said.

"He's also called Rob," Carly added. "I expect he's attracted some notice on the police blotter."

Carly and Mary Lou chatted while the librarian left to search. Mary Lou was on the arts side of the paper, as she was in Springfield. Carly was always a little envious that, every summer, Mary Lou got to spend a couple of months in the Berkshires covering the Boston Symphony Orchestra at their summer home in Tanglewood. Now, she got to cover the theater scene, which was kind of in its infancy. Mary Lou spent her time going to see pre-Broadway shows and plays; it could not have been more different than Carly's life.

Minutes later, the librarian returned with a stack of documents. Smiling, she handed them over.

"Here you go. Guess he's been a busy guy."

Mary Lou took the stack, thanked the librarian, and handed the stack of papers to Carly.

"Thanks so much," said Carly. "I owe you one."

"Professional courtesy, and I'm glad to help. I'm dying to know where you're going with this."

"I'm not sure at this point that I actually know; we'll see." Carly looked around and asked if she could use one of the desks.

"Sure. Have at it."

After Mary Lou left, Carly first glanced at the headlines:

"Convicted Drug Dealer Nabbed for Robbery"

"Murder Suspect Points to Co-conspirator in Trial"

"Bank Robbery Suspect Convicted."

It didn't take Carly long to see that Rob Gold had been involved in a number of high-profile crimes, including being implicated in a murder in Newton. For that crime, two other guys ended up going to prison for life while Rob managed to avoid any charges. But with the bank robbery, he was convicted and served five years. Rob's record went back all the way to the late '50s, and it looked like he started as a burglar with breaking and entering. In 1973, Rob got a five-year sentence for breaking into a post office. When he was asked why he went to the post office, Rob said: "To mail a letter."

Carly leaned back in her chair and took a breath.

"Whoa! Who is this guy?"

She had to wonder why such a bad guy like this would want to go after the cops. Choosing to summon the media also seemed a risky move.

She heard her father's voice in the back of her head: "There are good guys and bad guys in this world, and it's far better to be one of the good guys and spend your life fighting for what's right." William Howell had been a cop for years and was now an FBI agent. From an early age, Carly had been taught to do the right thing, that it was both honorable and admirable to find the bad guys and make them pay for their criminal behavior.

Now, she was faced with a guy, who had a long history on the wrong side of the law, accusing cops of doing wrong. How did he get away with murder? Could she believe him? Carly thanked the librarian and left the newspaper office, feeling energized and excited about the potential this story had. Carly was eager to report in to her boss and get his take.

The next morning, when she got to the station, Carly practically ran upstairs to report back to Jim on the late-night diner meeting and the results of her research at *The Globe*. The office was as basic as you could get: a big, open room with a desk at either end and a room divider separating them. There was a window of glass that allowed the employees to look down and see the newsroom below. Jim had spent much of his career in Louisiana--where he was from—going after corrupt politicians; more than a few in his home state. Jim had built a reputation for his reporting, and Carly knew she could learn a lot from him. Today, Carly needed Jim's approval to continue work on the story.

"This story is too intriguing not to pursue, and I believe I can handle it," Carly told Jim with a confidence she knew she needed to have.

Jim listened intently, then said: "Go for it...but be careful. This is new territory for you. I've worked with guys like this back in Louisiana—mob guys, in fact. Some of these guys are real smooth operators."

Carly paid attention, even as her thoughts wandered to Rob Gold's gold jewelry.

Jim continued: "This kind of guy can draw you in, seduce you with his charm until you can't tell right from wrong. You're playing with fire, but I am confident you can handle it. I'm here to help as needed, but those above the two of us on a higher pay grade are always nervous about these kinds of stories that challenge the powers that be, so don't screw it up."

Carly turned around and went back to her desk and reviewed her notes from the *Globe* clips. Jim supporting her working on the story meant a lot to Carly, though it scared her a bit, too.

CHAPTER THREE

After growing up in Indiana, as middle America as you can get, Carly worked hard and graduated from Northwestern University with both an undergrad and a master's degree in journalism. From grade school on, she stood out both for her good looks and for her quick wit and laser-like ability to get to the heart of a subject. Carly's skills helped her quickly move up the ladder, from her first job as a general assignment reporter to the more prestigious job of City Hall reporter at the *Springfield Union*—though Carly thought she should be working at *The New York Times*. Carly uncovered corruption in Springfield City Hall, with city councilors who had gone after money from contractors who were doing business with the city, and she won numerous awards and was known as a hotshot. That reputation helped Carly land what she thought of as a dream job: a researcher and investigative reporter at, arguably, the best television station in Boston—WBRN.

Since landing the job, Carly and Jim had broadcast some hard-hitting stories, like taking a close look at the way City Hall operated under Boston's powerful mayor and how he took care of his friends with no-bid contracts. It was the first big story for Carly and brought a level of recognition and respect within the newsroom and within the city of Boston. Her name became known, and that made Carly feel proud and also reinforced her ability to do this job.

She also did some on-air reporting on the weekends and got to do her stand-ups and establish herself as an on-air presence. She loved being on camera and getting known around town. This story had the potential to be an even bigger one; Carly knew it, and now, so did Jim.

When she was hired, Jim said Carly got the job because of a proven ability to root out a story. Carly was relentless. She had to be if she expected to uncover what others were actively hiding. As Jim's number two, Carly was grateful he gave her a great deal of independence and latitude. She was determined to justify Jim's faith in her.

No sooner had she gotten the thumbs-up from her boss than Carly's desk phone rang. "Good afternoon. It's Rob, checking in on your progress on my case."

Carly hesitated, then said: "Truth is, I've done a little more digging around about you, and I have some questions."

"What are you saying? You don't want to do the story?"

"Before moving forward, I need to verify certain facts," Carly said before launching into her questions.

"Were you an informant against two other guys who were convicted in a Newton murder? Seems like it. Otherwise, how come they were convicted and you weren't charged?"

"We're not going there. Not now. Maybe not ever. That is long over. And if you're telling me you're hesitating, don't bother, sweetheart! Do you really think you're the only reporter I can give this story to? You'll be sorry." Rob hung up.

Carly held the receiver in her hand and stared at the phone, unnerved by Gold's reaction. What had just happened? Clearly, she had hit a nerve. Carly needed to breathe and think. Saying nothing to Jim, she walked out of the office and into the fresh air. In front of the building, the steady rumble of traffic on Route 128 was almost meditative. Carly stared at the cars, one after another passing by. Then, she walked to her car in the parking lot, got in, turned on WCRB to listen to a little calming classical music, and sat there for a few minutes, breathing deeply while debating the options. It was tricky, Carly had to admit. This was all going to be new ground for her: her main source being a known bad guy with a record. How could Carly trust anything Rob told her?

After a half hour, Carly headed inside and grabbed her stuff. She needed to pay her good friend, Mike Holder, a visit. They were like sister and brother: no romance, just a truly deep and trusting friendship. Mike and Carly once worked closely together at the *Springfield Union*. These days, to make ends meet, Mike was bartending in Cambridge while writing plays about love and loss. He was steady and wise and funny, and Carly also loved hearing his colorful stories of his sexual escapades. Mike was also there as a sounding board for Carly's own relationships. They were best of friends, and neither was currently involved in a relationship, so they teased each other, but drew the line at sex; Carly, at least, didn't want to take a chance of ruining her friendship with Mike.

The place Mike worked, Henry V, was down a small, red-brick alleyway in the heart of Harvard Square. It was in "The Red House," which was set back from the street, with a restaurant on the first floor and a bar upstairs. Mike especially liked the gig because it gave him a steady stream of colorful customers from whom he could extract characters for his plays. Mike was also good at the job. He loved talking to people, and he had regulars who came for the conversation as much as for the booze.

There was nothing fancy about the bar; it had just enough space for one bartender, and Mike commanded the room. He was about six feet tall, with a brown beard and closely cropped hair that was clearly starting to fall out. Mike was attractive and had a certain way of charming women with his wit. On this afternoon, Mike was wearing a blue shirt, tucked into his chino pants;

comfortable and unassuming. Mike was a good listener and insightful in observing human interactions. Carly always felt like, in some ways, Mike was teaching her his own approach to people and relationships.

Polished wood lined the bar, and the bottles of liquor were neatly stacked on shelvesbehind Mike. As it was late afternoon on a weekday, the bar wasn't too busy. There was one other guy sitting at the bar and a table of two couples. Jazz emanated from the speakers: Miles Davis, Bill Evans, and Oscar Peterson. Mike not only made the drinks, but he also controlled the music and the vibe and made sure it was laid back. No disco music was allowed.

When Carly cozied up to the bar, Mike came around to give her a hug.

"Hi there, babe. You sexy thing, you. Take a seat and let me pour you a drink."

Carly found a chair at the bar's far end, hoping to remain inconspicuous so no one sat next to her and could overhear her conversation. Mike was doing his drink-mixing aerobics, and he knew what she wanted, putting a vodka and tonic down in front of her. Carly held the drink up: "Salud!"

Carly gave Mike a rundown of the last two days.

"Kind of crazy, huh?" Carly asked. "What should I do? From what I have read, he seems to be a bit of a bad guy. Like, he might have even literally gotten away with murder! Should I trust him? *Can* I trust him?"

"What's your gut tell you?" asked Mike. "You're usually right about people stuff."

"My first instinct is to go for it, but to be very careful—whatever the heck that means in a situation featuring drug dealers and crooked cops."

"Remember when we were working together in Springfield, and we tracked down the bribes paid to that city councilor for a fat public works contract? Remember? We went out to the city dump at night to find the machines that were purchased without going out for bid. What did you do? You dug through the garbage at the dump. That wasn't playing it safe. Carly, bad cops are worth rooting out. And maybe, just maybe, it takes a bad guy to catch a bad cop. Just take it slow. Make this Rob guy prove his story to you. Are you seriously going to let another reporter steal this story from you? This could be your ticket to that network job you want."

That statement hit a nerve. Carly really did want to work for one of the big national networks, and Channel 8 had a history of grooming reporters for the network. Up until now, Carly's work had been somewhat overshadowed by Jim's; he got the credit for some of the stories she'd worked long and hard on.

"You hit the nail on the head," She told Mike. "This could actually be the first major story that's mine...all mine."

Carly realized that Mike had done exactly what she had hoped he would: give her the encouragement she needed.

"Go for it," Mike urged. "You want it. You can handle it."

"Thanks, Mike. I knew I could count on you. You're the best."

Carly finished her drink and soaked in the music . . . the mellow music of Bill Evans. Mike had turned her on to him, and she loved listening to him. Bill Evans' piano mastery, together with the bass fiddle and skimming of the drums, was soothing. Finally, after a half hour or so of just relaxing with the music, Carly got up and went over to give Mike a hug before leaving and heading home.

Carly lived in a second-floor, one-bedroom apartment in a brownstone on Commonwealth Avenue, the grand dame of streets in Boston, with its iconic tree-lined mall that runs from the public garden in the center of the city all the way to Newton. She knew she was lucky to have found such an apartment right in front of the Prudential shopping center and the upscale Newbury Street—Boston's equivalent of Madison Avenue. Her rent was an affordable $300 a month. The door to her apartment was adorned with a number of locks that Carly quickly unlocked, then she entered, hung up her coat, washed her face, brushed her teeth, changed into her nightgown, and called it an early night.

The next morning, before she went to the office, Carly called her father at his FBI office, which he ran, in Indianapolis.

"Good morning. FBI. This is William Howell. How can I help you?"

"Dad, it's your daughter. Good morning! I know this is a kind of out of the blue call, but I need your advice."

Howell was devoted to his daughter—his only child—and the two were very close.

"Sure. Go ahead, sweetheart. I'm all ears."

Carly filled her father in on Gold, explaining a bit about his background and what he wanted her to do. Because she emulated her father in so many ways, Carly had a sense of what he would say, but she wanted to hear it directly from him anyway. She knew her father was overprotective of her and wouldn't want her to get herself in any kind of dangerous situation. So, she wasn't surprised with Howell's swift reaction.

"This sounds dicey to me. I know you are a great reporter and can handle almost anyone and anything—guess you got that from me," Howell laughed. "But seriously, these types of sociopaths can really be bad guys, and they don't care about anyone else but themselves. Stay away from this jerk. Let someone else do the story. What's his name again? I'll see what I can find out."

"Thanks, Dad, but I don't need you to do my job. This is my story, and I've already done some research, and I know he's a bad guy. I still think I can handle it, and so does my boss."

"Okay then. But I may go ahead and do some digging on my own, anyway. I don't mean to rain on your parade, but you called me, and I want to make sure you don't get hurt. What's his name?"

"Thanks, I guess. His name is Rob Gold. Let me know what you find, but I'm going to go ahead in the meantime. Love you."

"And I love you more than you will ever know. Be careful out there."

Carly hung up and walked around her apartment, replaying the conversations with Mike and her father in her mind and trying to balance what Mike told her versus her dad. She knew she had to muster as much courage and determination as she could. This job would test her, and that fact was both invigorating and unnerving. Carly had one more stop to make before deciding.

CHAPTER FOUR

The very next day, once she went through her messages and read the papers at the office, Carly went into Jim's office and said she thought she would go downtown and check out the sandwich shop that Rob Gold had told her he owned in the Financial District. Jim gave Carly a thumbs-up sign, and she was out the door. She knew she was lucky that Jim gave her as much freedom and license to pursue a story without interference. That freedom gave her a confidence that she needed. When Carly got down to the Financial District, it was 1:30 p.m., and the lunch hour was almost done. The brick buildings in this neighborhood were squeezed together, one after another: small sandwich shops serving the nine-to-five folks, bigger office buildings crowded next to each other. The narrow street was one-way, with cars parked bumper-to-bumper on either side. She crossed her fingers that she could find a parking spot with a view of the shop, and she did. Carly smiled to herself—good parking karma.

From her car, she watched a steady flow of office workers file in and out with sandwiches in tow. *Okay*, she thought, *he runs a legitimate business—at least under daylight.*

But Carly also wanted to know what Rob's life looked like at night. Was he doing any business out of the restaurant at night? In other words, was the drug business happening at night? She decided to find out. She went home and waited till about eight, after the nine-to-fivers had gone home, then headed back downtown.

The Financial District was pretty deserted after work hours, making it even easier to find a place to park at night. Carly parked across the street from the restaurant again. The shades were drawn, so she couldn't see if anything was going on inside. From her vantage point, Carly had a good view of the back door, and she spotted a couple of men walking in and out. Carly was a little nervous, and her stomach echoed that with some rumbling and a little agita. Carly realized she had forgotten to eat dinner. *Too bad the place isn't open*, Carly thought; she could have grabbed a sandwich.

Suddenly, there was a knock on the passenger side window. Startled, Carly looked over to see Rob smiling at her, and she rolled the window down.

"Funny seeing you here. Just hanging around? Do you want to talk?"

Carly reached for the ignition.

"No. I'll be in touch."

"Look, I owe you an apology," Rob said. "I jumped all over you when you expressed doubt about the story."

"Yeah, you did."

"I shouldn't have. Sorry."

With that, Carly nodded at the passenger door. No sooner had Rob slid into the front seat next to her than he reached out and put his hand on her thigh. Carly felt her body tense up, and almost reflexively, she took hold of Rob's hand and returned it to his side of the car and glared at him. Rob smiled nervously.

"Let's keep this professional," Carly said, laying down the rules. "I have a way of doing stories. The first thing is for me to find out if there's really a story."

"I get it. How about this: let's go see my lawyer. He might be able to answer some of your questions and ease your mind."

That endeavor sounded productive to Carly.

"I'd like that. When and where?"

"Meet me outside 250 Atlantic Avenue tomorrow at four o'clock."

"I'll be there."

Rob took Carly's hand and gave it a squeeze. Carly pulled her hand back and waved her finger, chiding Rob. Still, she smiled back.

CHAPTER FIVE

It was the middle of the day when Carly drove down to the harbor and entered the city's North End. The wind was whipping off the ocean, so it felt colder down near the harbor than anywhere else in the city. As Carly approached attorney Chris Kelly's office, she noticed a Coast Guard ship anchored across the street. She also faced a massive brick building—Lincoln Wharf—with its arched stone windows and a regal eagle sculpture at the top of the building watching guard. The building blocked the view of the water, something that was true all along the waterfront. *Kind of a missed opportunity*, she thought. And yet, to Carly, the harbor was one of the best things about Boston. Growing up in Indiana, she never knew what it was like to be so close to the water: to listen to the lapping of the waves, see the reflection of the sun making the water sparkle, and smell the salt-water. Carly loved being near the water.

Rob Gold's attorney had an office at the corner of Hanover Street and Atlantic Avenue. The office was a far cry from the elegant Boston Brahmin firms like Ropes & Gray. Instead, the modest two-person law firm was strategically located in the North End, the "Little Italy" of Boston, with its windy, narrow cobblestone streets, scores of Italian restaurants and coffee shops, Paul Revere's house, and the Old North Church from which Revere hung his lantern to announce: "One if by land, two if by sea . . ." The area was infamous for resident mafia kingpins like

"Jerry" Angiulo, who maintained a strong presence in the neighborhood. The neighborhood was centrally located near the harbor and was at walking distance from City Hall and Faneuil Hall, a revitalized set of buildings just behind City Hall that the mayor had worked to make a tourist destination, with shops and restaurants to draw people to the harbor.

After Carly walked through the building's open front door, she found herself in a generic open space with two standard metal desks. There were no oriental carpets or high-end furniture, nor a secretary or waiting room. The firm was as bare bones basic as it gets.

Carly saw a light on in an office at the end of the hall and made her way down there. In a totally nondescript room, she found Rob Gold and his attorney, Chris Kelly. Dark curtains hung from the floor-to-ceiling windows, and there was a desk lamp that provided most of the light. Kelly had his feet on his desk and hands behind his head. He looked comfortable and relaxed. With reddish hair and a pair of dark rimmed glasses, Kelly looked the part of an experienced lawyer. There was a twinkle in his eye and a smile on his face that made Carly think he was a charmer. Kelly took his feet off the desk and stood up; he was tall, well over six feet.

Rob made the introductions.

"Chris Kelly, Carly Howell."

"Hi there, sweetheart," Chris said with a wide grin.

"Sweetheart, really? I'm not your darling, so let's just use my name, okay? My name is Carly Howell, but you can call me Carly."

Chris took a step back and sat back down in his chair. "Whoa! Listen to her," he said as he looked toward Gold. "A real women's libber, huh? You're not going to burn your bra, are you? Just kidding. Please excuse me."

There was small talk about Boston, about the mob, about Chris's history as an assistant attorney general. After ten minutes or so, Chris finally got to the police raid at Rob's apartment that started the story, as well as how blatant the cop had been about taking the money from the shadowbox.

"Do you know how often cops steal from their targets? A lot!"

Chris then added to the drama. Turns out, soon after Rob's arrest, one of mobster Whitey Bulger's numbers guys set up a meeting with Rob at the Parker House. In all his time on the streets, Rob had never had a direct encounter with anyone working for Bulger. Both suspicious and nervous, Rob had asked Chris to sit nearby in the hotel dining room so he could overhear their conversation.

The Parker House is one of the most historic hotels in the country, and though it was rebuilt, it is still the oldest hotel in the United States. The Parker House sits on the Freedom Trail, and legendary figures from Charles Dickens to Henry Wadsworth Longfellow, Oliver Wendell Holmes, and many others had stayed there. In fact, John Wilkes Booth stayed at the Parker House eight days before assassinating Abraham Lincoln. Much later, John F. Kennedy announced his candidacy for Congress and had his bachelor party at the hotel. The Parker House is also known for its famous and much copied "Parker House rolls." The dining room is a massive, stately room, where waiters are known for doting over their regular customers, and service is a hallmark of the restaurant. The Parker House's dining room is a place to see and be seen, but there were large booths, too.

The meeting was set up for two p.m.; after lunch, when there weren't many folks dining. After Rob and the guy were seated, Chris managed to slyly maneuver into a table close enough to hear some of the conversation. As Chris now told it, the guy had quickly gotten to the point, saying to Rob: "Don't press charges against Detective Cross, and we'll take care of you." The "we" he was referring to was the well-known and much-feared gangster Whitey Bugler, whose brother William, or "Billy," as he was known, was the Senate president. Carly knew that her boss, Jim, was always on Bulger's trail, and the tales of the murder and mayhem he caused were well-known.

"That should have put the fear of God into you, no?" asked Carly.

"I took it in stride," Rob said. Carly was surprised by his answer. How could anyone take anything related to Whitey Bulger in stride? There were too many murders and other crimes tied to him and his gang.

"I warned him to take it seriously," Chris added.

"Sounds like good advice." Carly couldn't really tell whether Rob was truly that confident or if he was putting on a show for her benefit.

"Given the forces aligning against your client, wouldn't it make more sense for Rob to let this go and move on?" Carly asked Chris. "Why take a chance?"

"It's not something one can easily ignore, realizing that you, too, could become a target of Bulger if you failed to do what he wanted. Rob would be taking a chance either way. It was also a signal that the police and the mob might be working together in this instance." Chris turned and asked Carly: "And what do you make of this?"

She sat motionless for several minutes while she processed all that she had just been told.

"I agree with you," Carly finally said. "They clearly do not want Rob to take the stand against Dalton Cross. And I'm guessing that, if Rob drops it, the cocaine charges from the raid go away."

"You got it." Chris gave Carly a wry smile.

Rob and Chris maintained that there was an active ring of corrupt cops working with drug dealers in Boston. Money and drugs flowed between the two. All parties involved profited mightily; money in their pockets, the legal system be damned.

Chris winked at Carly. "Boston's bad rep for police corruption and organized crime is well deserved," he said.

"Maybe so, but how do you prove something when everyone involved is happily on the take?" Carly asked.

"That's the $64,000 question. I do think that getting you and the sources of your TV station involved will help considerably."

"I need so much more, not just talk," Carly said. "All I've got for now is your word against the police. And Rob's a convicted felon."

"Nobody's perfect," Rob interjected with a wink and a smile.

"You're on the right side on this," Chris said.

"Believe us," said Rob.

"Okay. I'd like to be able to. Here's one thing that might really help me. It would be great if there were a way to confirm the money being behind the shadowbox. Is there any way that could be confirmed?"

"Let me think about it," Rob said, then quickly added: "I may just have that answer for you. My friend, Brian, who lent me the money, would be the perfect guy to talk to. I will talk to him and get back to you."

CHAPTER SIX

When she got back to the station, Carly started plotting her strategy. Just then, her phone rang; it was Rob on the other end. There was no "Hi, how are you," no small talk. Instead, Rob said, "Meet me at my friend Brian's donut shop in Dorchester, Tasty Donuts, tomorrow, Saturday, around ten, okay? It's easy to find, just off the Southeast Expressway. And great donuts, by the way."

"That sounds great," Carly said, though she would have to restrain herself from actually eating the donuts; she was careful of her diet so that she could maintain her figure. "I'll be there."

Carly didn't know exactly where the donut shop was, but she quickly found it on a map. Dorchester, one of the first towns founded in the Massachusetts Bay Colony in 1630, was once home to the Jewish community of Boston but was now heavily African American, with abandoned buildings all over the neighborhood, from brick fronts to wooden triple-deckers and small mom-and-pop shops scattered along the main streets. Carly didn't know the neighborhood well at all.

Saturday morning brought a sunny day with a cool fall breeze. There was already a little chill in the air that was a reminder that winter was not far behind. Carly grabbed her blue wool coat and drove to the donut shop. She parked her car, gathered her notebook and purse, and walked to a nondescript building set back a bit from the street with a parking lot in the front. The donut shop was a one story red brick with two windows and a neon arrow sign that flashed "Donuts." When she entered, Carly saw a young woman in her twenties behind the display case. The sugary smell was wonderfully overwhelming, and the donuts looked tempting.

"Can I help you?" the young woman asked.

"I'm looking for Brian," Carly said. "I think he might be expecting me. My name is Carly Howell."

"Oh yes. He mentioned you might be coming by. Wait here, I'll go get him."

The woman returned momentarily with a short, balding guy. He was a little pudgy, too. *No surprise, given the store*, Carly thought.

"Good morning! I'm Brian. Rob told me you would be coming by. Why don't you follow me back to my office?"

Brian led Carly to the back of the shop. As soon as she entered, Brian closed the door behind her, and that made her feel a little more nervous than she already was. Brian's office was nothing fancy: a metal desk and a few chairs, a small table, and the aroma of donuts hanging in the air. Rob was already there, sitting at the desk with a big smile on his face like the Cheshire cat...like, somehow, this was a game he was playing.

As soon as Carly walked over to the table, she saw it: lines of cocaine laid out on a mirror, ready to be inhaled. Her heart started racing, and she broke into a sweat. She wiped her forehead, hoping neither Rob nor Brian noticed.

Fuck, Carly thought to herself. *What am I doing? What did I get myself into?* Carly had never seen or done cocaine. That's not to say she was totally unfamiliar with the occasional marijuana joint. Carly did, after all, go to college at the height of the anti-war, drug-friendly late sixties and early seventies.

Carly's father's voice resonated in her head, warning her to stay away from drugs: *Don't do it! Don't go down that road!*

Clearly, this was a test. If Carly stomped out of the store, that would likely be the end of the story. But if she stayed, she was putting herself in a compromising position. A voice in her head said: "A reporter should never get this involved."

Rob raised his eyebrows at her. "Thought you might want a little morning pick-me-up," he laughed.

There was no time to consider all the alternatives. Going through Carly's mind was a simple choice: *Do these lines and get the story, or say no and walk away.*

But Carly's father's voice was even stronger. She could not bring herself to crossing this line, and if that meant that it was the end of the story, then so be it. This situation sure did confirm to Carly that Rob was, indeed, a cocaine dealer, and maybe the cocaine the police found during the raid really was there despite Rob insisting that it was "planted."

Carly watched as Rob, then Brian, took turns snorting the lines. Then it was her turn. She politely declined and waited for their reaction.

"Seriously," Gold said. "You think you are better than we are?"

"No. But I just can't do drugs with subjects of a story I am doing. I can't."

"Hey Brian, whaddaya think?"

"Give her a break," Brian said, and Carly took a breath.

"Why should I?" Gold asked.

"Because you want her to do the story. Let's keep our eyes on the prize."

Thank goodness for Brian, Carly thought to herself.

"Okay...but this doesn't make me happy," Gold said, reluctantly relenting.

When Brian and Rob were done with their snorting, the two of them sat down at the small wooden table and offered Carly a seat, which she took. Carly was at one end, Rob at the other, and Brian on one side. There was a pot of coffee and Styrofoam cups there for the taking, as well as a plate of donuts. Carly poured herself a cup of coffee and left the donuts alone. Brian turned on the radio to lighten the mood, and with songs like "Hotel California" by the Eagles and "Stairway to Heaven" by Led Zeppelin, it did. Then, it was time for Carly to begin asking her questions.

"Okay, then . . . Let's start from the beginning—how do you two know each other?"

"When you live in the same neighborhood and are both in the food business, it's not much of a stretch to think that we would have run into each other," Rob said.

That seemed an easy answer..too easy.

"So, how and why did you become such good friends?" Carly asked.

"At first, I asked Brian to supply my sandwich shop with donuts, and he agreed, and they were a big hit," Rob said. "Over time, we would visit each other's shops, and we would occasionally go drinking in the neighborhood. We came to trust each other."

Carly looked over at Brian and asked: "And you trust Rob?"

"I do," Brian said emphatically. "Why would I be lending eight thousand dollars to a guy I didn't trust?"

Good question, Carly thought.

"Mind my asking you why you lent him the money? I'm not sure I would do that for my good friends."

"He asked," said Brian, as if there need not be any other reason.

Carly remained skeptical.

"Did Rob tell you what he was going to do with it?"

"He said he had a tax issue and that it would be a fairly short-term loan. It took me a while to get it all together for him."

"So, you are confirming that there was eight thousand dollars and that it was you who gave the money to Rob?"

"Yes, and yes."

"We would often help each other out with cash—right Brian?" Rob asked.

"Yeah. There were times when I needed cash and he would loan me money. We were both pretty much running cash businesses and tended to have a lot of it lying around," Brian said.

"When you say a lot of it, what do you mean by a lot?" Carly asked.

"On a good week, I take in between $7,000 and $9,000."

"And Brian, here, likes his cash in hundreds, don't you man?" Rob asked.

"I definitely do. Takes up less room in the pockets!" Brian laughed out loud, and Rob joined in.

"Did you sign an IOU or anything or was this all on the honor system?" Carly looked at both men.

"I placed the bills face up in a pile and wrapped them with two rubber bands and put them in a brown paper bag and gave them to Rob when he came by the store. That's the last I saw the money," Brian said.

Listening to the back and forth between the two men, Carly

could tell that Brian and Rob were truly friends. Their easy rapport was a sign of trust, and it made Carly feel a bit more confident in the story Rob was telling her; she needed that.

"One more question—was Brian your friend who was in the Caddy when you were stopped and frisked by the cops on the night of the raid?"

Rob looked a little surprised by the question.

"No! I was with a guy who helps me at my shop and helps with other stuff as well," Rob said.

"Yeah, I don't drive a Caddy. Just your basic Buick," Brian chimed in, smiling, and gave Rob a quick wink.

"Well, unless there is anything else I should know, I guess I should be going." Carly stood up and headed for the door.

"Feel free to call me with any questions you might have," Brian offered, not getting up.

"Thanks, that is much appreciated."

Gold bolted to his feet and grabbed Carly's arm.

"Wait a sec. Before you leave, I want to make sure you are still with me on this."

"At the moment, honestly, I'm still a bit skeptical...but I appreciate your setting this meeting up for me. I will continue to investigate, and I can't say where that will lead me."

"We're telling you the truth," Rob said in an almost pleading voice. *What else would he say*, Carly thought. Rob was pushing this story hard, and that, in itself, gave Carly reason to question the story.

CHAPTER SEVEN

Carly sat up in bed, startled, and glanced at the clock; it was three a.m. A recurring nightmare haunted her; it might have been the phone call with her father that triggered the nightmare this time. Carly could always recall the dream in vivid detail:

Carly's phone rang, and she picked it up.

"Hello?"

On the other end of the phone, Carly's mother was hysterical: "Your father has been shot. He's alive and in the hospital. I'm on my way there now."

"What happened?"

"I don't really know anything," Carly's mom said as she cried into the phone.

"I'm coming home," Carly said as she broke into tears.

"Okay, dear. Love you."

"And I love you. Give my love to dad, please. I hope he will be okay."

Carly loved—no, revered—her father. She prayed silently: *Please. Please. Let him stay alive and recover.*

When Carly got to the hospital emergency room, she was directed to the room where her father was. Her mother was at his side, holding his hand. Carly's father's eyes were closed, and there were wires and tubes everywhere.

Carly's mother turned to her, and Carly could see how red her mother's eyes were. She hugged her daughter tightly, then said: "We got lucky. He was shot in the shoulder, and the bullet lodged in his chest, but not near any vital organs. He'll be okay, though the recovery will take a while."

"Oh, thank God!"

Carly walked to the bedside and took her father's hand.

"Dad, I am here. I love you so much."

Carly's father was still out of it from the anesthesia from the surgery, so he didn't open his eyes. She pulled up a chair and sat next to her mom.

"Thanks for coming," Carly's mom said. "It will mean a lot to your dad, and it means a lot to me."

"Of course. I couldn't not be here."

Carly realized in that moment, as she held her father's hand, that she had been drawn to journalism because of the values her father had instilled in her: to speak truth to power, to uncover what is wrong and elevate what is right.

While this was all a bad dream, the truth was that Carly's father had been shot and had survived, and she also knew that, as long as her father remained an FBI agent, her mother would be on edge, and, Carly had to admit, so would she.

Carly was shivering a bit and got out of bed and went to the bathroom to rinse her face and clear her brain. Afterward, she went into the living room, sat down on her couch, stared out the window into the darkness of the night, and reflected on where she was and what she was doing. Carly convinced herself that she was right to pursue the story, though she was nervous about trusting a guy like Gold.

CHAPTER EIGHT

Carly's next step was to try to find out who in the District Attorney's office was prosecuting the larceny case against Cross. She had a couple of sources in the office, but she thought it was even better to ask Jim because he had stronger relations with the Assistant District Attorney, who was a source of his.

"Can you see if you can find out who is trying the case against Dalton Cross? I would really like to talk to him."

"Of course. What are the charges that Cross is facing?"

"Grand larceny," Carly said.

"I will call my guy over there and let you know what he says."

"Thanks."

The DA was a guy named Sean Callahan, who was known for his flamboyant attire and slap 'em on the back style. He was more often seen at community bingo games and church suppers, shaking hands and campaigning, rather than trying cases in court. He was a politician first and foremost.

Carly also knew that Callahan had a close relationship with the mayor and the upper echelons of the police department...maybe too close. Maybe, like any DA, he was very protective of law enforcement, and that made it very difficult to bring a case against a cop.

So, Carly was not at all surprised when she learned from Jim that Callahan had appointed a low-level assistant district attorney named Tommy Blake to the case. From her sources and Jim's within the DA's office, Carly learned that Blake was not a Boston native. He wasn't part of the political world of the DA, nor was he necessarily aware of the true levels of power in this city—the overwhelming power of the mayor above all. Blake was described by one of Jim's sources as "an innocent," and Carly suspected that Callahan had assigned Gold's case to Blake for exactly that reason. Blake was likely in over his head, and, perhaps, the hope was that he would lose the case and Dalton Cross would be found innocent.

Carly was pleasantly surprised when Blake agreed to meet her. After arriving at the office building across from the historic stone courthouse and City Hall and going through security, Carly took the elevator to the third floor and followed the signs to Tommy's office. The hallway was lined with portraits of former district attorneys; unsurprisingly, they were all white men. Carly wondered how long it would be before a woman would hold the job. When she found Tommy's office, Carly knocked on the door, and Tommy opened it and let her in. Carly was a little surprised to see the tight quarters and stacks of files piled high on his desk. She wasn't sure how Tommy could ever find anything in that mess. But then, she also knew she was more than a little obsessive when it came to keeping things neat. Carly's friends often made fun of her because of her organizational skills. There was never a dirty dish left in her sink, and she arranged her clothes in her closet according to color.

Tommy Blake was a wiry guy with dark hair and a mustache. He stood about five feet nine inches tall and wore a white shirt and rep tie, with his suit jacket hanging from a hook on the back of his office door.

Carly had dressed to look professional, with a touch of style: a short black skirt with a pastel flowered shirt and black leather boots that hugged her calves. Carly's shoulder-length blonde hair was well-coiffed, and she had just enough makeup to highlight her blue eyes. Checking herself before leaving home, Carly thought she looked damn fine.

"Come into my spacious office," Tommy said with a smile, giving a first indication that he had a sense of humor. There was one other chair in his office, and he motioned to Carly to have a seat. "I don't usually get called by reporters because I work on kind of low-level cases—the stuff that doesn't exactly make the front page of *The Globe*."

"Well, there's nothing low-level about Dalton Cross's case, that's for sure," said Carly, settling in and pulling out her trusty notebook. She crossed her legs, letting just enough thigh show, and rested her notebook on her lap. Carly wasted no time: "So, where do things stand with the case? Does anything you've learned throw any doubt onto the charges that Gold alleges?"

Tommy was not giving too much away. "We are moving in the right direction. The people we're looking at are very good at being sneaky; they've been doing it for years. Gold was certainly not the first drug dealer to be robbed by the police by any means."

Carly had to admit that was a bit of a shock, really, to hear from an assistant DA. . . like somehow, it was just accepted that cops steal from their targets.

"When you say, 'not the first one,' do you mean not the first one to be shaken down or robbed by the police? It's a pattern? Is that what you are saying?"

"It's clearly a pattern."

That answer was intriguing, and Carly felt a jolt of energy. This might be an even bigger story, she thought, with broader reach. But for now, Carly had to focus on this case. "Have you gotten any cops or ex-cops to corroborate the charges made by Gold?" she asked.

"Actually, there was a member of the raid that night who did see Cross take the money. He reported it to Lieutenant James and is, supposedly, leaving the police department and transferring to the fire department."

That was news to Carly; she wasn't even sure that Chris or Rob knew about it.

Blake got up and pointed to a stack of documents that was a foot high on the floor by his desk. "I requested all DCU search warrants for the past two years. I figured that would give me a picture of who the cops were after." Blake pointed to the stack of papers, and Carly took a moment to take it all in. Certainly, all that legalese wouldn't exactly make fun reading.

"And do the warrants indicate any trends?" Carly asked. "Who in the DCU is asking for most of these?"

"Well, those are astute questions—ones I asked myself. My survey of these records clearly indicates some of these guys are much more inclined to use a search warrant to gain entry wherever they want to go."

"And what about Dalton Cross? Did his name come up in this pile of warrants? Does he have a lot of search warrants under his name?"

Blake hesitated, then said: "I'm not sure I can really tell you that. This is all off-the-record, right?"

"Yes. Definitely. I should have made that clear before we even started. I know this, my interviewing you, is not an everyday occurrence, and I appreciate your willingness to even meet with me, even off-the-record."

"Well, perhaps not surprisingly, Dalton Cross is at the top of the list, followed by Bobby O'Rourke and John Parker."

"I heard that there might have been an informant in this case.

Did you talk to him?"

"I certainly do not want to expose an informant to any danger, so let's steer clear of that question for now."

Carly was feeling confident that she had come up with the right questions to get a better picture of this case and where things stood. *So, there was, indeed, an informant as Rob and Chris had alleged*, she thought. "Have you interviewed any members of the DCU?" Carly asked. "I guess that would be obvious, right?"

"Yes, I will speak to some of them. But I know that these guys will do anything to cover each other's backs. But I do want to ask a couple of these guys about all the warrants. Even hinting at a pattern might help my case against Cross."

"What about any conversations with Gold, his wife Eileen, and sister-in-law Katherine? At least the two women should be pretty believable."

"Well, of course I've talked to them. His sister-in-law Katherine (Kate) Maloney is a nurse; couldn't be nicer. Frankly, I don't think there's any love lost between her and Gold. I think she is fully aware of what a shit he is, but he is married to her sister, and she's loyal to her. And the bottom line is Kate saw what she saw and is willing to testify to it. She will be a strong witness."

"And Gold?"

"He's a scumbag. His charm may work on some folks. But I'm not fooled by it," Blake continued. "He is despicable. He's murdered, robbed, dealt drugs. It makes me wonder what would lead someone like his wife to stay with him. Eileen Gold can't be that naïve to believe her husband hasn't done all the things he has been convicted or accused of."

Carly remained quiet. Blake might be right about Rob Gold, but she also knew that, without Rob, there was no story; she needed him.

"Are you cool with my staying in touch with you? As you might be able to tell, I'm sticking with this story until the end."

"As long as we can keep our conversations between us. There's a lot on the line."

"Got it," Carly said as she got out of the chair, took her coat, and put her hand out. "This has been really helpful, and I hope that we can stay in touch."

"Yes," Tommy said. "You got it."

As she walked out of Blake's office and headed back onto the street, Carly felt that the meeting had gone even better than she had imagined. Tommy was so forthcoming with what he was willing to tell her, and there really was a story there. Carly also decided that she had to try to set up a meeting with the two sisters to hear firsthand what they witnessed.

CHAPTER NINE

Carly was successful in convincing the sisters to meet with her. She decided on Amrhein's in South Boston. The oldest bar in South Boston, Amrhein's had been around since 1890 and was known for its hand-carved wooden bar. City Councilor Dapper O'Malley from South Boston used the restaurant as his office away from City Hall. The bar also had a good-sized parking lot, which would make the tedious job of finding a parking space a lot easier. And none of the women were from the neighborhood, so they wouldn't be recognized. Carly arranged to meet with the sisters at two p.m. the next day.

Carly was nervous; she wasn't sure Eileen and Kate would be as forthcoming as she wanted them to be. She knew it would be up to her to quickly establish a rapport and trust.

Carly was good at gaining people's trust; it was part of what made her a good reporter. Half of the art of reporting is being able to elicit information from people that they may not have an interest in sharing. It takes the ability to first establish a rapport by talking about mundane kinds of things—the weather, the city, being a mother, being a nurse, everyday life. It also involves encouraging people to keep talking, and that takes a certain curiosity and ability to come up with questions to be answered without being too aggressive or demanding. Establishing rapport was a kind of verbal dance, and Carly loved it.

Carly wasn't trying to put either of the sisters on the spot; she just really wanted to hear firsthand what each of them had seen during the raid.

She arrived at the restaurant first. When she saw two women walk in, she knew it was them. Eileen Gold was a thin, unremarkable looking woman with no distinguishing features that would cause you to immediately recall her looks. She was about five foot four with shoulder-length medium brown hair, dressed in a navy-blue wool coat and a red knit hat. As the sisters approached the table, their eyes met, and Carly had the feeling that Eileen was more than a little hesitant.

Eileen's sister Kate was more attractive. She had light brown hair, with a shorter cut, and was dressed more stylishly than her sister, wearing a green and pink plaid poncho and tan bell-bottom pants. Kate also had a jaunty bounce to her walk.

Carly caught the sisters' eyes and waved to them. They were almost alone in the restaurant anyway. Kate and Eileen walked over, Carly introduced herself, and the sisters followed suit. The sisters then sat across from Carly, and after ordering some food, Carly started the conversation.

"I know you both have already talked to the police and to the assistant district attorney trying the case about what happened the night of October 18. And I know that this is asking a lot of you to meet with me. But we have the same goal—to get to the truth and to make sure that, if the detective committed a crime, he pays for it. So, it would really help if you could tell me what you saw or didn't see since it's at the heart of the prosecution of this case."

Eileen looked at her sister and then at Carly, then Kate spoke.

"We want to make sure, first, that whatever we tell you remains between us. Obviously, it's scary to be accusing a police officer of wrongdoing, so the more support we can get for our story to be believed, the better off we will be."

"I completely understand, and what we say is between us. I hope you understand, the more ways I can confirm what happened, the more accurate the story will be, so thank you," Carly said. She wanted to try to put the sisters at ease, even though she knew that was almost impossible given the circumstances.

"Kate, you are the one who saw Cross take and pocket the money, right? Can you go through it one more time? I apologize for asking you to repeat it."

Kate dabbed her lips with the napkin before speaking.

"Because of Rob's schedule, Eileen is often alone, and we're close, so I often come over during the evenings to keep her company and to visit my niece, who is a great kid. On that night, Eileen was in the kitchen making some tea, and my niece and I were sitting at the kitchen table with her, when, suddenly, there was loud banging on both the front and back doors. Even before we could answer the doors, these men burst in—five from the front and five from the back, with guns out and pointed at us. One of them was doing the talking and said they were Boston police detectives, and one of them flashed a badge. Eileen was freaking out but tried hard to remain as calm as she could. She asked me to please take my niece upstairs so she didn't have to witness anymore.

Imagine the trauma that just the entry inflicted on her? That's something she will never be able to forget. She talks about it almost every day, and it makes her cry. I was scared to death and took her hand, and we started to walk toward the stairs.

That's when I saw the detective take the shadowbox off the wall and feel all around the frame and under it. There was a hidden drawer, which I had no idea about, and when he found it, he grabbed what was in it and stuffed it in his pocket. From where I was standing, I could see it was money...wads of it. I had no idea how much was there, though. My niece saw it too. She looked at me and said: 'Did you see that?' I put my finger up to my lips to keep quiet and kept going to the stairs. Then, the detective turned around and saw us watching, and he gave me a furious stare and said, 'What the fuck are you doing?' I told him I was taking my niece to her bedroom, and he yelled, 'Get the fuck out of here. You're not supposed to be here.' I noticed in that moment that my hands were shaking. The two of us quickly went upstairs to her bedroom. My niece and I shut the door and just sat together on the bed hugging each other. She was crying. I held her tight and whispered that everything would be okay. She lay down, and I felt like I had to go back down to the kitchen with my sister; I didn't want to leave her alone.

When I got back down to the kitchen, I told Eileen what had just happened and what we had witnessed."

Carly took careful notes. Kate's confirmation was crucial to Rob's allegations. "Eileen," Carly asked. "Did you know there was this secret drawer in the shadowbox and that there was money in there?"

The sisters looked at each other.

"I had no idea. None," Eileen said. "That shadowbox has been there forever, and the only reason I even put it on the wall was to have some dried flowers to brighten up the living room. I may have known about the drawer at some point but totally forgot about it. I had no idea, frankly, that Rob knew about the drawer either," Eileen added.

Carly turned back to Kate. "What happened after you went back to the kitchen?"

"From there, it was impossible to see what was going on in the living room, so I don't know everything that the detective did. But another man came in the front door and introduced himself as Lieutenant Henry James. As soon as he walked into the kitchen and introduced himself, I told him what I had seen and even asked him to make the cops line up so we could search them. No surprise, he said no," Kate said.

Carly's next question to Eileen had been eating at her: "Mrs. Gold, how surprised were you to learn about the hidden money?"

Eileen glanced at her sister before answering, "I was very surprised. I had no idea Rob even knew about that space. And yes, I had a sense he was involved in other stuff besides the sandwich shop. But he takes good care of me, and I know better than to ask a lot of questions."

Carly couldn't decide if Eileen was being blind to her husband's drug dealing or just naive. It was difficult for her to believe that Eileen Gold could be married to Rob for more than a decade without knowing what he did to earn money. Carly knew that her next question veered into private territory, but she felt that she had to ask anyway: "Were you ever afraid of Rob?"

Eileen, once again, looked at Kate. The two sisters kept secrets; that was clear.

"No," Eileen said quietly.

"Didn't it frighten you that your husband had been in jail for armed robbery?" Carly asked.

"Rob always told me that what he called 'his days as a criminal' were behind him. He vowed to stay out of trouble."

Wow. Carly understood that Rob could be charming, but she could not wrap her mind around the idea that one person could so completely fool another into believing what was clearly fiction.

"Have you ever had to testify on his behalf before?" Carly asked Eileen.

"Once, yes. It was for breaking and entering, and I was called as a character witness. I knew absolutely nothing about it, so there was nothing I could say. I think the testimony lasted about five minutes, and I was dismissed."

Carly didn't want to push too hard on this first meeting, but she just had to ask: "Do you think that Rob deliberately keeps you in the dark about his activities beyond the sandwich shop, so you never have to lie?"

Eileen pondered her answer before offering it, "Well, I couldn't testify to something I don't know about, if that's what you're getting at."

"How do you spend your time, Eileen? What do you do for a living?"

"I spend a lot of time at home with my daughter, who is Rob's stepdaughter. I was married previously for five years. I also work about twenty hours a week as a receptionist at an auto repair shop in Dorchester. I can walk there, so that is convenient."

Carly leaned back in her chair and looked at both sisters before meeting Eileen's eyes. "You must be grateful to have such a supportive sister," she said.

Kate chimed in, "Eileen is my older sister, and I'd do anything for her."

Eileen reached over and grabbed her sister's hand. "The feeling is absolutely mutual. We have always been a very close-knit family." The sisters looked each other in the eyes, and Carly could tell that the emotions were genuine.

Carly changed directions, saying: "May I ask how you and Rob met?"

Eileen seemed to take a breath and then looked wistful as she remembered the moment. "It was a bar in Dorchester: the Eire Pub. It was eight years ago, a summer night. I was sitting at the bar, and Rob came and sat on the stool next to mine. He gave me a big smile and said: 'Hey beautiful. How are you this evening?' It was how we started our conversation. He has a gift for gab, and we stayed at the bar for a couple of hours, and then he offered to drive me home. I let him. When we got to my house, he looked into my eyes and said that he really hoped we could continue our conversation, and he reached over and took my hand and kissed it. I thought that was a sweet gesture, and I agreed. We dated for almost two years before he popped the question. He and I got along well, and he loved my daughter as if she was his own. I'd fallen in love. By then, we were already living together, so it was kind of expected. We had a low-key wedding, just family and a few friends at St. Mary's Church. Neither of us is particularly religious, but for my mom's sake, we wanted a church wedding. I didn't know any of Rob's family. He was adopted, and his adopted parents are dead. After the wedding, we moved into the Dorchester apartment, where we've been ever since."

As Eileen told her story, it struck Carly that she was reciting facts without a hint of emotion. It seemed a little weird. If Eileen were telling someone the story of how she had met and fallen in love with her husband, she would likely have more emotion about it—hopefully happiness, but definitely not a lack of feeling. No doubt the reality of an illicit life with Rob had taken its toll on Eileen.

Carly knew she needed to find out whether and how much Eileen knew about the cocaine dealing; she had a hunch she did. Could Eileen really have been living with this guy all this time and not know he was a cocaine dealer? Could she be part of it too? Carly had to ask: "And what did you, or do you, know about Rob's dealing cocaine?" As soon as she asked the question, Carly could hear a pin drop!

The two women looked at each other for what seemed an eternity. It didn't pass the smell test that Rob could have been dealing cocaine without her having some idea of what was going on. For all Carly knew, Eileen was helping Rob in a criminal enterprise: making deliveries, letting strange people into their apartment. Eileen Gold had to know something about her husband's illicit business practices.

Eileen gave Kate a quick look, cleared her throat, took a sip of coffee, and said: "I had no idea about it."

"Did you ever see cocaine in the house?" Carly asked.

"There's not really anything I can say. If there was cocaine in the house—and mind you, I am not sure there was, since the cops could have planted those drugs—Rob kept it hidden. I didn't know where or how, but I never saw drugs."

Kate leaned over and put her arm around Eileen's shoulder.

"I think we're probably done here," Kate said.

Carly nodded. "I hope you don't think that I was being too tough on you. My job is to find out the truth. Sometimes, that means asking uncomfortable questions."

There was no answer from the sisters. They gathered their coats and purses and stood up from the table to leave.

"Thanks very much for your willingness to meet," Carly said. And with that, the sisters departed without a word.

CHAPTER TEN

Carly was sound asleep in her Back Bay apartment when the doorbell rang. She jumped out of her bed and looked at the clock; it was two a.m. Who could possibly be ringing her doorbell at this hour? Fear ran through her like an electric shock.

Then, as she grabbed a bathrobe and made her way to the door, Carly realized who it might be. No one else would dare wake her up if it wasn't an emergency.

Carly looked through the peephole and saw Rob, fidgeting in the hallway.

"Just a minute," she said, running back to her bedroom and throwing on a pair of jeans and a top. She came back and opened the door with more than a little hesitancy.

"What could you possibly want from me at this hour?" Carly asked as she unlocked the dead bolt, the door lock, and the bar that was a third line of security.

Rob was undaunted by Carly's stern tone. "I have something for you."

"Okay, but it had better be quick." She hesitated before letting Rob in. Now, he was invading her space, and that frightened her.

Rob was rearing to go; he had likely dipped into some of his product.

It was one thing for Carly to meet Rob at his diner or Brian's donut shop...but showing up at her home was crossing a line. She had no place to hide here, and that reality hit her.

"What's so urgent, and how did you get past the front door?"

Rob laughed as he walked in and took a look around Carly's apartment. "It helps to have certain skills," he said. "I was just meeting a friend over in Watertown and thought I'd stop by." Rob was glib about it, like there was nothing out of the ordinary about this visit in the wee hours.

"I've got a present for you." Rob took out one of those little glassine envelopes seen at a jewelers. In it were two gold chains.

"These are for you," Rob said proudly as he put the chains in Carly's open palm.

"You know that I can't accept these. Journalists can't accept gifts. It would compromise my objectivity."

Rob had a Cheshire cat grin as he said: "You can do whatever you want with them, but I'm not taking them back; they're yours."

Carly tried to hand them back, but instead, Rob gently pulled her close to him. Rob Gold gave her a quick kiss on the cheek, a move that caught Carly entirely off guard.

She pushed Rob away, then said: "What are you doing? You can't just come into my apartment at any time of the day or night and think you're going to start something."

Rob stepped back, and without apologizing, he said: "You know that I am very attracted to you."

"You're married."

"It's okay," Rob reassured Carly. "This can't go very far. But it doesn't mean I don't find you sexy. I do."

Carly had to admit to herself that she was also attracted to Rob, even as an inner voice screamed an alarm. She escorted him into her living room, keeping her distance as the two sat on opposite ends of her brown velvet couch.

Truth was, it had been a long time since Carly had felt the warmth and care of a man. She'd had occasional one-night stands with guys—and, admittedly, some of them had been married. No surprise; nothing stuck. The fact that Rob Gold was so clearly unlike any guy Carly had ever been with was titillating. She was intrigued and excited by the danger, even as her inner voice voiced serious objections: "Don't do it, Carly! There's zero chance you won't regret it later."

"As long as you're here, let's get some work done, or I've got to ask you to leave. And in the future, don't stop by without telling me you're coming."

"Okay. I hear you." Rob moved closer and kissed Carly on the cheek. "By the way, you should know that the drug control unit is, no doubt, watching my every move. Just be aware of that."

"What? Are you telling me that you just led the DCU to my apartment?"

"Don't worry. They're following me, not you," Rob said, sounding a bit sulky; he was leaving without getting what he came for.

With relief, Carly closed the door behind Rob. She couldn't believe what just happened.

Needless to say, it wasn't easy falling back to sleep. Carly rolled over to one side, then the other, her mind going a million miles a minute. She had to consider how much trouble Rob Gold was bringing to her door. While he might be a sexy charmer, he was also a criminal, possibly a sociopath. Carly went through a kind of checklist of Rob's qualities to convince herself she should keep him at arm's length despite needing him for the story. He had superficial charm. *Check.* He was manipulative and cunning.

Check. He could lie with the best of them. *Check.* He lived on the edge and clearly had no remorse for anything he'd done. *Check.* And he was clearly willing to cheat on his wife. *Check.*

Carly had only known Rob for two weeks, but he had managed to work his way into her head and was making sure she was going where he wanted with the story.

But Carly had her own motive for pursuing the story—to find out, if she could, just how corrupt the police department in Boston was and how high up it went and to make the story the kind of blockbuster that would help cement her reputation as a star reporter.

Carly also knew that she couldn't be completely open with her boss Jim about just how she was going about researching this story.

CHAPTER ELEVEN

Dalton Cross, who had been charged with larceny after the raid, and his partner Tim O'Malley, who had also been in on the raid at Gold's, parked their unmarked police car with the engine on. It was November in Boston, after all, and the heater was set on high. The two officers sat in the car on Commonwealth Avenue within eyesight of Carly's apartment building. They had the radio on, but softly, so as to not give themselves away in this quiet part of town.

Drug cops: the street is their office, and their hours are whatever they have to be.

A fifteen-year veteran of the Boston police force at thirty-five, Dalton Cross didn't have that harsh veneer many cops take on. He looked more like your friendly next-door neighbor. Cross was also kind of a fashion fiend, and he liked making a statement, particularly with his many colorful sweaters; they were his signature and had earned him a reputation for his dress within the unit. On this night, Cross was wearing a maroon sweater with a white stripe across the top and light grey wool pants; dapper, he thought. Cross loved the job and his band of brothers whom he spent more time with than his family. In fact, they felt more like his family. Cross was recently divorced, so that gave him more availability to be on surveillance whenever he felt like it. Late nights and early mornings were Cross's favorite times of the day. He was a coffee fiend and could drink six cups a day and still be able to sleep when he finally did hit the pillow. Cross liked being on the street where the drug deals were happening. He knew after years of catching the dealers that, if he were well-positioned on the street where he was surveilling a drug dealer, he could often find him actually doing business. Cross could also use his camera, which he kept with him in the car at all times, to record whatever he saw.

Cross had been watching Gold ever since the raid, and now, he and O'Malley were sitting across from Carly Howell's apartment on Commonwealth Avenue, one of the most iconic streets in Boston, with its beautiful walking path dividing it. Lights on the trees made the darkness of the season a bit brighter.

"How long do you want to wait out here?" Cross asked his partner, who was getting antsy and clearly wanted to end this surveillance.

"I leave that to you," O'Malley said. "What do you think we'll see?"

"Got a tip that Gold might show up at Carly Howell's place. Apparently, the creep's been stopping by the reporter's apartment."

"I get it. But we've already been here for about two hours, and there hasn't been any action for a while. I wonder whether it's worth our time."

"Let's give it another half hour, then we can call it quits."

Their car—seized in a drug raid—was a relatively new model: a dark blue Chevrolet Impala with no distinguishing markings. Cross took pride in his appearance and was a very neat guy, so unlike a lot of these nasty lent-out cruisers, which rapidly filled with empty coffee cups and food wrappers, this one was immaculate. Cross did smoke though, so he left the driver's window rolled down a bit to air out the car.

At two a.m., just as the officers were about ready to leave . .

.bingo!

Rob Gold pulled up and parked his black, shiny Lincoln on the street, where he was lucky to find a parking space, and went up to her front door.

"There he is," Cross said. "Damn! I can't believe he's actually stopping at her apartment."

Just under an hour later, the officers spotted Gold emerging from Carly's apartment building. Cross noted the time he'd come and left, thinking that, at some future moment, he might be able to use this visit against him or her.

Cross would stop at police headquarters in the morning to fill in Lieutenant James, his boss and the head of the Drug Control Unit. "Time to roll," Cross declared. "We got what we came for."

Cross was not a fan of Lieutenant James. In fact, he couldn't stand the guy.

James had a reputation as an honest cop who lived by the code to uphold the law—not to break it. In fact, before being transferred to the Drug Control Unit, James had served in Internal Affairs, the unit charged with investigating police corruption and wrongdoing.

The detectives under his supervision, like Cross, were highly skeptical of James because of where he'd come from—and, obviously, they had reason. He was playing it straight while most of them were more than willing to use their positions to line their own pockets, which meant breaking a law here and there if they needed to.

James had been put in charge of the unit exactly because there was suspicion among the higher ups that the Drug Control Unit wasn't living up to "department standards."

Like everyone else who was in on the drug raid at the Gold residence, James was livid that this no-good career criminal had exposed a level of corruption in his unit that he wasn't aware of and seemed to relish in it and rub it in their faces.

James tended to spend his days at his desk, going through paperwork while his men were out on the street. He was there for them, but he didn't intrude in their work—a "hands off" approach.

The next morning, after their surveillance—well, really more like early afternoon—Cross knocked on the door to James' office, then walked right in.

"I got news on that low-life drug dealer Rob Gold."

"Let's hear it. I'm all ears."

"Well, after a tip, we were watching the apartment building where the reporter at Channel 8 lives on Comm. Ave. in the Back Bay. Guess what we saw? Gold going in around 2 a.m. and staying for about an hour. Interesting, right?"

"Absolutely. Thanks for the info. I'll take it from here."

A couple of days later, Carly was at her desk, reading *The Boston Globe,* when the phone rang. "Carly Howell speaking, good morning."

In a low baritone, Hank James said: "Ah, yes, Carly, this is Lieutenant James. I think you know who I am."

"Of course. What can I do for you, or, more importantly, what can you do for me?"

"Any chance we could have lunch?"

Carly was totally taken aback. She knew Lieutenant James was Dalton Cross's boss, and she was surprised he would take this step. And why all of a sudden, Carly wondered. But she put that thought in the back of her head because she was thrilled by the chance to learn what made James tick and what he might be willing to tell her about the raid, Dalton Cross, and Rob Gold.

"Sure. That would be great. You name the time and place, and I will be there."

"Do you know a restaurant called Richard's near police headquarters?" James asked.

"No, but I am sure I can find it."

"Let's say tomorrow around two—after lunch, but before the cocktail crowd comes in. It's likely to be pretty quiet at that time."

"Looking forward to it." Carly put down the phone and turned to find her boss standing beside her desk.

"Guess who just called? Lieutenant James. He wants to meet me."

"That's great," Jim said, leaning against the edge of Carly's desk. "You know, we haven't talked much about where you are with the story and what you've managed to find out."

After Carly filled him in, Jim said: "Sounds like you have a good handle on how to dig out the facts here. And I don't want to get in your way, but I am here for you and happy to help you interpret and dissect what you learn. You want to be careful that folks aren't leading you down the wrong path or trying to divert you from the truth."

"Believe me, I'm leery of all facts in this case, especially since Rob Gold is involved. He is one smooth operator, that's for damn sure."

"Smart criminals are like that. They're good at getting folks just where they want them to be. It will be interesting to see how much the Lieutenant is willing to tell you. Take good notes."

"You know I will!" It was Carly's habit, anyway. As a reporter, she always had a notebook. Carly was highly doubtful that the DCU head would allow her to tape their conversation (in Massachusetts, both parties must agree to be taped), but she was confident that she would get it all down on paper.

CHAPTER TWELVE

The closer Carly got to the Hancock Tower—the glass-enclosed skyscraper designed by I. M. Pei, in the heart of the Back Bay—the windier it always was. And it was already a very windy day; Carly could feel it. Her hair was blowing around, and there wasn't much she could do about it; she didn't have a hat. Carly wasn't alone, however, as other Bostonians rushed along the sidewalk, scarves covering their faces and hair blowing all over the place.

Carly found a parking space right in front of the restaurant and hurried inside. She scanned the dimly lit restaurant until she spotted a guy she thought might be the lieutenant, sitting alone in one of the booths, tapping his fingers on the table and with a drink in front of him.

Even in the middle of the day, the bar was smoke-filled, which Carly hated. As soon as she walked in, she heard the Temptations playing on the jukebox; Carly loved Motown, especially the Temptations. She went over to give the playlist a glance; one of her favorites, "Smiling Faces Sometimes," was there. Carly put in her quarter . . .

"Smiling faces, smiling faces tell lies and I got proof . . ." The lyrics always reminded Carly of her college days, plus they were fitting for the moment.

Carly stepped up to the bar. Perched along the bar were a

couple of casually-dressed men. The bar itself was undistinguished, with rows of the requisite liquors and two bartenders busily making cocktails. Carly took an empty seat and ordered a vodka and tonic.

"You bet, beautiful," the bartender said, quickly bringing her the ice-cold drink. Carly took a sip and gazed over at the table, where the guy she suspected was Lieutenant James shuffling through some papers. When James looked up and gave her a slight wave of the hand, Carly took her drink and headed over to his table.

She had dressed to impress. The straight pencil skirt was just tight enough to show off her toned buttocks, and she had a black and white mohair sweater that accented her buxom chest. Carly liked her gold jewelry but didn't want anything that was too ostentatious, so she had on a modest gold bracelet and some black and gold earrings pressed against her ear lobes. She was wearing her favorite cologne—a smoky fragrance called Caleche. Her hair was neatly coiffed in a flip, and she had put on just enough makeup to highlight her blue eyes, with some red lipstick to accentuate her TV-friendly smile.

As Carly got closer to the table, the lieutenant stood up and said in a deep, baritone voice: "Welcome to my home away from home." Smiling, James motioned Carly to take a seat. "This is a place where we Boston cops feel comfortable."

As she looked around, Carly noticed that the bar was overwhelmingly men, not necessarily in uniform, talking in small groups of three or four. Lieutenant James was dressed in civilian clothes as well: an open collar blue shirt that matched his eyes and a grey sport jacket. Carly took a seat, and after a few pleasantries, said: "I have to tell you I was pretty surprised that you called and wanted to meet me."

"It's not something I can ever remember doing before,

frankly," James said. "But the charges brought by Rob Gold against the department are serious ones. These allegations have made a lot of folks in the upper echelons wonder about what the heck is going on with the Drug Control Unit, and that's my baby. This Gold charge caught us—at least me—totally off guard. I was present at the Gold apartment that night and saw nothing of the sort that is alleged. And I need not tell an experienced journalist like you that Rob Gold is not exactly a model citizen. I'm frankly not sure why anyone would believe a thing he said." James took a breath and looked up, meeting Carly's eyes. She was taken aback by the lieutenant's lecture and insinuation because, so far, she hadn't even asked a question. Carly decided to calm the lieutenant down a bit with more nonthreatening questions.

"Tell me about yourself. You're not from Boston, right? So, how'd you get to be head of the Drug Control Unit?"

"I know, it's rare for someone from outside to rise up in this police department. I didn't exactly take a direct route getting there. I was in the Coast Guard and got stationed in Boston, probably before you were even born." James smiled, and Carly thought his accent might be from upstate New York—complete with the hard "a."

"When I got out, kind of on a whim, I took the police exam and passed with flying colors and decided to join the department. I was on the street for a few years and then went through the ranks and became a lieutenant. Before the DCU, I was in Internal Affairs."

James had an easy manner about him and didn't seem to be too full of himself. He was handsome, too, Carly had to admit to herself; his deep baritone was enticing and very sexy. She guessed the lieutenant was in his fifties.

"And when you were in Internal Affairs, did you investigate any instances of corruption among the drug cops?"

"You want the truth?"

"That would be refreshing, yes."

"There were allegations about the DCU, but never enough proof to move forward. And, of course, now that I'm in the unit, I keep a vigilant eye out for it. I've never seen any of it."

"So, you think it's a stretch to believe that this incident may have happened, no matter what you think of Gold, right?"

James lifted his drink and swirled it around so the ice cubes clanked in the glass. "It is possible that such a thing could happen. There are such things as rogue cops. But this is not a pattern of behavior in the Drug Control Unit."

"So, you believe your guys. Didn't one of them come and tell you that he saw Dalton Cross taking money from the Golds' apartment?"

"How do you know that?" James asked, looking surprised. "Yes. That's true. I gave a deposition to the assistant district attorney to that effect."

"So, it's very likely that Gold is, indeed, telling the truth. And given what you know, how could you think this instance was the only one. Isn't that giving these guys a pretty big benefit of the doubt?" Carly asked.

"I'm not going to draw any broad conclusions until I have seen the evidence. Show me!"

It was a Catch-22. How could James discover a pattern without an investigation?

"Do you think this was Cross's first time taking something of value from a drug dealer?" Carly asked bluntly.

James got defensive: "Let me ask you a question: Why the heck would you believe a convicted lowlife like Gold?"

Carly straightened her spine and looked straight at the lieutenant.

"His character is beside the point. He's not an employee of the Boston PD. Like you, I'm trying to sort out fact from fiction. That's not easy to do, is it?"

"Much of what these guys do on a day-to-day basis, they keep to themselves. It's their sources, their raids. I walk a fine line between overseeing the unit and making sure we are 'staying within the lines,' letting each officer have the flexibility and room to nab their prey—if you get my drift."

"You're in a tough position, it sounds like to me," Carly said with an air of understanding. "Since you came from Internal Affairs, do you think the guys may not be as open with you as they might be with someone who doesn't have your background?"

"I've never felt any overt hostility from the guys, but they each have their own little groups of confidantes and friends. We're not exactly one merry band of brothers."

"What is Cross's reputation within the department and within the DCU?"

"He's been a pretty good cop. Like me, he's not a native. He's from Bangor, Maine. Not sure what brought him down to the city. I do know he's been a cop most of his adult life."

"Do you know if he has any ties to the District Attorney? Would anyone up the ladder be trying to help him out?"

"Well, why would you say that?" James let his momentary shock show.

"If I tell you, I'll have to kill you," Carly said, laughing.

"Ha." James took a sip from the glass and looked at Carly with his sky-blue eyes. Sarcasm: Carly loved it but knew not everyone appreciated that kind of humor. When she found someone like

James, who clearly used it himself, it was a point in their favor. And Carly had to admit that she found herself being drawn in by James' charm and good looks. When Carly was done with her questions, she and the lieutenant continued eating their lunch, finishing their cocktails, and making small talk about the Celtics and anything else Carly could think of; she took it upon herself to keep the conversation going. When they were done, Carly got up and put on her coat.

"I want to thank you for meeting with me. I hope you got a sense of my earnest desire to get to the truth. And if you did, I am wondering if we might meet again?"

"I would certainly hope so. You have definitely enticed me to want to get to know you better." James looked at Carly with his deep blue eyes and smiled broadly. She was a little taken aback by his flirtiness, but it didn't turn her off; quite the opposite, in fact.

"Well, then, I'll be in touch," she said.

Carly was a little surprised to find that there was an immediate, undeniable physical attraction between her and James, but maybe it shouldn't have been so unexpected. It fit her pattern: another married guy was coming onto her, and she was taken in.

CHAPTER THIRTEEN

Carly knew that investigative reporting might sound sexy and dangerous to those who enjoy its results or look at it from the outside. The profession carries an aura of intrigue, sprinkled with a touch of danger. But the truth is that investigative reporting, like law enforcement itself, can often be tedious and boring, with hours and hours spent sifting through documents stacked in places like the Registry of Deeds or the district or superior courthouses. The "down and dirty" of government is not easy to illustrate. Cameramen at Channel 8 hated getting involved in these investigative stories. More often than not, the job involved shooting pieces of paper and trying to make them look interesting.

Carly and Jim were hardly the most popular unit at the station, so they were largely left alone and given broad license to pursue whatever stories they thought would pay off, and they were not housed in the main newsroom. Carly did not like her and Jim's office. She felt like they were intentionally set apart, which was true. Carly was a people person. She wanted to be where the action was, and she also wanted to be "on-air." Carly often came out of the cocoon to find out what stories her colleagues were working on, as well as to schmooze with them.

Carly did get lucky during the summer of 1979, when she got a gig as a stand-in on air weekend reporter. It was a chance for her to "show her stuff" to an audience and establish her cred as an on-air reporter, all thanks to President Jimmy Carter and the oil shortage, when prices spiked and car owners were either left without gas or waited in endless lines at the gas pumps. This crisis impacted everything from tourism to daily life, and the station coverage was all over it...but the station was also down one on-air reporter.

That discrepancy gave rookie Carly the chance she had longed for: to be on-air as a weekend reporter. That was probably how Gold even knew who Carly was or what she looked like. Since the weekends did not interfere with her "day job" of investigative reporting, Jim didn't have a say in whether Carly could take the job or not. In fact, Jim took personal pride in Carly's on-air appearances, like she was his protégé. He also had confidence in Carly, in her abilities and her dedication to getting whatever story they were after. And there was no deadline on when Carly's stories had to be finished, which gave her the freedom to work on the weekends for the newsroom. Carly knew she could turn a head or two both on-air and off, and she used that to her advantage. Her blonde, shoulder-length hair was worn in a shag style, a la Farrah Fawcett, with lots of layers and brow-skimming bangs that made her eyes pop. Carly had taken makeup tips from the cosmetics counters at various department stores and skillfully learned the right amount to highlight her high cheekbones and lipstick to accentuate her smile. The late 1970s were also the time for shoulder pads in blazers and sweaters, and they helped highlight Carly's waist and figure.

She also made sure she had a great rapport with the cameramen at the station and knew how to make them feel important. They were a team, and a smart reporter never took the cameraman for granted. Cameramen could screw up a story and make a reporter look less than their best.

Depending on the story, a reporter and cameraman might spend long hours together in the car, traveling to and from shoots or waiting for events. Conversations could hop from various subjects: the internal dynamics of the station; what was happening at Boston City Hall; who sold the best lobster rolls; what was happening with the Red Sox, Celtics, or Bruins; and who was "getting it on" with whom. Carly favorite was a cameraman named Larry, as he was more willing to do the investigative stories than some of the other cameramen.

"It's a challenge I like," Larry told Carly early on. "While these stories might not lend themselves to grand camerawork, they are important, and it's up to me to make sure that the public understands the story and why it matters. I like that challenge."

Larry and Carly did not necessarily agree on music and who liked what. Larry had a definite penchant for the Eagles, who were on top of the charts. Carly much preferred Donna Summer or, even, better the Jackson 5 and loved singing along with the music. While Larry and Carly were in the car, more often than not, the police radio was in the background so they could hear if there was any kind of emergency they should know about.

Jim didn't insist on daily updates of Carly's progress, but she knew he was there as needed to act as a guide and to steer her in the right direction or be a sounding board. Carly did the same for Jim when he was preparing a story. She greatly valued and felt fortunate that they had such a good working relationship.

With all that had been going on, Carly knew she owed Jim an update.

"What do you think? Time for a little download," Carly said.

"I have been wondering what you've found out, but I didn't want to get in your way," Jim said.

"And I appreciate your faith in me. Truth is, I've learned a lot, but I'm not sure how it all adds up yet."

Jim leaned back in his chair and put his feet up on the desk and his hands behind his head. "I haven't been going behind your back, so don't take this the wrong way, but my sources have told me that the DA is on the police department's side and wants to make sure that this doesn't go too far up the ladder."

Carly let that statement sink in. "I knew it. That puts another piece into place. But Tommy Blake isn't taking these allegations lightly either. Even though he's a relative newcomer, he's keeping his head down and working the case the best he can."

"Tell me about the meeting with Gold's wife and her sister."

"I tend to believe them. I don't think they're making up what they said and what they saw, though I wish there were another way to corroborate the story."

"The only other way, frankly, would be to get one of the cops to talk to you. What about Lieutenant James?" Jim asked.

"I did have a meeting with him the other day at a cop hangout. He called me and asked to meet. I was floored that he did that."

"Did you charm him with your smile?"

"I did my best. It was a first meeting, though, and I didn't want to come on too aggressively. I wanted to keep him talking and trusting me."

As she was relaying the conversation to Jim, Carly knew that she was going to have to work even harder to get Lieutenant James to open up more; she was up for that job.

CHAPTER FOURTEEN

Around noon, with hunger gnawing at her, Carly walked downstairs to the newsroom to find her friend and news producer, Rhonda. Rhonda was busy getting stories ready for the six o'clock news, and Carly asked her if she wanted to go out for a quick bite.

"Sure. Great idea."

The two women drove down to what was the main street in Needham and went into one of their favorite sandwich shops. Carly already knew what she wanted: a Greek salad with tuna. Rhonda chose a turkey sandwich. The women then found a booth and sat down.

"I realize we haven't talked in a while," Carly said.

"You're right. I guess between us, the jobs are a little all-consuming," Rhonda said. "What are you working on? Is it still that drug raid story and the cops?"

"Yes. It's not only occupying all my time at work, it's also invaded my brain. Now I'm having nightmares because of it."

"You know, you can't let this stuff take over your life."

"I keep telling myself that, but it's not working. I even had the drug dealer show up at my door in the middle of the night."

Rhonda looked at Carly in shock. "Are you serious?"

"Would I make it up? I even let him in, which I regret doing.

He's a slick operator, that's for sure. But enough about me. What are you up to?"

"Work has been busy, but I've managed to go out a couple of times with a new guy"

"That's great! How did you meet him?"

"I met him at one of our favorite bars—Charlie's. He works for the city in Parks and Recreation."

"Tell me more. What does he look like?"

"He's cute: about six-feet tall with dark brown hair and brown eyes. His name is Scott, and he's from New York. He came to Boston to go to BU, then got this job right out of school."

"Well, I can't wait to meet him."

"Next time we're together at Charlie's, maybe."

"Sounds like a plan."

Carly and Rhonda ate their lunch and lingered for a little while before going back to the station.

"I can't tell you how much I needed to just get a change of scenery, even if it was just for a few minutes, to get a break from this story and hear about someone else," Carly said. She realized how important her friends were and how she had neglected them during the past few weeks. Carly resolved to reconnect with her posse. She also made a vow to herself that she would not let Gold back into her apartment. If a meeting needed to happen, it would be someplace public. Rob might not like that, but that was too bad. Carly also realized that, from now on, she would be a little more paranoid, watching to see if she could see any cars that were parked out front or following her when she was walking in the Back Bay.

CHAPTER FIFTEEN

It had been a couple of weeks since Carly's first meeting with Lieutenant James, and she decided it was time for another visit to Richard's.

Carly took a seat at the bar. Even though she had only been to the bar once, Richard, the owner and bartender, didn't even have to ask what she wanted to drink. As soon as he saw Carly, he put down a vodka and tonic and gave her a wide grin. A group of four guys were playing cards at a round table in the middle of the room, and billows of smoke rose from their cigarettes. Beers all around, playing cards, peanuts, and other assorted snacks littered the card table. The men waved at Carly, and she waved back, though she wasn't at all sure who they were or why they were waving.

Just then, Carly spotted Lieutenant James walking through the door. He ambled over, his well-pressed khaki pants sitting low on his hips. James wore a light blue, button-down collared shirt covered by a navy-blue V-neck sweater. His light brown hair, specked with grey, was swept to the side.

Carly tried to hide how glad she was to see the lieutenant, but couldn't resist giving him a smile.

The lieutenant walked over to the bar, put his hands on Carly's shoulders, turned to say hello to the card game, and then turned back to Carly. James stayed standing, his foot on Carly's chair, and his hand resting comfortably on the back of the chair. To see James better, Carly swung her legs around, and they touched Hank's. She could feel her heart beating a little faster with anticipation.

"Like the sweater," Hank said.

Carly had put on the black sweater with a low neckline, keeping Hank in mind.

"Let's go over to a booth," Hank said as he headed with the drinks to the far side of the bar, which was fairly empty.

As they sat down and started sipping their vodka and tonics, Hank caught Carly off guard when he said: "DA Callahan asked me to come over to his office."

"Really? Can you tell me anything about the meeting?"

"He just wanted my side of the story. I told him exactly what I've been saying all along: I did not see anyone take any money, and I believe my guys."

"How did he react?"

"I think he was pleased that my story remains my story."

"You'll clearly get called as a witness," Carly said.

"No doubt about it."

Hank seemed to be in a pretty good mood, almost playful. He surprised Carly again when he said: "How about if I settle up the bill, and I'll meet you outside in your car?"

Carly hesitated, knowing that she was taking a risk, but not knowing how big of one. Other issues aside, Carly was convinced she that could do her job and be objective about the corrupt narcotics cop story...even if she gave into her desires.

Carly looked up, and her eyes met with Hank's.

"Deal."

Carly finished her drink and left the bar without another word.

Carly's red Honda was parked just outside the restaurant, and she waited a few minutes. Sure enough, Hank came sauntering over to the car. Carly opened the passenger door, and Hank slid in and over to her, giving Carly a long kiss. The stick shift in the middle made the kiss a little awkward, but he managed to get over it. Carly wanted to keep the vibe going, so she drove just a short distance to the public garden. She parked the car and motioned with her open arms for Hank to get out.

"Let's go sit over there on that bench for a bit," she said.

As soon as he and Carly were seated, Hank said: "I can't help myself when I'm around you. You turn me on."

Carly was flattered and a little taken aback.

"And I'm attracted to you, too...but I have a hard time getting past the married part. That just doesn't feel right." After her various exploits with married guys, Carly really wanted to be careful about getting involved with another one again.

"It's okay, I can assure you." With that, Hank reached over, put his arm around Carly's shoulders, turned her face toward his, and gave her a long, hard kiss.

Carly opened her eyes and looked at Hank. "I hadn't planned this," she said.

"Sometimes, stuff happens when you least expect it," Hank said.

Carly thought about that statement as she took Hank's hand and led him back to the car.

Doubts lingered in Carly's head as she parked the car down the block from Richard's. Hank gave her one last kiss, then jumped out and said: "Good night. Sleep tight."

CHAPTER SIXTEEN

"Manny, Rob here."

Rob's voice reflected a certain urgency. He was at The Hen after hours, taking care of business for both the deli and his drug ring, which had taken a hit after the raid.

"We need to make a quick trip to New York. You in?"

"*Hola*, Rob. You know I'm here for you whenever." Manny was Rob's right-hand man who helped with the cocaine: storing it, packaging it, and getting it to customers. He was the guy who picked Rob up the night of the raid.

"We'll need to use your wheels. The cops are all over me for this drug cop thing, and I don't want to take any chances. They're watching my every move. A car is parked on the street in front of my place with two guys in it, even late at night."

"Got it. When and where should we meet?"

"Come down to The Hen around midnight. Park a block away, though, at the corner of Milk Street, and I'll find you. We've got to go to Queens. Should be about four hours down and four back."

"I'll be there *amigo*."

It was good for Rob to have a friend whom he could count on. Manny Salvato was a small-time dealer who hailed from Columbia, and he depended on Rob for his supply of blow to sell. Gold's network was solid. He had a few guys whom he considered "his guys," meaning they dealt drugs they got from him. The guys knew where their income came from and weren't about to do anything to screw with it or with Rob. Solid! And Manny was Rob's number one guy. The two men had met when they were both serving time, and they bonded behind bars.

Even though the DCU had Gold under a microscope, he knew it was time to refresh the coke supply Cross and friends had taken when they'd raided his house. All the while, Rob maintained to Tommy Blake and Carly Howell that the cocaine found at his place had been a set up. He would continue that fiction, but the reality was that he was a businessman and needed more product to sell. Rob wasn't making anywhere near enough money at The Hen.

Rob was lucky that he knew the federal drug authorities were much more interested in busting up heroin rings rather than cocaine rings. Gold had never been interested in heroine; he did just fine dealing blow.

Only once before in his drug career had Gold traveled down to his suppliers. It was his introduction to the group that sold him the cocaine, and he wanted to meet the suppliers face-to-face. The meeting took place in a Latin restaurant in Jackson Heights, Queens on an April night.

There were four guys, plus Rob. It was a pleasant enough night, and the business was fairly easy and straightforward. The cartel guys gave Rob the rules and the money requirements. He agreed, shook hands, and that was that. But after that, the well-established routine was that the suppliers brought the drugs from New York City to Rob in Boston. Now, with all eyes on him, Rob felt that it might be too risky to take deliveries at the sandwich shop.

Manny drove his late model black Cadillac downtown to the Financial District around midnight. Rob was on the lookout for the car, and at the corner of Milk Street and Broad Street, he spotted the car and jumped in. At that time of night, the streets were deserted, and the few streetlights did little to enliven the neighborhood. What little traffic there was consisted mostly of delivery trucks and an occasional cab trolling for business. Rob could feel the adrenaline rushing through his body; he was hopped up on his product. As soon as he got in the car, Rob offered Manny some cocaine. Manny snorted a little and headed out.

It was a foggy early November night, with the occasional drizzle. *Perfect weather for this mission*, Gold thought. Gold let Manny choose the music on the radio, and unsurprisingly, he found a station that played Latin music, which Gold didn't even know existed. There was almost no one on the road at this hour, so they made it down to Queens in record time: under three and a half hours on I-95. When they got to the address, Gold used the directions he had gotten from his contact. The two men were in an industrial area with a bunch of what looked like abandoned buildings or dilapidated brick warehouses. The street lighting was spotty, so it was dark, and Rob thought that was a good thing. The buildings were scarred with graffiti, and there was building after building with windows broken or knocked out. Neither Rob nor Manny saw anyone on the street at this hour, but that wasn't surprising. Rob watched carefully for the address and directed Manny to pull up to an abandoned, one-story brick building that hugged the Hudson River. The building wasn't easy to find without streetlights, and Rob had never been to this particular spot before. He checked his watch when they got there—four a.m.

Rob had a confident swagger that he used whenever there was a need to play the tough guy, and this was one of those times. Dressed in neatly-pressed, dark grey pants, a black shirt, and a mid-length black leather coat, Rob blended into the background of the streets, which was his goal.

Before leaving Boston, Rob had stuffed his favorite North American Arms .22 caliber handgun in his coat pocket. He hoped he wouldn't need it, but it was better to be safe than sorry. Manny also had a weapon.

The building the men were about to enter was mostly used as a chop shop for stolen cars. Graffiti dotted its outside walls, and the tangy reek of gasoline and oil wafted over the desolate area. When Rob and Manny found the door and opened it slowly, it made a creaking sound. They could hardly make out anything in the deep darkness. It was pitch-black and deadly quiet inside, and no one working on any cars at this hour.

Fear struck Rob in the gut, and he and Manny waited a minute to see if anyone would step out of the darkness.

"Shhh," Rob motioned to Manny as they listened for a sound. Then, Rob nudged Manny and whispered: "Ask if anyone is there?"

Manny obliged: "¿Hay alguien ahi?"

Nothing. And then, after about a minute . . .

"*Vien aqui*," answered a voice from the darkness.

Rob motioned to Manny to follow him, and together, they walked slowly toward the voice. As they got closer, a bright light came on, blinding the men for a moment. Rob and Manny could just make out the form of a man standing just on the other side of a car, its trunk open.

Rob took a deep breath; he hoped he was ready for whatever was about to happen.

"*Bienvenido*," the man said as he stepped toward them, extending his hand to Rob.

As the man emerged from the darkness, Rob could see that the guy was medium height and had a stocky build, with a thick neck and deep dark eyes that gave nothing away. He wore a navy, velvet pantsuit with white trim and stripes down the pants. And, like

Rob, the man let his gold jewelry show. It was hard to tell if he was packing a weapon, but Rob could only assume he was.

"Beautiful countryside, isn't it? Especially this time of night." The man had a strong accent—half Columbian, half Queens. "I'm Carlos. I'll bring you to the man you came to meet. But before we go further, take off your coats and hand them to me."

"Damn." Rob had hoped this would not happen. But there was no need to panic . . . yet.

Rob and Manny tossed their coats toward Carlos, who caught them and went through the pockets. Carlos found the weapons and took them out, holding them up with a big grin on his face.

"You think you are clever, *amigos*?" As Carlos laughed, the sound reverberated throughout the building. "Keep walking."

Rob and Manny did as Carlos asked. The sound of their shoes on the cement floor was audible; the click, click of their heels echoed throughout the building. With one hand, Carlos pointed Manny's gun at them. With the other, he held out a small flashlight to track the way ahead.

Rob's throat was dry as a bone. He needed a drink of something, but he wasn't about to ask Carlos for one. He and Manny hadn't really planned an exit if necessary—other than the standard "Run!" As he and Manny walked, Rob squinted into the blackness, looking to see if he could spot a door or any kind of exit sign, but it was way too dark.

The men reached a big, heavy metal door. Carlos tugged it open and stepped away to let Rob and Manny inside.

This room was lit from a light bulb hanging bare from the ceiling. In the center of the room was a well-dressed gentleman with dark, Ray Ban aviator sunglasses. He sat on a big black leather chair, an Uzi resting on his lap, and a big black and brown dog seated next to him. Rob thought the dog looked like a

Rottweiler.

Formal introductions were dispensed with. Carlos waved the guns so his boss could see what the men had brought with them.

"Welcome to little Columbia," the seated man said without warmth.

Rob stood there, speechless, watching and hoping that he and Manny could get the hell out of this meeting with their lives.

The dog was growling as the seated guy started to talk: "Well, here we are, Mr. Gold. You, owing me serious money for drugs you no longer have, and now you want me to sell you more drugs? How do I know you are good for it? How do you intend on making up for the lost *plata*?

Rob had played this scene over and over in his mind on the way down to New York and had prepared his answer.

"You know that I have never had anything like this happen before. I have been a reliable partner with you, haven't I? This was a set up, no question in my mind. I know that may not make any difference to you, but I need you to know that I am not playing games. I'm good for the money and will prove it to you. You sell me more cocaine, and I will take less for me so you can make up the loss on the fourteen ounces."

The man didn't answer right away, and Rob's heart rate tripled. He could literally feel his heart pounding in his chest. His weapon was taken away; this could be the end. Too bad he brought Manny down here to die with him.

The seated man finally said: "You're not getting another chance, got it? Screw this up, and your life, as well as that of your wife and daughter, will be on the line."

"I know, I know." Rob could feel his stomach turning over, and he struggled to not toss his cookies in front of this guy.

"I get it. I won't let you down again. I promise," Rob said in a pleading voice, putting his hands together in a prayer posture.

Then the guy spoke: "The only reason I am doing this is because you have always been a trusted dealer." The man then gave Carlos the order: "Show him where the product is. How much do you want this time?"

Rob didn't answer immediately; he had been trying to do that calculation while driving down. Rob was confident that he could sell whatever he got, but at the same time, he needed to be a little more careful than usual. In fact, Rob had already arranged with another friend of his to put the drugs in his garage; that would be a transaction that Manny would handle. Talk about trust.

"How about twenty ounces?" Rob asked. That way, he figured, he could make up the loss.

"*Bien,*" the man said.

Rob was a little surprised that he agreed so quickly. Maybe he should have asked for more. Too late.

Carlos motioned to follow him, and he took Rob and Manny out of the room and further into the bowels of the warehouse. He used a small flashlight to illuminate the path. There was no doubt these guys wanted to make sure Rob saw as little as possible.

They arrived at another door, which Carlos opened. Even in the darkness, Rob could see piles of plastic bags neatly stacked. He had been in this business for a long time, but he had never seen a stash this big in one place; it was something to behold. In the darkness, the whiteness of the cocaine almost glowed. The plastic bags went all the way up to a twenty-foot ceiling.

Carlos counted out twenty packets and put them in a bag. He handed the bag to Rob, and Rob passed it to Manny.

Then, Carlos grabbed Rob and put a gun to his head and held

it there for what seemed like forever, though it was likely only for a minute.

Is this how it ends, Rob thought. Carlos turned him around and forced them to head back the way they had come. Now, the warehouse seemed endless, like they were never going to get out of there.

"Scared you? Didn't I," Carlos laughed.

Rob knew that Carlos had the upper hand. He could feel his hands damp with sweat, and a few drops dripped from his forehead.

In a few minutes (or what seemed like hours), Rob and Manny were back at the front door. Carlos opened it, shoved them out, and yelled: "*Vamanos*! Get the fuck out of here! You are lucky, you know? Don't piss this away or you'll be sorry."

Rob and Manny hurried through the fog to their car. Manny turned on the ignition and got the hell out of there.

A few miles later, Rob took a deep breath and looked at Manny.

"Man, we were very lucky. But you know, we have got to sell this shit as fast as we possibly can, and I am going to count on you."

"Don't worry, man. We'll be fine. This will work out," Manny assured him.

"It had better or I'm a dead man."

As they got on the highway, Manny and Rob saw red lights flashing and sirens blaring, and Rob thought they were coming for them and this was the end. Rob slowed down and took a deep breath, then held it. The cops were behind him for a mile or so, but just as Rob thought they were going to pull him over, they sped up and passed him.

"Oh my god," Rob said.

Manny held his hands up to his heart and said: "*Gracias dios.*"

CHAPTER SEVENTEEN

Carly had a method of reporting that involved checking in regularly with her sources so she could be sure she wasn't missing anything and to find out if there was any new information she should know about. With Chris, she had decided that once a week was a good place to start. Around three p.m. on this the first Thursday in December, Carly drove down to the North End, where she knew she would find Chris and, likely, his main client these days—Rob. Carly kind of wondered whether Chris, in fact, had any other clients. It was late afternoon, and the sun was already low in the sky, and the wind was whipping off the water. Carly was snug and warm in her blue, wool, knee-length coat and beautiful multicolored scarf tied around her neck. Carly also had on tan, leather, knee-length boots with a good size heel. She looked good, Carly told herself.

Carly approached the front door, knocked on it, and opened it without waiting. As soon as she did, Carly could see Chris and Rob, sitting in Chris's office, and they, in turn, motioned for her to come in. As Carly walked down the hallway to the office, she made the decision to abstain from snorting any coke, even though they might give her a hard time about it; better to keep her wits about her and not cross that line.

Chris smiled broadly when he saw Carly. "Well, look who's here: the one and only award-winning journalist Carly Howell. How the heck are you?"

"Good, thanks for asking. Guess I don't need to ask how you are."

"Ha! No better way to relax after a hard day at the office."

Rob reached an arm out to pull Carly toward him and gave her a quick kiss on the cheek. "Found out anything new?" he asked.

Carly hesitated because she wasn't at all sure how much of what Tommy had told her she should share with Gold; it wasn't like she worked for him. Rob Gold was just part of her story. And while both Tommy and Gold might be on the same side against crooked cops, Tommy was no fan of Gold's.

"I know they are looking through all the search warrants for the past several years to see if there is a pattern with the cops. What about you two? Have you learned anything new?"

Chris' eyes glistened as he asked: "Would it surprise you to know that I learned from a cop friend of mine that several of the guys in the DCU have brand-new cars recently purchased from the same dealer? I think it might be worth paying a visit to that dealer—a Cadillac dealer on the Lynn Way—to see what we might be able to learn about how these cars were paid for."

Chris almost couldn't restrain himself about finding out about this, though Carly figured it was probably partly the cocaine talking.

"Makes sense." Carly wondered if Lieutenant James had any idea that his guys were using money that they had taken from their targets to purchase luxury cars. Maybe the lieutenant was a little too trusting, thought Carly. Or was *she*?

CHAPTER EIGHTEEN

When Carly got home, she couldn't wait to call Hank to find out if he had any idea about the cars. She also realized as she dialed his office number that her feelings for him were deepening.

"Hank, this is Carly. I have information I think you are going to want to know about. Rather than meeting at Richard's, do you want to come by my apartment when you get off from work?"

"Well, that sounds like an invitation I can't possibly refuse. See you around seven."

"Do you know where I live?"

"Hello? I am a detective after all."

Carly laughed. "Right. Of course."

As soon as she got off the phone, Carly walked over to the kitchen and looked in the refrigerator to see what she had and what she might need to entertain Hank. She needed to get some snacks and some tonic water for the drink of choice. Carly rushed out and walked down Newbury Street to DeLuca's and got some cheese and crackers and tonic water. As soon as she got home, Carly took off what she was wearing and put on a new outfit: a pair of black, wool bell-bottoms and a sweater that accented her figure.

With everything ready, Carly put out the hors d'oeuvres, refreshed her makeup, and sat down on her couch, then put on her favorite music—the Temptations—on the record player and sat back and let herself relax just for a few minutes.

At seven on the dot, the doorbell rang. Carly buzzed Lieutenant James in. There he was, standing on her landing, one hand on the door frame, the other on his hip.

"Well, hello." Carly smiled and ushered Lieutenant James inside. He quickly removed his coat, then his holster and gun, placing them on a nearby chair. James then took Carly by the waist and pulled her close and gave her a kiss on the lips.

"Let me give you a quick tour," Carly said as she walked James across her living room, with its chartreuse, wall-to-wall carpet, and pointed out the floor-length windows to the aboveground swimming pool in the alley that was visible from her living room. Given the season, the pool was drained and empty.

"My landlord likes to rent to cops and stewardesses. Makes for some lively gatherings with beer on tap." Carly would occasionally partake in the party-like atmosphere beside the pool. Not too many apartments in the Back Bay, or anywhere else in the city, had such a perk. And the rent was reasonable. The apartment had a large living room/dining room with a fireplace, a small kitchen and bath, and one bedroom; it was compact and efficient.

Carly invited Hank to sit on the couch facing the fireplace and offered him the *hors d'oeuvres.* He declined but was all in on a vodka and tonic. Carly realized she had never seen Hank eat anything.

"Can we talk about the case first, if that's okay with you?" Carly asked.

"Okay, though I don't know that there's much more I can tell you."

Carly drew close and turned toward Hank, looking straight into his baby blues. Suddenly, she had the upper hand and was feeling confident. "Did you know that three of your men recently bought fancy Cadillacs from the same car dealer in Lynn?"

Shocked at Carly's words, Hank shook his head. Carly realized that he also looked a bit pissed off.

"I'm impressed by your tenacity," Hank said.

"Thanks. Coming from you, that's a real compliment."

Hank looked at Carly with those electric blue eyes and swung his arm over her shoulder, and she let him.

"I take it we're done with business?" Hank smiled, leaned in, and gave Carly a quick kiss that she didn't resist.

First, Rob Gold had paid Carly a visit, now it was Hank. Anything for a good story, Carly told herself...but knew it was about much more than that. After a really bad relationship she had while in college with a guy who was verbally abusive, Carly was more than a little reluctant to commit to a long-term relationship with another man. She hated the confrontation that her last relationship had resulted in. Carly had kept the incident to herself and hadn't shared it with anyone but her old college roommate. But married men, somehow, felt a little safer...or so Carly had convinced herself.

The first kiss led to a longer, more intense one. Carly felt herself letting go. He can kiss, she thought to herself as she took in Hank's tongue and danced around it with her mouth. Hank pulled Carly closer, and she let his hand go under her sweater to find her breasts. Hank was a smooth operator.

Carly moaned and fought to regain control. "What about your wife?"

Hank lurched back. "Why bring her up? I'm here now, aren't I? Do you really want or need to know more?" The deep bass of his voice was seductive.

Hank had gotten Carly excited. Her crotch was tingling, and

she reached for Hank's zipper and unzipped his pants, then she reached her hand in and pulled out his dick. Carly slid down Hank's torso and brought him into her mouth, then moved up and down. It didn't take long for Carly to massage Hank to an orgasm.

Hank let go with a "Yes! Yes! Yes," then lay back with a big sigh.

Hank reached for Carly's crotch, and he was ready to pull down her pants when Carly took his hand and moved it away. She had decided that, while she was turned on by the lieutenant, she couldn't let him screw her; that was a line too far.

"Maybe at another time, but not tonight," Carly said. Hank then abruptly stood up.

"Thanks," Hank grinned. "You turn me on for sure." Carly was turned on too, but she was satisfied that she had resisted the temptation.

Hank made a quick stop in the bathroom and then headed for the door. On his way out, he gulped down what was left of his vodka and tonic, picked up his gun, and was ready to go.

"Thanks for the tip. I will check into the car dealership," Hank said.

"Next time, we can compare notes." Hank gave Carly a kiss on the cheek and then opened the door and was gone.

Once Hank left and Carly was tidying up, she couldn't help thinking how crazy this all was. Lieutenant Henry James was letting himself be seduced by a reporter trying to find out whether one of his men was crooked. He didn't think anything of it, apparently, and Carly was letting all this happen too. Her adrenaline was free-flowing. Carly acknowledged that this story was more exciting and intriguing than any story she'd ever worked on before.

CHAPTER NINETEEN

Tommy Blake knew from various informants that he'd spoken to in the corruption case against Cross that the Rob Gold shakedown had, by no means, been an isolated case. It was almost a given that, where there were drug dealers with wads of cash and little incentive to rat out crooked cops, the latter were eager to take whatever they could from their prey.

Being the diligent prosecutor that he was, Tommy couldn't just look the other way. After considering the idea for a long time and not discussing it with his boss, who likely would have nixed the idea, he quietly began to set in motion an idea he had developed of how he might catch one of the other members of the Drug Control Unit in the act of being on the wrong side of the law.

Because he had to bypass the Boston Police Department, Tommy turned to the FBI, which led him to one Bill Cole, who'd led the FBI in Boston for more than a decade. Though Tommy had never met him before, he set up a meeting with Cole to lay out what he had learned and what he wanted to do. Tommy hoped the FBI would partner with him in this effort.

Tommy arranged to meet Cole, who was eager for the meeting the next night, in the North End at a restaurant Cole suggested—Roman's—in Creek Square. The restaurant sat on a narrow corner of cobblestone streets and brick buildings tucked closely together. When Tommy walked in the restaurant and told the host whom he was meeting, he was led into a back room with one guy, whom he assumed was Cole, sitting alone at a table.

"I hope this is a hidden enough spot for you," Cole said.

"Yes, thanks," Tommy said.

As soon as he sat down, a waitress came over, and Tommy ordered a cappuccino, then wasted no time in telling Cole what was happening. Cole was familiar with the Cross case. "I've been following this closely. It's not every day that a convicted drug dealer has the balls to go after a cop," he said.

"But the whole point is, Cross is not the only cop who is using his position to steal from his targets. I have gotten tips from other dealers that the cops are often on the take themselves and using drug busts to steal," Tommy told Cole. "I am hoping that, if we can catch one or two more of these guys in the act, it would be a way of shining a light on the corruption that could convince the powers that be that there needs to be some serious house cleaning done at the police department."

Cole was not surprised by Tommy's statements. "We get tips all the time about these guys," he said. "But we've never really been able to catch any of them, so yes, a sting might be a way of catching one of them in the act." Cole took a long sip of coffee, then continued: "By the way, you might want to order a cannolli. They make the best."

Tommy took Cole up on the suggestion and ordered two, one for each of them. "Do you have any detectives in particular that you think we might start with?" Cole asked. "Anyone you've heard mentioned in talking to your informants?"

Tommy suggested they might start by targeting a detective whose moniker came up most often among informants—Bobby O'Rourke. Local drug dealers had given Detective O'Rourke the nickname "The Thief." He was the kind of cop who gave cops a bad name.

"I've got informants left and right telling me how bad these guys are," said Tommy. "And this O'Rourke guy is at the top of their list."

"Okay. I see where you're going. What's the game plan?"

"I have an informant—a known drug dealer; his name is Jimmy Leonard. I've been talking to him ever since I got the case, and I think he can be trusted on this front. We can give him enough cocaine and cash to entice O'Rourke. Leonard will let O'Rourke know when a deal is going to go down, and we'll be there in an unmarked car—nearby, but close enough to see the deal when it happens. When we know that the money has changed hands, we swoop in and corner O'Rourke. Make sense?"

"That's good, Tom, especially for someone who doesn't usually do this sort of thing. There is no guarantee, of course, that the money will change hands, so we just have to go into it with a healthy dose of might *or might not* happen. You okay with that?"

"Sure. I get it. I know I'm a little overexcited about this. You're right to inject a cautionary note into the picture."

"And how much do you trust your source?"

"I don't think he would put his own situation in danger by making this up, but we'll see. We're not exactly dealing with upright citizens."

"Great. Thanks. Fingers crossed."

CHAPTER TWENTY

Cole and Tommy didn't have to wait long. Within the week, Tommy received a call from his snitch, and he immediately called Cole.

"It's happening tonight," Tommy said, sounding nervous. "A deal's going down in East Boston, along the harbor, on East Pier Drive. It's set for three a.m. Leonard says O'Rourke will be there. It's like a dead zone down there at night. No one is ever around. There should be about a kilo of cocaine and about one hundred thousand dollars changing hands. Our man will be there with his gun drawn and his hands out."

Tommy felt his heart pounding in his chest; the bust was really happening. "I've got to notify people on my end, but we'll be there down the block, waiting. What kind of car will the drug dealer be driving? Do you know?"

"Black Buick Rivera convertible with white wall tires."

"Thanks," Tommy said.

Tommy then decided to phone Carly to let her know. "Get your hands on a camera and head down to East Boston, East Pier Drive, at around one or two a.m. We'll be in a dark grey Chevy Malibu. The dealer will have a black Buick sedan. At that time of night, there shouldn't be too many cars. But stay out of sight. The deal is supposed to go down around three."

Carly was extremely surprised that Tommy was involving her. "I can't thank you enough," she told him over the phone, sounding almost as excited as he was.

"Don't thank me yet," Tommy said.

Carly could feel herself getting really excited, and her stomach started to get a little upset.

She hung up the phone and went into Jim's office for some advice.

"Do you think there's any chance in hell we could get a cameraman to volunteer to do this in the middle of the night?"

"Sure. These guys are available. You never know when there's going to be a fire or a murder. I am sure if you talk to a couple of them, you will find one who will want to be part of this story. Who do you have the best relationship with?"

Carly thought a moment, then it clicked. "Larry Sanders. He's been great to work with; very helpful and supportive. He gets how I work, and I think he might be up for this."

Carly headed down to the assignment desk to try to find Larry, but he was out on an assignment, supposed to be back in an hour. It was only four p.m., so there was still plenty of time. Carly kept her fingers crossed.

While anxiously waiting for Larry's return to the station, Carly couldn't concentrate on anything else and found herself idly watching the TV screens in the newsroom, which, at this hour, had mostly soap operas on. Carly never could understand the draw of soaps.

Finally, after what seemed like forever, Larry walked back into the newsroom, camera under his arm. Carly rushed over to him and ushered him to a private corner, then gave him the background and the details of the criminal deal that was supposed to go down.

"Count me in," Larry said, giving Carly a thumbs-up.

Carly was jazzed. She had never seen a drug deal happen in real time, so she understood what Tommy had been feeling—that rush of adrenaline.

At around six o'clock, Carly left the station and went back to her apartment for a few hours of sleep, as if that were even possible. Finally, she gave up. Sitting on the couch, Carly looked out at the alley, with the backs of the brick townhouses facing her. It was peaceful and quiet outside, and Carly thought about her father and how he had set up and carried out scores of stings during his career. She wondered whether it eventually became routine or whether it was always an adrenaline high? Carly also thought about all the things that could go wrong and how this would be the most dangerous situation she had ever gotten into on a story.

Carly turned on the television. It was nine p.m. on a Monday, and luckily for her, *Lou Grant* was on—the TV show about a television newsroom. She watched just long enough to start dozing off, but there really wasn't enough time for sleep now, so Carly lay there, anxious for the alarm to go off. She took a quick shower and put on her black, wool coat with a red, plaid scarf and went downstairs and waited in the small lobby till she saw Larry's car pull up in front of her apartment. Carly got into the passenger seat and noticed that Larry had a large thermos and cups.

"If that is coffee, thanks for that," Carly said.

"We will probably be very glad we have it," Larry said.

At one a.m., it was pitch-black in East Boston. It was the middle of December, and the temperature was twenty degrees with the wind blowing off the water. Carly could hear the lapping of the Boston Harbor on the shore and, as she sat in the car with Larry, a mist blew in, making it harder to see anything clearly. And then the wind picked up, audibly whipping along the shore, even with the car windows rolled up; it made Carly shiver.

A large portion of the East Boston neighborhood had been demolished to make way for the expansion of Logan Airport. Local residents had resisted but ultimately couldn't stop it. That left swaths of the area abandoned; the perfect place for a drug deal!

Unlike most other neighborhoods, the number of streetlights was minimal. Carly and Larry had turned off all the lights in the car, and with no motor running, it was getting cold inside. They had brought blankets—Larry's idea—and they had the thermos of hot coffee; *thank goodness*, Carly thought.

Suddenly, after what seemed an eternity, a black Buick sedan approached. Carly and Larry both ducked as the car cruised by. Carly's heart was beating so fast that she was afraid it was going to burst.

After the Buick passed, it pulled over about a block away— well within sight.

"Larry, are you ready?"

The question, though whispered, sounded outrageously loud to Carly as she spoke. "The camera's ready to go. I just hope we're close enough to be able to get a halfway decent shot. It may not be the clearest video ever, but I think we'll get what you need." They had to hope that Tommy and the FBI were ready, too. While Leonard had told Tommy the make and color of the drug dealer's car, Carly and Larry had no idea what car O'Rourke would be driving.; it didn't take them long to find out.

They spotted the approach of a new model, silver-grey Caddy. *Of course, it's probably one of the Caddies that the DCU folks recently bought*, Carly thought. The Caddy passed close by them, and Larry ducked, motioning for Carly to do the same. Larry raised his camera and recorded the scene as Carly peeked over the dashboard.

The silver car pulled up next to the black car. Its driver—built like a fullback—got out, his gun drawn. Next, they recognized Boston police officer Bobby O'Rourke exiting the vehicle too. A short runt of a guy, O'Rourke also had his gun drawn.

Carly couldn't make out any of the back and forth, but she could see bags of cocaine being transferred from one car to the other. Then, one of the guys emerged from the black sedan and walked over to O'Rourke—Larry and Carly could see it as if it were daylight—and passed an envelope to him. The whiteness of the envelope glowed like neon in the night gloom.

Sirens wailed and lights flashed as the authorities rushed in with two unmarked cars.

FBI Agent Cole jumped out of his car, aiming his revolver at Officer O'Rourke and shouting at him to drop the envelope. O'Rourke did as he was told.

Carly could hardly contain her excitement. "Holy shit! Did you see that? That's amazing. It's like we're in some movie."

Larry was grinning ear to ear without halting his filming. "I just love it when things happen as they are supposed to. You owe Tommy Blake big time."

"You're so right." Carly couldn't wait to get back to the station and review the footage.

CHAPTER TWENTY-ONE

Tommy sat in the car, frozen to his seat; he was blown away. "Damn, it worked," Tommy said to himself. He had actually managed to pull this bust off. A Boston undercover drug cop had been nabbed in a drug sting under his direction; they had O'Rourke cold.

Cole shoved O'Rourke against the car with an audible thud. Talk about turning the tables: this was one guy who could not complain about police brutality. Now, two Boston cops had been observed on the take, proving Tommy's informants were right.

Tommy would have to tell his boss about the night's events ASAP. D.A. Callahan was unlikely to be happy about what had just happened, but the evidence was there, and Carly should have the video; there was no denying O'Rourke's wrongdoing.

Within a few minutes, a few Boston Police cars—sirens blaring—pulled up next to the car O'Rourke was laid out against; they were not part of the DCU. They cuffed him and put O'Rourke in the back of one of the squad cars. Cole had a conversation with the cops that Tommy couldn't hear, then they took off to police headquarters to book O'Rourke.

Cole returned to the car and gave Tommy a high five. "Nice work, kid. I give you credit. This took guts to plan, especially since this isn't really your line of work."

"Thanks, Bill. I knew I was taking a chance, but I just felt in my gut that these informants weren't making this shit up. There are more of these bad cops, you know."

"If you say so. I guess it wouldn't surprise me in the least."

"Now what are you going to do? Obviously, with Channel 8 having been here, there is no way of keeping this quiet; it's going to blow up."

Carly and Larry were headed back to the station. "This is getting better all the time," Carly said.

"No shit. I am glad you asked me to take this assignment. We should try to get this on the air for the morning news." Larry picked up his pager and dialed the assignment desk to alert them to the story.

It was five a.m. when Carly and Larry got back to the newsroom, and other than one guy on the assignment desk who was listening to the police scanner, the newsroom was pretty dead. There were no editors to edit the film. Carly had to be patient—no easy feat; patience had never been one of her strong suits.

"When do any of the editors get in?" Carly asked Phil at the assignment desk.

"Not 'til about six o'clock. Can you wait?"

"Hardly." But Carly knew that had no choice. She started writing the script, knowing that the package would lead the news, and she would be sure to highlight the fact that Channel 8 was the only station there for the sting.

When Carly finished her work, she was exhausted; she needed to get some sleep. She left the station around seven a.m. and headed home for a few hours of sleep. As she unlocked her apartment's front door, her phone was ringing. Carly rushed to answer.

"Carly, it's Tommy. That was pretty fucking exciting, wasn't it?"

"I still can't quite believe our luck with all of it," Carly said. "You took a real chance, and you deserve a raise, I think."

"Somehow I don't think that will happen. My boss is not going to be happy about this, though I knew that going in. But what could I do? Knowing all the bad stuff happening out there and not doing anything about it is just wrong. How long can you hold the story before it airs?"

"It will go on soon. What are you asking?"

"I haven't told Callahan yet, and he is going to be really pissed off to see this first on the news."

"You've got a few minutes. Can you tell him now?"

"I've been trying."

Carly imagined Lieutenant James was also going to be exceedingly pissed about this story getting out, but she couldn't do anything to stop it—and she didn't want to.

The story aired at eight a.m., with a big banner headline across the screen: WBRN Exclusive.

Carly loved seeing that banner; it was bound to get people watching and talking. From her couch, she toasted herself with a big glass of orange juice.

The phone rang again, and Carly had a pretty good idea as to who was on the other end.

"What the fuck!" shouted Hank. "How could you do this behind my back? Do you have any idea what this will mean to me and my career?"

"I truly wish I had been able to tell you ahead of time, but I couldn't. You have tounderstand."

"Understand what? There's not a lot to understand. Whoever ordered this thing thought it was okay to do a drug raid without letting the Drug Control Unit know—and you were part of it. And we're not talking just anyone here; it's me. Hello?"

"I wasn't calling the shots."

"Who was, exactly?"

He'd find out soon enough anyway, so Carly told Hank: "It was Tommy Blake in the District Attorney's office, working with the FBI."

"This is making me look really bad."

Carly had sympathy for Hank. She believed Lieutenant James was an honest cop, but it was obvious that his unit was full of bad actors, and now that was out there for all the world to see.

CHAPTER TWENTY-TWO

Tommy knew he was in for a difficult conversation with his boss. On the surface, the sting and the arrest made the DA's office look good, but behind the scenes, District Attorney Sean Callahan would, no doubt, feel blindsided, given how close he was with the police brass.

As soon as he got to the office, Tommy went straight to the DA's office. Callahan's secretary, Mary, was sitting out in front of his office.

"Mary, I need to talk to the boss ASAP. What's his mood today?"

"It's early, but I've already heard him yelling at folks on the phone. Let me go tell him you're here. Can I ask you what the topic is?"

"It's about a sting that happened last night that I had something to do with.

"Wait here. I'll be right back." Mary knocked on her boss's door, then went in and closed the door behind her. She was there for about five minutes before she came out.

"He says you can go in. Good luck."

"Thanks, Mary; I expect I'll need it."

Callahan was a big man. He stood about six feet tall with a sturdy build, and he had that Irish look: rosy cheeks, blue eyes, and premature white hair. A heavy Boston accent declared to all that

Callahan was born and raised in this town. He favored suspenders and bold ties. Callahan served his time in the trenches and had worked his way up the ladder.

Callahan graduated from Suffolk Law School—where locals went to make their mark—and had a wide network of lawyers who found him interesting and always a hoot at fundraisers and get togethers. He had a good sense of humor when his mood allowed it, but today would not be one of those days.

Tommy took a seat; he was well prepared. Callahan's reaction was swift and exactly what he'd expected.

"You went behind my back. Who's running this office anyway: some young punk lawyer or me, the guy who was duly elected by the citizens of Boston to do the job? And who the fuck told Channel 8?"

"Sir, I had to do it this way. And there is clearly a pattern of abuse and wrongdoing by some members of the Drug Control Unit. You know that as well as I do. And I let Channel 8 know because I wanted there to be a record of the sting and the results."

"Who gave you the authority? This isn't going to go down well at City Hall. You know that, don't you? Did you consider the ramifications?"

"More than anything else. I was focused on making sure the sting had the desired outcome."

"I'd call it a definite overreach. Get the hell out of my office. I don't want to see your face," Callahan said.

"Yes, sir." Tommy took his papers and turned to the door, opened it quickly, and left without a look back at Mary. His heart was pounding out of his shirt as he made his way down the hallway to his office. Once there, even though the space was anything but private, Tommy picked up the phone to call Carly.

"Carly, it's Tommy. Can we talk off-the-record on background?"

"Of course. What's up?"

"Well, maybe not surprisingly, my boss is pissed as hell about all of this."

"You can't be surprised by his reaction, can you? I spoke to Hank James earlier, and you think your boss is pissed? James is furious. But the fact remains: this criminal behavior was going on under his watch. I guess there is no way we were going to make a lot of friends. But you have to keep your eye on the prize. At the end of the day, we caught a bad cop."

"You're right, of course," Tommy sighed.

"If Callahan were smart, he would grab this situation by the horns and make the most out of it. His office catching a bad cop red-handed? He should hold a press conference," Carly said.

"Now that's a good idea," Tommy said. "I am guessing you'll cover a press conference if it happens?"

Carly laughed. "Lights. Camera. Action."

Tommy thought a bit about where things stood and decided he couldn't just let this bust get swept under the rug. He had too much on the line: he had exposed a bad cop, and the residents of the city deserved to know about that. So, while he couldn't talk to the District Attorney about it, Tommy decided to go to his immediate boss: Dan McGill, who was as straight an arrow as you could find. Tommy had a good relationship with McGill and hoped he could make his case and let Dan then persuade the DA.

Tommy knocked on Dan's door and heard: "Come in."

Because of his elevated status within the office, McGill had an office to himself, with a window looking out onto the street. He also had an old wooden desk that looked like it had been in that spot for a long time. The desk was relatively clear of random papers. Dan was also a crisp dresser—with a starched blue, button-down shirt, dark suit pants, and a red striped tie. His head of red hair was neatly parted and combed.

Dan was widely admired. He could spar with the best of them and find just the rightquestion to ask at trial, getting to the heart of a crime. There was no doubt as to why Dan was the number two guy in the office.

"Dan, I really need to talk to you about this sting and what I think would be in our best interest as a department. I know the boss doesn't want to hear from me, and I get that. So, I'm hoping that you'll hear me out."

"Sure. By the way, while I don't condone going behind the DA's back, the sting was an impressive operation, and I commend you for pulling it off."

Tommy let himself breathe for the first time in what felt like days, then said: "I think that the best thing we can do is to urge Callahan to hold a press conference and make an example of Bobby O'Rourke and emphatically state that this will simply not be tolerated in Boston. He doesn't have to like it, but it will make him look good...and the mayor, for that matter. I also think the mayor should be at the press conference."

"If this were up to me, I'd agree with you. But I am not sure I can convince Callahan of this. He's got to protect his relationship with the police department, and this sting does not help that in any way, shape, or form. But I'll try. That's all I can do."

"Just so you know, there are a couple of other cops in the Drug Control Unit who I think are on the wrong side of the law. Can I go after them?"

"I will need to get the thumbs-up from the DA, which isn't going to be easy. Hopefully, if nothing else, he might see how this could help him in his upcoming re-election campaign. Always better to be seen fighting wrongdoing wherever it is."

"Thanks for hearing me out."

"You're welcome."

Tommy headed back to his office, sat down, and stared straight ahead. His head was swirling, and he couldn't even focus on the last forty-eight hours and all that had happened.

All Tommy could do was wait and see what would happen. There was no way he could focus on any other case he had before him, and there were many. After about an hour of rearranging papers and staring out into the abyss, Tommy got a call from McGill. He took a few deep breaths and said a few Hail Marys and walked down the hall and around the corner to McGill's office.

"Please sit down," McGill said. "You already know how pissed off our boss is, don't you? Well, multiply that by about a thousand! I have never, frankly, seen him like this. He was practically foaming at the mouth. After I got him to calm down, though, I convinced him that he needed to look at this from the public's perspective—he nabbed a bad cop in the act. And I presented the idea of having a press conference with the mayor. He was skeptical that he could convince the mayor but asked for a few hours to mull it over. Perhaps not surprisingly, he is also furious about Channel 8 being there. But you know that already, don't you? And while I don't condone giving the media this information, that ship has sailed, and he needed to know that because he needs to look like he is in charge and presenting this as a win for the people of the city. He asked for an hour to think it all through."

Within less than an hour, Tommy's phone rang. It was McGill again: "Tomorrow at eleven a.m., The DA, the Mayor, and, yes, the Police Commissioner will all be at a press conference at City Hall to formally announce the arrest and take questions. If you thought our boss was angry, that's nothing compared to how the mayor reacted. But he realized that, either you can be on the right side or the wrong side of this situation, and he is not about to be seen as being complicit with corruption."

Tommy was relieved. Even though he was in the doghouse with the DA, he picked up the phone and called Carly.

"You're going to be happy about this—the Mayor, Police Commissioner, and DA are going to be together at a press conference tomorrow at eleven at City Hall to announce the arrest and answer questions. You're the first to get the call. I assume you will be there."

Carly laughed out loud. "You could put money down on that."

CHAPTER TWENTY-THREE

Carly was aware that the sting would probably change her relationship with Hank—at the very least, in the short-term. She decided to let it ride out and not provoke him by calling. Carly also decided to forego her visits to Richard's for a while and to go back to enjoying her friends and her life before this story began.

Carly's circle of friends had been trying to get her to hang with them, and some of her closest friends had even been a little worried and nervous about the story she'd been working on. Carly had given them a taste of what the story was about, and now they'd also seen the coverage on TV.

There were a couple of disco clubs and bars that Carly frequented. She loved to dance, and guys liked watching her; it was a good way to put herself out there. Carly was pretty sure her friend Rhonda from work, who liked dancing almost as much as she did, was a good bet to accompany her clubbing that evening.

"Hey there, Rhonda! Any chance you are free tonight and feel like a little dancing? It's been a while and I am dying to get on the dance floor," Carly said.

"On a work night?" Then, after a momentary pause, Rhonda answered: "Okay, what the heck. Just as long as we are not going to stay out too late."

"Great! Let's meet up at 15 Lansdowne."

"Okay. See you around nine."

Now, there was the all-important choice of what to wear. Carly rummaged through her closet and drawers and decided on a dressy pair of black bell-bottoms that hugged her waist and a flowery blouse with yellows and reds. Carly put a black belt on to accentuate her waist and spent time on her hair and makeup, then she was out the door.

It was the end of December, and it was cold in Boston. Carly grabbed her coat and gloves and headed out onto Commonwealth Avenue and walked the few short blocks to the disco at 15 Lansdowne, where she and Rhonda had agreed to meet. There was a little snow along the sidewalks after a couple of small snowstorms, nothing like last year's "Blizzard of '78" that dumped two feet on the Commonwealth and shut down the state.

Lansdowne Street backed up to Fenway Park. It was a Thursday, and there was a line waiting to get into the club. Carly loved Rhonda's sense of adventure and her sense of humor. The two women could spend hours finding things to laugh about, and Carly needed that. Rhonda was also a great dancer and loved the dance floor almost as much as Carly. There was something about dancing that Carly couldn't resist; it was a chance to let go and groove to the music. She knew, too, that guys liked to watch and join in.

When they got to the disco, Carly and Rhonda checked their coats and looked around, the lights swirling from the ceiling and the music rocking the place with *Love to Love You Baby*. This club was always a fun place, and even on a weeknight, the crowd was growing and raucous.

The two friends walked up to the bar, which extended almost the length of the room, and ordered drinks—Rhonda had a gin and tonic, and Carly kept to her vodka and tonic, thinking momentarily of Hank; that drink might forever be identified in her mind with him.

Carly scanned the room and spotted a good-looking black guy with a light blue shirt worn tight enough to accent his toned middle and black pants. He stood about five eleven with a well-coiffed afro; he definitely stood out.

Carly glanced in the man's direction, and when she caught his eye, she took the first step: lifting up her drink to toast him. He saw the move and picked up his drink and sauntered over to Carly.

"I'm Frank Upton. Nice to meet you." Carly looked straight into Frank's dark brown eyes.

"I'm Carly. I haven't seen you here before. I know this will sound ridiculous, but do you come here often?"

"Ha! Good one. No. Not really. This end of town isn't always the friendliest to my skin color, but I thought I would take a chance. I've heard a lot about the place. So far, so good." Frank gave Carly a big smile that she couldn't resist.

As the music stirred Carly's need to dance, Frank moved right in and offered her his hand. They took to the dance floor, with Michael Jackson's *Don't Stop 'Til You Get Enough* giving the two of them just the right beat to let it all out. The dance floor was crowded, and the room was dark, with light effects adding to that pulsating disco mood.

When the music ended, Carly and Frank lingered on the dance floor.

"That was great," Carly said, overjoyed at feeling so free in being able to let go and move to the music with a good-looking guy. She couldn't really ask for a more perfect break from the story and all the pressure that had been building up inside her. "I'm up for another," Carly told Frank.

"Me too!"

Frank and Carly stayed on the dance floor for three more songs, and the chemistry between them became palpable; Carly was loving it. But then, Carly realized that she had lost track of Rhonda. Scanning the dance floor, Carly spotted Rhonda across the floor, dancing with a tall, thin guy. Carly was relieved, knowing her friend was enjoying the evening just as much as she was.

"Let's take a break," Carly's said, her voice barely audible above the music. Frank nodded, and they walked together back over to the bar.

"What can I get you to drink?" Frank asked.

"Thanks! I'll have a vodka and tonic."

"Make that two vodka and tonics." Frank did the ordering and paid for the drinks, which was a welcome surprise. Carly was always ready to pay her fair share, especially with someone she had just met.

Frank started the conversation: "May I ask what you do?"

"I am an investigative reporter at Channel 8."

"Really? Well, that's impressive. I kind of thought that, maybe, you were a lawyer or something."

"Why? Do I look that stiff?" Carly laughed, and Frank smiled. "And you? What do you do?"

"I work for the City of Boston in the Department of Neighborhood Development. I've only been there for about a year. I came up from New York, where I was doing similar work for City Hall. Can I ask what you are working on?"

"You can," Carly smiled. "But if I tell you, I will have to kill you."

Frank and Carly laughed and enjoyed the conversation, then danced well into the night. Carly could feel herself slightly buzzed by the end of it.

Carly and Frank went outside for some fresh air, a relief from the smoky bar they'd been in for several hours. Carly took a deep breath and looked up at the night sky, with the stars and the moon shining down. She also saw the nearby Citgo sign flashing its lights, a beacon in the Boston skyline.

Carly turned to Frank. "I really enjoyed that."

Frank took Carly's hands and looked into her eyes. "You are a great dancer and really fun to talk to—not an easy combination to find."

"Thanks," Carly said, wondering what his next move would be.

"Can I call you?" Frank asked.

"Absolutely."

"Let's do this again soon, okay?"

"Sure." After Carly wrote her phone number on a piece of paper from her notebook and gave it to him, Frank pulled her closer, then leaned down and kissed her lips. Carly let the kiss go on until their tongues were touching.

Frank and Carly stayed there, kissing for what seemed like a long time. She felt a tingling throughout her body. Then, Frank stopped, smiled, and said: "We will do this again soon. I am sure of that and can't wait."

"Call me, for sure," Carly said.

After going back inside to say good night to Rhonda, Carly walked back along Commonwealth Avenue, taking in the brisk, cool air, the night sky, and a wonderful feeling of anticipation. When she got home and took off her coat and clothes and put on a nightgown, Carly sank into her couch. She wondered if she was having way too good a time with the various men in her life without having to make a commitment to any one of them...kind of like what a guy usually gets to do.

Carly had no regrets. She had strong feelings for Hank but knew it couldn't go anywhere; he was married. Carly was attracted to Frank and hoped they'd go out on an actual date. She was feeling pretty damn good about herself.

CHAPTER TWENTY-FOUR

The room outside the mayor's office was packed with reporters. Windows on one side looked out toward Faneuil Hall; it was a spare room. There was a podium at the far end of the room closest to the mayor's office, and chairs were set up in three rows, and there were risers for the cameras. This room was where the mayor usually held his press conferences. Carly had arrived early to stake out the best spot. Her cameraman, Larry, was right there beside her. This was their time to shine, and other reporters came up to Carly and congratulated her on the story.

Mayor Christopher Black was not at all happy to have to be doing this press conference, Tommy had told Carly as much. But she knew that he had no choice. Now was the time to put on a show, taking credit for exposing a bad cop while acknowledging the good work that the vast majority of cops do every day. Yeah, yeah, yeah—Carly had heard it all before and knew what was coming, but she had the advantage of knowing what had been behind this scandalous and sensational bust.

Even her competitors at Channels 4, 5, and 7, as well as at *The Boston Globe,* had given Carly kudos for the story. As she walked in the room, *Boston Globe* investigative reporter Bob Mooney gave her a thumbs-up.

"Thanks," Carly said, smiling. "We got lucky."

There was a buzz among the standing room only crowd room

as they waited for the mayor and his entourage to make their entrance. The podium was stacked with microphones. Following the mayor as he emerged from his office was Bill Cole of the FBI, then came the Police Commissioner, and last was DA Callahan.

"Good afternoon and thanks for coming today," the mayor began. "As you all know by now, yesterday, one of the detectives of the Boston Police Department was caught taking cash during a drug raid in East Boston. It was the work of an assistant district attorney, Tommy Blake—working with the Federal Bureau of Investigation—that led to this bust and to the arrest. I think all of us who have watched the Channel 8 video are shocked and saddened by this turn of events. Any time there is wrongdoing by a member of the police force charged with enforcing the law, it is deeply disturbing. I want to make one thing clear: we will prosecute this case to the fullest extent of the law, and for that, we can thank our District Attorney. Detective O'Rourke has been put on administrative leave without pay."

Carly realized that was news she had not known about before this press conference.

"But I also want to be clear that the vast, vast majority of those committed law enforcement individuals working for our police department are good and honorable men and women; they deserve our respect and support. This case will proceed as any other would. The District Attorney will name a prosecutor, and the case will wind its way through the court system."

The mayor stepped away from the podium, and District Attorney Callahan stepped forward.

"Good afternoon. My office is already working with the FBI and the Boston Police Department to further investigate the case and develop the facts and evidence necessary to prosecute this case; it will be no different than any other. I can assure you that we will bring in any expertise we do not have in-house to ensure that we have what we need. Dan McGill, my deputy, will oversee the prosecution."

Next up was Bill Cole from the FBI:

"Good afternoon. As the mayor said, it was our office that worked with the District Attorney's office to set up the sting operation; we are satisfied that it achieved its purpose. We have pledged our full cooperation with the District Attorney's Office, and we will follow through with that. This case is not about one law enforcement office versus another. This is about rooting out the wrongdoing and prosecuting those who would rather line their own pockets than uphold the law and maintain the honesty and code of conduct that is a hallmark of each and every member of law enforcement."

"I can also tell you that, since this bust and arrest, we have been flooded with calls about other cops stealing from their targets. We are investigating each and every one of these calls, and you can expect further arrests in the not too distant future."

Whoa, Carly thought. This was big news, and it might even be the lede of her story.

Finally, the Police Commissioner stepped to the podium: "The Boston Police Department is comprised of men and women who believe in justice, who put their lives on the line to help their community, and who believe in upholding the law. That is why it is shocking and extremely disappointing to have one of our own allegedly caught in the act of stealing. I can tell you on a personal level that it struck at my very core when I learned of this arrest. There is no excuse, and the Police Department is committed to doing whatever we have to do to ensure that this is an isolated incident."

The mayor stepped back in front of the microphones. "We have time for a few questions. Let me first recognize Carly Howell of Channel 8, who broke the story."

All eyes turned toward Carly. "Thank you, Mr. Mayor. I would like to ask you how surprised you were to learn of this arrest and whether you think this is an isolated incident?"

"Carly, was I surprised? You bet I was. In every police department, there are likely a few bad apples...but I expected Boston to be different; it's not. And whether I was shocked or surprised does not matter now. Our job—all of our jobs—is to get to the bottom of this and to root out the corruption. I know that the Police Commissioner and I are both committed to this mission. Any other questions?"

A reporter from a competing television station—WBZ, Channel 4—stepped forward. "Will anyone else lose their job because of this arrest?"

"It is too early to be able to answer that question. The first thing we have to do as a city is take a hard look at the Drug Control Unit and how it is run, and that may lead to others. We just don't know."

Then a reporter for the *Boston Globe*, Bill Lerman, got the next question. "My question is directed to the Commissioner. Had there been any complaints leveled against Officer O'Rourke before the arrest?"

"I hope you understand that, for privacy reasons, I cannot publicly discuss personel questions."

The mayor stepped back to the microphone. "Thank you. That will conclude this press conference. If there are additional questions, please contact the press office, and they will be glad to help you. Good afternoon."

Carly decided to use Bill Cole's remarks about potential further arrests as the lede to her story set for six o'clock. Despite qualms over Hank and his hurt feelings, Carly was feeling pretty good about what she had done, and she and Larry packed up and headed back to the station.

"We make a damn good team, Larry. I couldn't have done this without you."

As she and Larry drove back to the station, Carly played the press conference back in her mind, and having decided on Bill Cole's quote, she knew she had her lead. For Carly, it was always about the lede. Ever since she was a newspaper reporter, she had loved writing a good lede. After figuring out a good lede, the rest of the story kind of wrote itself.

CHAPTER TWENTY-FIVE

Back at the station, Carly called Chris Kelly.

"Hey there, Carly. Where've you been? We miss you. Why don't you come by for a little pick-me-up?"

"Thanks. Do you know what's been happening?"

"You mean with that dirty cop O'Rourke? Of course. Everyone's buzzing about it, and Rob is feeling damned good about it. Obviously, he's known for a long time how corrupt these guys are, and now there's proof."

"How do you think this will this affect the case against Cross, or will it at all?" Carly asked

"Good question. I think it can only help. Of course, it's not yet clear the bust will be allowed to be introduced at trial. It's kind of a sideshow to the charges against Cross. Why don't you come down to my office? Gold is here, and you know what that means?"

Indeed she did, but to maintain some level of dignity and self-respect, Carly would not indulge in the habits of Gold and Chris; she could enjoy their company without snorting cocaine. On some level, it amazed her that Chris could have let himself be taken over by Gold...but he had: he was less in the driver's seat and more a passenger on this wild ride.

Carly wrapped up her story and handed it to the editor, then put on her coat and headed out.

Before walking into Chris's office, Carly took a few seconds to just breathe in the air. The North End and the waterfront were a different world from the station's suburban location. Sea air permeated the neighborhood, weaving through old brick buildings and the small bars and restaurants lining its cobblestone streets.

Carly walked through Chris's office door, and both he and Rob Gold were in the front office and ready with high fives.

"Great work, Carly," Gold said with a broad smile on his face. "Now maybe the judge will be more likely to believe that a cop can steal from someone just as easily as a thief. These guys are no better than the criminals. Believe me, I know!"

"Let's go back into Chris's office. There's a little something on his desk you will enjoy."

They shut off the lights in the front office and walked back together, where lines of cocaine were laid out. Carly politely declined but encouraged Chris and Gold to go ahead. It didn't take much for Chris to start telling tales that sounded like total fiction, but Carly played along with it, if for no other reason than Chris was a hell of a storyteller, even if he used exaggeration as his main tool. Carly couldn't always tell whether he was making stuff up or not, and so took it all with a big grain of salt.

Rob still couldn't believe it. "What does it take for a relatively low-level assistant district attorney like Tommy Blake to go out on a limb like he did?"

"He's kind of bulletproof because his boss knows that to fire him now would look very suspicious," Carly said.

Chris, who once worked in the AG's office, understood: "It took balls!"

"No shit," said Rob "Now what happens? There are other members of the Drug Control Unit who are just as bad as O'Rourke. Do those guys get caught too?"

"Tommy may have blown his wad with this sting," Chris said. "But even getting one of these guys off the force will be a win for him and for the DA—even if Callahan doesn't want to admit it."

"Is there a trial date already set in your case?" Carly asked.

"There is," said Chris. "We are scheduled to go to court February twelfth. That's when we will hear opening arguments."

"Have your learned anything new?" Carly asked.

Chris weighed in: "Cross, it turns out, was looking to retire to his home state of Maine and had put money down on some property near Rockport."

"Guess I know where he got the money for that."

Chris and Gold let out laughs in unison.

"Actually, I don't know why I'm laughing," Gold said. "Ain't nothin' funny about cops ripping off their targets."

Carly felt a little naïve as she asked Chris: "What else does Tommy Blake have besides the testimony of Eileen and Kate?"

"Well, I am pretty confident that he will be able to demonstrate a pattern of corruption that will have Cross as 'Exhibit A.'"

"Will any of the informants testify, particularly the guy who was there that night and told the cops that the cocaine was there?"

"I think it is very likely he will be called," Chris said. "But I don't know that he will be much help since he was not in the apartment when the money was taken. If he is given immunity, which I imagine he will, he might testify about a general criminal pattern and if any money was ever taken from him. And they will still likely have to, somehow, hide his identity."

"But I can tell you that I just submitted an affidavit to the court that includes a report by Lieutenant James that one of the detectives who was in on the raid and who saw Cross take the money is leaving the department because of it," said Chris, who was definitely lit up and on a jag. "That should tell you something, shouldn't it?"

"I guess it does. Have you tried to talk to this guy?" Carly asked Chris.

"I have asked...but to no avail. No surprise, really. I wouldn't talk to me either. He has nothing to gain and an awful lot to lose."

"How about giving me his name and I will try and see if I can get him to talk," Carly said.

"Sure," Chris said. "Robert Ross. Go for it."

While Chris and Carly were talking, Gold was busy laying out more lines, and he waved his arm to usher them over. Carly watched and wanted to partake, but she knew that she couldn't. She kept hearing her father's voice in her head, and above all else, she didn't want to disappoint him.

But Carly came away with a name, and she would do what she could to try to get Robert Ross to talk to her.

When Carly got to the station the next day, she called the police department and asked to speak to Ross. She waited as the phone rang, and then she heard a voice on the other end: "Hello. This is Detective Ross; how can I help you?"

"Detective, my name is Carly Howell, and I am a reporter for Channel 8. Can we talk off-the-record?"

There was a long pause, then: "Let me call you back when I get off my shift."

"Sure," Carly said. "Here is my number." Carly gave him Ross office number.

Carly felt a rush of adrenaline pulse through her. She made the call as a long shot, but now there was a real possibility that Ross might actually talk to her and confirm the stolen cash. And sure enough, when Ross called back, he told Carly that he was just about fed up with his fellow detectives, especially Cross, and he just couldn't deal with it anymore. So, it was far better in Ross's mind to leave than to have to make excuses and lie.

Carly was grateful for Ross's willingness to stand up and speak the truth.

CHAPTER TWENTY-SIX

After the story ran about the arrest of Detective O'Rourke, Carly got call after call from anonymous sources who told her of other incidents in which O'Rourke or other drug cops had taken money or other valuables from them. Carly needed to talk about the calls with Jim, who knew a lot more about anonymous sources than she did...like how much to trust them.

When Carly filled Jim in on what she was hearing, his reaction was definitive: "Shouldn't really surprise you. This kind of shit happens all the time. Once the door is open, others will walk right through and allege the same thing."

"I am clearly experiencing that," Carly said. "But here is my question—how can you tell who is telling the truth and who is not?"

"Ah, therein lies the rub: you can't always know. If you're reporting it, you can always just say that we have been flooded by uncorroborated reports of alleged wrongdoing at the hands of Boston drug cops."

"We've clearly tapped into a pattern, and I am convinced that it is worth digging around and meeting with a couple of these sources to hear their stories. This story has legs, and I want to be sure that we are not leaving anything on the table. And if there are more bad cops, we should do what we can to expose them. Don't you agree?" Carly asked.

"Absolutely! That doesn't mean you will necessarily be able

to prove the wrongdoing, but just calling attention to it is worthy of your time and effort. I have to say, I am impressed by your determination to stay with this story," Jim said. "You have done a great job here and I'm proud of you."

Jim's approval made Carly feel great.

After talking to Jim, Carly was more motivated than ever to keep digging, so she decided to follow up with one of the informants whose story sounded very credible. The phone rang twice, then she heard a voice say: "Yah, hello! Who's calling?"

"Hi, this is Carly Howell from Channel 8. You called me and let me know you had information about drug cops and police corruption. Can we talk? I would love to hear what you have to say."

"Sure. You're not going to believe it."

"Given what I just witnessed in East Boston, I'm not sure anything would really surprise me at this point."

"Let's meet at J.J. Foley's in the South End. Do you know where that is?"

"Of course. What time?"

"Let's say four o'clock."

"I'll be there. How will I recognize you?"

"I'll be wearing a Red Sox cap. I'm tall with light brown hair. Your good looks will give you away, and I look forward to meeting you."

At four p.m., the streets in the South End were quiet. Carly hurried down them, entered the bar, and looked around. Though it was a fabled hangout, she'd never stepped foot in the place. A long wooden bar ran the length of the restaurant, with dark wooden tables filling out the floor. It was early, but there were already several guys at the bar, smoking and drinking. It suddenly occurred to Carly that, in this town, there might be a bunch of guys wearing Red Sox caps. She walked up to the first guy she saw wearing one, and the man looked at her and smiled. Carly figured this was the guy she spoke to on the phone.

"Hi there. I talked to you earlier, right?"

Carly got lucky.

"Yup. That was me. Let's go to the booth over there." The man pointed to a darkly lit corner.

"Sure."

"Can I get you something to drink?"

"I'll just take a Diet Coke. Thanks."

For an instant, Carly imagined what Hank James would think about all of this and whether he truly had no idea about his men.

"I'm glad you are willing to talk to me," Carly began the conversation. "I just want you to know that you can remain anonymous if you prefer, but it would help me if I knew your name, at least. I don't have to use it, but it gives me some confidence in your story."

"Okay, as long as, for now, it remains between you and me. I'm Craig Hanley."

"Thanks, Craig. I appreciate it. Please, go ahead."

Craig was about thirty or forty years old—hard to tell exactly. He stood about five nine, with a sturdy build. He was neither thin nor heavy—just average. His most distinguishing feature was his green eyes that stood out even in the darkness of the bar. He was wearing tan corduroy pants, a blue, buttoned-down, collar shirt, and a leather bomber jacket—and, of course, the Red Sox hat.

"I have a small construction company in Quincy, and we work in and around that city and Milton—mostly residential. I've had the opportunity to do a little buying and selling of drugs on the side. Nothing big. I know full well that, every time I make a sale, I am putting myself at risk. So, I'm no angel, and you have to take that into account. Up to you if you believe me or not."

Carly was impressed that Craig would be so candid. How did he know that she wouldn't turn around and rat him out?

"Last year, about this time of year, in between deliveries, I stopped at a friend's house in Dorchester for a quick drink. It was cold and dark, and the street had little traffic. When I left the house and started to walk back to my car, I saw a dark car parked right behind mine with its motor running. I didn't think much of it until I opened the driver's side door, and then, suddenly, I felt someone behind me and the muzzle of a gun in my back. 'Don't move,' a guy said. I was frozen in place. I had no idea what was going on. Was this a robbery?

'Step outside,' the voice in the dark said, and I did as I was told. The next thing I knew, this guy was tearing through my car: under the seats, in the glove compartment, and wherever else he could. I had a couple of ounces of cocaine and a couple ounces of marijuana and about $1,000 stuffed in the glove compartment. He took both and the gun, then walked away. But as he turned, I got a good look at him, and sure enough, it was the same guy that they just caught in that sting in East Boston. Bobby O'Rourke—that his name? He looked at me and said: 'Turn the fuck around. You never saw me. Got it? You want to stay out of jail? Forget this happened.'

I did what he said, but before I did, I got the license plate number of the car, and the next day, I traced it through the DMV; it belonged to the police department."

"Wow!" Carly wasn't sure what else to say. "I really appreciate your candor and your willingness to tell me this story. It corroborates what I've heard about O'Rourke, but it's totally different when you hear it from someone on the other end. Thank you."

"I just want to see this guy go to jail. Look, I've done some bad shit, but this guy is a rotten cop and deserves to pay for that."

"And, frankly, it takes folks like you who are willing to come forward," Carly said. "Did you ever hear from other folks of this happening to them?"

"Yes! It is a part of what we all take for granted on the streets. It's ironic, though, when you think about it. I'm not so much worried about other drug dealers robbing me; I'm worried about crooked cops. What does that say?"

It was an irony, indeed...but one guy wasn't enough. Carly needed more names, more people to talk to who could back up Craig's story.

"Look, I've gotten a few calls from guys like you who say they were also victims of O'Rourke. Do you know any other folks who could corroborate these stories?"

"Actually, I might. Let me make a few calls, and I will let you know what I find out. It's less a question of do they have similar stories than are they willing to talk to you. Maybe, though, if I can assure them that this is all anonymous and their names need not be made public, I can convince one or two to talk to you. I will get back to you."

"Thanks. I truly appreciate it." And then, Carly pushed Craig: "Would you be willing to do an interview on camera if we blurred your identity and voice?"

"I would need to think about that."

"Understood. But it would really help the story and rooting out these bad cops," Carly said.

With that, Carly grabbed her coat and walked out of the bar

and to her car parked across the street, then headed back to her apartment. She felt like she had tapped into something that would help support the story, and she was determined to stick with it. She was also confident in her powers of persuasion in getting Craig to do an interview. Carly knew that she had to do what she could to persuade him. Craig's word was worth something, but an on-air (if disguised) witness to the corruption was something else entirely. She was hopeful that he would come through with another source, and it also made her want to call a couple of the other guys who had left messages to see if their stories were similar and if there was somebody more ready than Craig was to come forward on-air.

When Carly got home, she called her dad. It was seven p.m., and she figured her parents would be at home, either relaxing or watching television.

"Good evening," Carly's father's voice was reassuring.

"Dad, it's your daughter calling to get a little advice."

"Well, go ahead, darling."

"I am still working on that story about the drug cop. Once it went on the air, I got a bunch of calls from other guys, claiming they'd also been subject of illegal busts by the same rotten apple cop. So, here's my question: what made you trust a source?"

"Hold on a minute. I'm going to go into my office. Your mother doesn't need to hear this."

Moments later, Carly's father picked up the phone and told his wife to hang up the phone in the living room. Then, he launched into it: "This is tricky, for sure. You can never really be one hundred percent sure of any informant. You don't know what their motivation might be. But the fact that you got multiple calls from different individuals all basically wanting to tell you a similar story should give you some confidence in what he's saying."

"If I can get these guys to go on the record, it will help

reinforce the story about these bad cops."

"I think that makes sense, dear. I am proud of you and impressed with your reporting of this story."

"Thanks, Dad."

Carly thought to herself about the things that she had done during the reporting that her father wouldn't approve of, which gave her pause.

"Don't hesitate to call anytime for any reason. I am always here for you."

"Love you," Carly said.

"Love you more," her father said.

When she went to her office the next day, there was a message from Craig: "Please call me. I have good news for you."

Carly immediately dialed Craig's number, and he picked up right away. "Carly, I've thought about your offer to disguise my identity, and I have decided that it is worth getting this bad cop off the streets, so I am willing to do the interview."

Carly almost couldn't restrain her excitement at that news. "That is great! I can't thank you enough, and I can assure you that no one will be able to recognize your voice, and your image will be blacked out. Give me some times tomorrow that would work out and the location, and I will arrange to be there with a cameraman."

"Let's say five o'clock tomorrow. Come to my house, which is on Brooke Road, near Turners Pond. And I know a couple of other guys who would likely be willing to talk to you anonymously."

"You got it. We will be there, and I want to thank you for your willingness to do this. Helping get a bad cop off the streets is not easy but very important," Carly said.

Carly was practically jumping up and down with the adrenaline rush that the call had given her, and she knocked on Jim's door and gave him the news.

"Wow!" Jim exclaimed. "Your powers of persuasion are impressive, and this will be a very important interview. The editors shouldn't have a problem disguising his voice and image."

CHAPTER TWENTY-SEVEN

Carly decided that she had a responsibility to dig as far as she could into the potential wrongdoing of the Boston Police. She had a sense from what she already knew and the calls of informants that there was, indeed, a pattern, but she needed more proof. She decided to go to the Police Department and request any and all records of complaints of wrongdoing by the police and the outcome of any and all investigations in the past five years. She had a feeling even before she began the pursuit that it would be a long slog.

Carly was told she would have to file a Freedom of Information Act (FOIA) request. The request might take months, but it was the right and necessary thing to do.

As soon as Carly got back to her office, the message light on the phone was blinking, and a message was waiting. She thought maybe it was another one of the folks who had called her about O'Rourke.

"Yes, hello, Miss Howell." The familiar baritone sent chills down her spine. "This is Lieutenant James. I wonder whether we might have a conversation. Please call me back."

Carly had kind of figured she wasn't ever going to hear from Hank again, so she smiled at the thought of seeing him. She picked up the phone and called him back right away. On the third ring, Hank picked up.

"Yes?" That's how he answered every call.

"Hello! I am returning your call, which I have to say I was more than a little surprised to get."

"I bet you were. You sure have gotten me in a tough place, but you're not to blame for the situation I'm in. It hasn't been an easy few weeks, I can tell you that."

"No doubt. Why did you call?"

"I just need to vent to someone and thought you might be the logical person. Do you want to get together? I'd say we could go over to Richard's, but I don't think it's a good idea for folks to see us together.

"No shit." Carly regretted that statement as soon as it came out of her mouth. "Do you want to come over to my apartment?"

"I thought you'd never ask."

"Tonight? I leave work around five thirty, so any time after about six o'clock will work. Let's say around seven o'clock."

"See you then."

Carly hung up, filled with anticipation at seeing Hank, even though she knew it was bound to be at least a little awkward. She also knew that she had to watch her mouth and not give away any new information she'd gotten from either Tommy or from Chris or Rob; she was walking a tightrope.

Carly straightened up her desk—she was very neat, making sure that everything was stacked in piles—and packed up her papers, put on her coat, and headed out of the station. On a good night, the drive took about a half hour to get home. This night traffic was pretty light. Carly stopped on the way at a neighborhood liquor store—no shortage of those—to pick up some vodka and snacks. There was no way she wanted to make a real dinner—so peanuts and chips would have to do. Hank wouldn't care; she'd rarely seen him actually eat anything.

When Carly got home, she barely had time to put on a little makeup and straighten up the living room. She took some room spray in a lavender scent and sprayed it around.

She put on a George Benson record to set the mood, then waited. Within a half hour, the doorbell rang, and Carly buzzed Hank in. She opened the door, and Hank stepped over the threshold, grabbed her by the waist, pulled her close to him, and gave her a long kiss that had an immediate effect on Carly's body.

"I've missed that," Hank said with a smile.

"Me too. Come in!" Carly laughed as she motioned for Hank to enter the apartment. She realized on one level how bizarre and crazy this was, but she was too curious and captivated by his charm and, deep down—if she was being honest with herself— she'd really missed him.

"Let me guess, you'd like a vodka and tonic." Carly flashed a smile at Hank, which worked its magic.

"That's exactly what I want. How'd you know?"

"Call it my reporter's instinct."

"I'll give you that. I will say that, while it's pretty tough being on the receiving end of your work, you're definitely making an impact throughout the department, maybe even throughout the city."

Carly had to admit that she was flattered.

Hank followed Carly into her tiny kitchen, which had barely enough room for one person, let alone two. He watched as Carly took the vodka out of the freezer and made his beloved drink, then made one for herself.

"To what do we toast?" she asked.

"Let's toast to both of us getting to the other side of this story."

"You've got it!" They tapped each other's glasses, and each took a sip. The cool drink hit the spot. Hank offered Carly his hand, which she accepted, and they walked together back into the living room and sat on the velvet couch. Carly was, frankly, amazed that Hank could be as calm and seemingly unfazed by everything that had happened.

"Why did you call?"

"I really need to talk to someone. I truly wish this whole thing hadn't happened on my watch, and it may even cost me my job, but the actions of my guys—guys who I put my faith in—is just plain wrong. Before I say any more, I assume I can trust that this is all off-the-record?"

"Yes, you can."

"I'm feeling a little like a sucker who just didn't see the signs or ignored them, which is hard to accept given I was working in internal affairs before this. It's not like I don't know something about bad cops. None of the guys in my unit had come on my radar before I took the job. I also think that, in retrospect, I may have been a little too hands-off in managing the unit. I figured these were all qualified, experienced cops and they didn't need me micromanaging them. It's not my style, anyway."

"And now what do you think of these guys?"

"This is nothing I can or will testify to, but some of these guys are taking advantage of their jobs, and I hope the truth comes out at the trial or trials. Not all the guys are bad, but there are enough of them to really give the whole department a black eye. No question! Bobby O'Rourke is at the top of that list."

"Who would have ever thought that Gold would be on the right side of this? Have you already been feeling the heat within the department? Are they coming after you, too?"

"Too soon to tell, but no question they are circling the wagons down at headquarters, and it wouldn't surprise me if I am being looked at as a fall guy. After all, they need one desperately." Hank took a deep breath and a long sip of his drink, then looked straight into Carly's eyes.

Carly reached out and touched Hank's thigh. The spark was felt by both of them, and he took her hand and moved it to his lap. Carly took the prompt and, without a word, unzipped Hank's pants, moved her head and mouth, and reached into his pants and took hold of him. It didn't take long for the long strokes from Carly's hand and the rhythmic, up-and-down movements of her mouth to have the desired effect.

Hank let out a low groan, brought Carly up to his lips, and kissed her long and hard, then his hand started to move toward her crotch. Carly was definitely turned on and wanted to have sex with Hank so badly, but she had made a pact with herself not to let this happen. Carly took Hank's hand and held it tightly for a moment, then kissed it and put it down. She wanted Hank badly, but she knew deep down that she would be leaving herself in a very compromised position. Still, Carly was left wanting for more.

CHAPTER TWENTY-EIGHT

The sting and arrest of Bobby O'Rourke sent a shockwave through Dalton Cross's defense team, including David Boone. "Holy crap!" is how Boone put it after hearing the news reports.

Boone gathered his team of lawyers—all men—into the conference room of his law firm to talk strategy and tactics as the trial date drew near. Cross was there, too, sitting quietly and listening closely to his legal team. Boone had a full floor in a downtown office building, right across from City Hall and the courthouse. His corner office was decorated in a masculine style, with a heavy wooden desk and one wall's wooden bookcase filled floor to ceiling with law books. Boone knew that he was not the neatest guy in the world, and there were stacks of papers on his desk and on the floor next to it. His secretary, Louise Gross, sat right outside and had been with Boone for almost twenty years. Louise had a friendly demeanor but was a fierce protector of her boss, and no one—that's no one—got to walk into Boone's office without Louise allowing it.

On this morning, the legal team was seated around an enormous wooden table with green shaded lights running along the center of the table, resembling a library reading room.

"Guess there's no way we are calling O'Rourke to testify," Boone said with a laugh. No one else found the joke particularly funny, certainly not Cross.

"We weren't going to call him as a witness anyway, were we?" Cross asked.

"Nah. But now the prosecution can bring it up to show there is a pattern in the department, and you are only a piece of it. We've got to hope that the other guys in your unit are more interested in saving their own asses and supporting your story. Of course, there is one guy in the unit who says he saw you taking the money: Ronnie Ross. How well do you know him?"

"We're not good friends, if that's what you mean. He's clean...squeaky clean. I heard he's leaving the police department and going to the fire department, so he doesn't have to get involved with any of this."

"That doesn't bode well for us," Boone offered. "He may feel that, once he's gone, he has nothing to lose by turning on you. But we'll have to wait and see if they list him as a witness."

"Let's go over the plan of attack. I've got a few tricks of my own, and afterwards, those bastards will be left trying to figure it out." Boone moved his chair back and went to stand next to a blackboard. A tall guy, he was dressed in a three-piece grey suit with the vest unbuttoned and the red tie loosened.

"First of all, my opening statement will build you up and your reputation and all the good work you've done in your time on the force. You'll come across looking like a boy scout. Trust me!"

"We've also got Lieutenant James and his deputy, both of whom were there that night and neither of whom is going to say anything damning—especially now with the O'Rourke case. They will likely say they saw nothing. We also have at least two other members of the unit who were there and who will back you up. I will go after Gold's wife and her sister with everything I have, making them look like they don't know what they're talking about and like they're in on the action with Gold. And, of course, I'm ready to tear Gold apart, whether he testifies or not. My hunch is he probably won't. They don't have much to gain and a lot to lose putting that jailbird on the stand. Does that sound like a plan?"

The legal team nodded their heads almost in unison; that was how things worked at the law firm. Boone was in charge, and his team was there to back him up—perhaps occasionally challenge him, but that was a pretty rare occurrence, and it was obvious that no one would be challenging Boone that day.

Cross had been paying close attention. He leaned into the table, rested his head on his hands, crossed them in front of him, and said: "Sounds good." Cross was tired of all of this, and it showed on his face. After more than twenty years on the force, to have this case in front of him...it had already taken a toll.

Boone put his hand on Cross's shoulder and said: "You and I need to spend some quality time together in the next several days so that you know every potential question that could be asked and are prepared with a good answer."

The meeting lasted for an hour. Boone did a good job of making his team feel like they could win this case. Dalton Cross appeared less confident. After all, his future was in the balance, and knowing the truth of what happened that night.

CHAPTER TWENTY-NINE

Since Carly started working on the story, she had gotten a police scanner for the office and one for her apartment; it was a good way of listening to what the police were up to. She didn't listen all the time, but on this night, while snuggled up on her couch, wrapped in a throw her grandmother had knitted for her and reading a novel, she heard it: "Cop down. Shot in the buttocks. We are taking him to MGH Emergency." That news made Carly sit up and listen more closely. She turned on the radio to WEEI, the CBS all-news radio station. She waited to hear them report it, and it didn't take long. "We are just learning that a Boston police officer has been shot and was taken to Mass. General Hospital. We don't have any details yet. We will keep you updated as we learn more."

Carly listened for a while longer, but there was no update, other than repeating the initial report. She decided to call it a night, but she couldn't wait to learn more in the morning.

The next morning, as soon as she got to the office, Carly turned on the police scanner. No sooner had she done that than the phone rang.

"You're not going to believe this," Tommy said on the other end. "Did you hear about the cop shot last night? Guess who it was? Yup, Cross. He says it was an accident. He says he went out for a cup of coffee in the South End, and while he was in the restaurant, he saw what he suspected was a drug deal going down outside. He ran into the alley, supposedly in search of these guys, and he saw one guy in the car and one guy standing by him. He yelled at them, but the car supposedly sped off, and he fought with the guy in the alley, who turned and fired a gun at Cross, hitting him in the thigh and butt. There was a massive response by the police, who saw no car and no trace of the guy in the alley. Cross ended up at MGH and got ten stitches. He's out of the hospital now."

"You can't be serious," Carly said. "I heard the report of the shooting last night."

"You can't make this shit up. There's a team at Internal Affairs investigating, but I'm pretty sure Cross set it up in such a way that they won't find anything."

Carly was incredulous.

"Do you think it was intentional? What was he hoping to gain from doing that...if he did do it intentionally?" The questions were running through Carly's head.

"Maybe he thought it was a way of retiring from the force because now there's already a buzz about him going out on disability and taking early retirement. I will obviously ask Cross about this when he takes the stand, but I expect him to stick to his story. It does open up a new avenue of questioning for me that can help throw doubt about just how honest and believable he is."

"Thanks for letting me know," Carly said. "I really appreciate it." Carly put down the phone and went into Jim's office with the news.

Without cracking a smile, Jim came back with: "Guess he'll be the butt of a lot of jokes," and he couldn't help laughing at his wit. Jim was a sarcastic kind of guy, and Carly appreciated that about him. She was also sarcastic, though sometimes, she found it came back to bite her. Not everyone, she learned, appreciated that kind of humor, especially from a woman.

"Ha. Very funny. Just when I thought this story couldn't get any crazier, something else happens."

"Well, the good news is it makes for a better story. You've got to report this today. I'll let the newsroom know."

Carly headed down to the newsroom to find Larry in an editing booth. "What pics do we have of Cross?" She proceeded to fill Larry in on the latest news, and he laughed out loud. "Unbelievable. I'll look through the tape and get a couple for you to choose from."

It wasn't hard to put the story together—just a quick, ninety-second script—and in the meantime, the station threw up a promo: *"Tonight on the six o'clock news—the cop at the center of the Boston police corruption case gets shot. Tune in tonight."*

Carly could only imagine what Gold and Chris were saying and doing about this. As soon as she was done with the story, she'd race to see them.

CHAPTER THIRTY

"Well. Well. Well. Look who's here. Let me guess," Chris said. "You heard the latest. You have to hand it to Cross. He's pretty creative, if he thought this was his way out."

"What a load of bull," Rob weighed in. "If anyone believes this, it will be amazing. The timing is just too coincidental. He did this for sympathy or for a medical leave."

Rob passed Carly a mirror with some lines of cocaine already laid out. Carly smiled and politely pushed the mirror back. "Thanks, but I need my wits about me. When I heard it, I couldn't help but laugh out loud. What are the chances that this is somehow admissible? And how might it impact the case against him?"

"There's no way Tommy won't try," Chris said before taking a deep inhale. "It may not get in, though, since it has nothing to do with what happened at Rob's apartment. It's anyone's guess as to whether the judge would let it in. Tommy will have to make a very strong argument."

"You know, by the way, that they've moved the location of the trial out of the Dorchester Court across the river into Cambridge?"

"No, I hadn't heard that," Carly said. "Why?"

"I think the feeling is it's better to get it out of Boston just because of all the baggage that comes with it. So, they've given it to a judge—Judge Summers—a nice Jewish boy who has a reputation as a very smart and fair judge."

"Have you been in touch with Tommy, or is that an obvious question?" Carly asked Chris.

"We haven't talked directly about this latest development, but I do intend to call him."

"Should we do it now?" Chris smiled and moved toward the phone to dial.

"Tommy, my friend, it's Chris Kelly. We heard the latest news about the incident with Dalton Cross and just wanted to check in with you and see what your view of this is and how you're planning to deal with it."

Chris didn't give away that both Rob and Carly were in the room, listening. While she could only hear one end of the conversation, Carly did get a better sense of the dynamic between the two lawyers, picking up that Chris and Gold were feeding Tommy information that they hoped would help with the case against Cross.

When the conversation ended, Chris put down the phone and looked at both Gold and Carly. "He knows what he's doing. He believes pretty strongly that this only adds to the picture of Cross as a cop who will do anything to save his ass—get it?"

Carly shot Chris a look and said: "Seriously?"

"So, will Tommy use this in his opening statement, do you think?" Carly asked. "And I assume Cross is not about to take the stand, right?"

"I would think Tommy would definitely mention it as a way of calling Cross's character into question," Chris said. "And Boone would have to be out of his mind to put Cross on with all the questions that would be hurled at him. It's always much safer to keep the defendant off the stand."

"I can't wait," Rob weighed in from across the room.

CHAPTER THIRTY-ONE

One of the best parts about living in the Back Bay, no matter the time of year, was being able to walk to the Public Garden or to the Esplanade and take in the beauty of the city. While it was winter and there was a chilling wind blowing, Carly decided she needed some fresh air. She bundled up in her down parka, wool Burberry scarf, and wool cap and headed out to the Esplanade. Carly could do a walking loop in about forty-five minutes; was her favorite walk, and she tried to do it at least three times a week. It was just about dusk, and the streetlights were on. While walking over to the river, Carly had a weird feeling that she was being watched or followed; it wasn't the first time she had had that feeling since she started working on the story. Carly had come to look behind her and around her as she walked. She was looking around at the cars parked along the street to see if she could see anything suspicious. And then, almost without warning, as she turned on to Berkeley Street and headed down about a block, Carly saw a black Crown Victoria with the motor on, just sitting on the side of the road, parked.

Normally, Carly wouldn't have even given it a second thought. But tonight, for some reason, she did. As she walked past the car, Carly tried her best to look inside, but the windows were tinted, and she couldn't really see who was in the car. She brushed it off and kept going. She walked across the pedestrian bridge, which spanned Storrow Drive and connected the Back Bay with the Esplanade, walked down the stairs on the other side, and headed down toward the Hatch Shell, where the Boston Pops performs its famous July 4th concert, with the "1812 Overture" and fireworks. There weren't too many people walking or jogging at this hour, but there were a few. Carly looked out to the river and could even see a few ducks or geese in the water and remnants of a past snowstorm dotting the grass. She stopped to take in the scene, and as she did, someone approached her from behind and pushed her as they passed by, then stopped, turned around, and looked back at her.

"Watch your step!" the man yelled at Carly. She almost lost her balance but remained upright. She tried to get a good look at the guy—she could tell it was a guy—but he was wearing a hoodie, so there was no way she could really see who he was. The man kept running, and Carly lost sight of him. *What was that*, she thought to herself? Was that just an accidental hit, or was it something more sinister? Carly couldn't tell for sure, but suddenly, her stomach started to churn, and she realized that she had to get back to her apartment as the sky turned dark.

She decided to take a bit of a risk and walk back the way she had come to see if the car was still there. As she approached Berkeley Street, Carly could see that the car was still there and that the motor was still on. She crossed the street so she didn't have to walk right by the car, and no sooner had she gotten close that one of the windows was rolled down, and a guy yelled out: "We're watching you, bitch."

Carly stopped and leaned back against a light pole. What the hell just happened? How much danger was she in? She needed to let someone know ASAP.

When Carly got back to her apartment, she couldn't get her coat and gloves off fast enough. She dialed Hank's number, though she kind of doubted he would still be in his office. The phone rang once, twice, three times, and just as Carly was ready to hang up, he answered: "Yes, this is Lieutenant James."

"Lieutenant, this is Carly Howell. You may remember me. I just got back from a rather terrifying walk along the esplanade where I was pushed by a runner, and then some guys in a Crown Victoria shouted out: 'We're watching you, bitch.' I have no idea who it might be, but it isn't the first time that I have had this gut feeling that I am being watched."

"I am very sorry to hear this," James said. "If it's my men, it is clearly unacceptable. Let me see if I can run it down and find out if it's one of my guys. It may not be so easy, but I can at least make a blanket warning to leave you alone."

"Thanks. I would appreciate that. I figured I could also just call 911, but it doesn't quite rise to an emergency . . . at least not yet."

"I can certainly understand how unnerving this is, and you shouldn't be going through this. It's not who we are or, at least, who we should be."

"That is an understatement," Carly said.

CHAPTER THIRTY-TWO

It was the first day of Dalton Cross's trial. Carly walked into the courtroom. She had her notebook and pen (she never traveled anywhere without both) and was wearing a navy-blue suit with a white blouse and a red, white, and blue scarf around her neck. Carly's goal had been to look very professional, almost lawyer-like, and she thought the red, white, and blue scarf added kind of a patriotic feel.

The courtroom was packed with Boston cops: some in uniform, but many in civilian clothes. Carly took a rough head count and concluded there were about two dozen in the room. The trial would make for good video, for sure. There was a "pool" camera shooting the trial. That meant all the stations would have to use the same footage. Carly was pretty sure the cameraman would get the public, but she went up to him and specifically asked if he could get a wide shot of the crowd; he said yes. Carly was confident that, no matter which other reporters were there, she knew the story far better than any of them. Others had written a story or two about the case, but they hadn't been in the middle of it like she had. If they only knew . . . Carly looked around to see if she could see Hank. She saw him tucked into one of the benches near the back of the courtroom. Carly caught his eye and smiled. There was no smile on his face, but James shook his head up and down to acknowledge Carly.

Dalton Cross was already seated at the defense table. Carly could only see the back of his head and couldn't really get a good sense of his demeanor. She assumed though that he had to be pretty nervous. Carly saw two lawyers were at his side: Boone and a second chair.

Boone was wearing his signature three-piece suit—a brown tweed with a green and white striped tie. He turned around to survey the courtroom and smiled at the gathered crowd. "His men" had turned out for their guy. All the cops had to make an impression on the judge and on Cross, who, for the first time in his life, knew he was facing potential serious consequences for years of using his position to line his pockets.

On the other side of the courtroom were Tommy Blake and two other attorneys who Carly had never met. Tommy, in a grey suit with a red and white striped tie, was standing behind the table. Carly could tell that he was nervous just from his pacing. Tommy turned around, saw Carly sitting on his side of the room, and gave her a slight smile and a thumbs-up sign. Carly reciprocated, ready for this show to begin.

The judge walked in, dressed in his robe, and the bailiff called the session to order: "All rise! The Court of Middlesex County is now in session, with the Honorable Albert Summers presiding in the trial of Suffolk County versus Dalton Cross."

Carly had never seen the judge before, but she knew that he was well-respected for his handling of complex cases. The judge appeared younger than she'd expected, and Carly was surprised when he actually smiled at the courtroom.

"Good morning," Judge Summers began. "We are here today to hear the case of Suffolk County versus Dalton Cross, who has chosen to be tried before a judge, which is the law in the Commonwealth of Massachusetts. This also means he may choose to have a second trial before a jury. Thus, as you can see, there is no jury present today, nor will there be. We have one camera that will be shooting the trial, and I fully expect that all of you in the audience will remain seated and quiet throughout. No outbursts will be tolerated. I hope I make myself clear."

"Yes sir," Boone said.

"Yes sir," echoed Tommy.

Carly was secretly hoping that, at some point, there would be an outburst by the cops in the room; it would make for much better TV.

"Mr. Blake, we will begin with your opening statement."

Tommy moved his papers around, stood up, took a deep breath, and began:

"Your honor, the people of Suffolk County believe that we have a strong case to present that will leave no doubt in the court's mind that the defendant, police officer Dalton Cross, knowingly and intentionally stole $5,000 from behind a shadowbox in the living room of citizen Robert Gold." Tommy looked to the defense table and pointed to Cross, who sat straight up, hands crossed in front of him on the table. Carly was disappointed that she couldn't see Cross's face.

Carly thought Tommy looked confident, and he was able to rattle off his opening without looking down at his notes. The eyes of the cops in the audience were zeroed in on Tommy, almost like a beam of light. The "heat" was there, focused on him. Carly hoped that Tommy wouldn't let the other cops intimidate him, which was their intention.

"Your Honor," said Tommy. "Members of the police force have taken a solemn oath to uphold the law, yet what we have here is an officer of the law intentionally breaking it and stealing for his own benefit. This should shock everyone and anyone who believes in the rule of law. It's that simple." Tommy continued: "On the night of October 9, 1978, ten members of the Boston Police Drug Control Unit commenced a raid on Mr. Gold's home. A police informant—whom we will call informant A—had gone to the Gold residence, allegedly to buy jewelry, which was a sideline of Gold's. The informant left the premises after he allegedly saw the jewelry, as well as an amount of cocaine, which Gold also showed him.

He then walked across the street to a drugstore and used a pay phone to let the police know that the drugs were there. The Boston Police Drug Control Unit responded with ten cops in two cars.

Members of the Drug Control Unit surrounded the apartment, and five of them entered through the front door, including Detective Cross. Lieutenant James remained in a car in front of the house and came in only after the raid was over. The detectives searched the house and found ten ounces of cocaine—with an estimated street value of $10,000. During the raid, Mr. Gold's wife, Eileen, and her sister, Kate, and Gold's nine-year-old daughter were in the house. Kate was asked by her sister to take her niece upstairs so she did not have to witness what was going on. It was as she walked past the living room to the stairs that Kate observed Mr. Cross—again," Tommy pointed to Cross, "take money from a shadowbox, which was hanging on the wall in the living room." He then pointed to the shadowbox, which was resting on a table directly in front of the judge.

Tommy methodically laid out the case against Cross in as much detail as he could. Having never before witnessed him in court, Carly was impressed. Meanwhile, she took copious notes, even though the whole thing was being videotaped; it was her training as a print reporter. Carly always felt more confident if she had her own notes on whatever story she was writing. In this case, she also knew she had a backup when it came to quoting people, and she could add her own observations and comments as the trial proceeded. It was disappointing, Carly thought, that, given the placement of the camera, the faces of the lawyers would not be visible to the television audience.

CHAPTER THIRTY-THREE

Next up was attorney Boone, who was notorious for his opening statements and his use of outlandish language. Today would be no different. Boone stood up and, in a loud voice, proclaimed:

"Your Honor, I am shocked—*shocked* that this case ever got to this point. The evidence against my client is weak, and my client is a pillar of his community, as well as a fine, twenty-year veteran of the Boston Police Department. He has devoted his life to protecting the public, to finding bad guys and taking them off the street, preserving our neighborhoods and the safety of the public. He deserves a medal, not a trial.

We will prove that Detective Cross is innocent of these charges and that a convicted felon like Robert Gold and unreliable witnesses like his wife and sister-in-law cannot and should not be believed. Plain and simple: they are lying. Based on the word of an informant who had been in the house and seen cocaine on the night in question, Detective Cross was one of a ten-member squad of the Boston Drug Control Unit who raided the home of Robert Gold, a known drug dealer, convicted felon, and genuinely bad guy. The detectives made a thorough search of the house and found ten ounces of cocaine, which is a serious amount of drugs, Your Honor, with an estimated street value of $10,000."

The aggressive attorney turned and looked Gold squarely in

the eyes before continuing: "Clearly, the Drug Control Unit, headed by Lieutenant Henry James, believed that Gold was a big enough drug dealer with a significant footprint in Boston that it was worth the raid to get him and the cocaine off the streets, and they did just that. It is no surprise that his wife and daughter and her sister are trying to cover for Mr. Gold; that's exactly what is happening here. They will tell you that they saw one of the detectives take money from the Gold residence. But I ask you, Judge: are you really going to believe the words of this despicable individual's wife, or are you going to believe the words of a fine, upstanding police detective who is doing his job every day to keep the streets of Boston safe and rid this city of scumbags like Rob Gold? We will prove beyond a reasonable doubt, Your Honor, that there can be no question who is telling the truth and who is lying to protect the criminal enterprise that the police are working hard every day to eliminate." Boone went on for a little while longer, building up Cross and tearing down Gold. From Carly's perspective, it was a good opening statement, but it was also unsurprising. No matter what Boone said, his style was made for TV. Obviously, Carly would have to use the statement in her story.

Once the opening statements were done, the ball was thrown back to Tommy to present the prosecution's case.

"Mr. Blake," the judge said. "The floor is yours."

"Thank you, Your Honor."

The first witness Tommy called was Gold's sister-in-law—Kate Maloney. She was wearing a conservative dark skirt and tan sweater; nothing flashy!

Once sworn in, Kate took her seat, and Tommy started in. Carly could sense a certain nervousness on Kate's part, which was completely understandable. First, Tommy established who Kate was and her relationship to Rob. When Tommy began asking her about what had happened the night of the raid, Kate remained calm and was extremely believable as a witness. She remembered that night's events in great detail and seemed almost anxious to tell her story.

"Please tell the court what you saw that night."

"I saw one of the men take a wad of cash from behind the shadowbox. He said: 'Look what I got,' and put the wad in his pants pocket."

"Do you see the person who took the money in the courtroom?"

"Yes. I do."

"Can you point him out?"

Kate looked straight ahead and pointed directly at Cross

"Are you sure?" Tommy asked.

"I am absolutely positive," Kate said with no hint of hesitation or doubt.

"Did you try to confront Detective Cross?"

"I did, but he pretty quickly told me to: 'Get the—you'll excuse the language—fuck out of the living room,' that I wasn't supposed to be there, and I should get back to the kitchen."

"What did you do?"

"I did what he said. I wasn't about to get into a fight with a police detective."

"Was there anyone else in the living room when you saw Detective Cross take the money?"

"Yes, there were two other men who I assumed were also detectives."

"Do you see them in the courtroom?"

Kate looked around at the crowd on the defense side of the

courtroom and pointed to two other men. Tommy made a mental note of the two men.

"Where was your sister?"

"She was in the kitchen, where she was instructed to sit throughout the raid. I was taking my niece, Jill, up to bed, at the request of my sister."

"What did Detective Cross do once you left?"

"He left the living room, and I couldn't see where he went."

"Did you tell anyone else about what you had witnessed?"

"I told my sister Eileen, of course, who hadn't seen him herself, and when the head of the Drug Control Unit came into the house and into the kitchen and started questioning me and my sister, I told him too."

"Can you point him out in the courtroom?"

Kate pointed to Hank, who was in the back of the courtroom. Carly turned around to see Hank's expression as he was called out; he looked dead serious.

"What did Lieutenant James say to you once you told him?"

"He thanked me for coming forward and said he would investigate the matter."

"Was there anything else you saw?"

"No. That was it."

"Thank you for this testimony," Tommy said.

Carly sensed Tommy's confidence that the trial was starting off as he had hoped, and, thus far, Boone had not really interrupted the flow. Carly worried, though, that it was only a matter of time, since she knew of Boone's reputation for drama.

CHAPTER THIRTY-FOUR

It was Boone's turn to cross-examine Kate.

"Tell the court what you do for a living."

"I am a nurse at Boston City Hospital."

"Are you married?"

Tommy yelled: "Objection, relevance?"

"I want to establish the relationship with Gold."

"Overruled," the judge said.

"No, sir, I am not."

"But you were married, weren't you? And your husband was a drunk."

"Objection."

The judge admonished him: "Mr. Boone, please stick to the issue at hand."

"Did you know your brother-in-law, Robert Gold, is a drug dealer? And what, exactly, is your relationship with your brother-in-law?"

Kate started to tear up at the implication that she—a fine Catholic girl—might be having an affair with her sister's husband.

"I am not sure how to answer that question. We have a friendly relationship as in-laws."

"No further questions." Boone let Kate go, with the idea of an affair left hanging in the air. Carly had never even considered an affair. She knew that, after just one witness, she had enough for the evening news.

Conveniently, Judge Summers called a recess for lunch, which gave Carly the chance to figure out which sound bites to use and quickly write a script for the evening package that she would put together later back at the station. Carly was in the courtroom and seated when everyone else returned. She tried to catch Hank's attention without success, but she caught Tommy's eye and gave him a thumbs-up.

The next witness was Eileen Gold.

Unlike her sister, Eileen appeared nervous as she took the stand. It was understandable, Carly thought. Being married to Gold was probably no picnic. Carly assumed that Eileen also knew a lot more about his drug dealing than she'd admitted to.

"Mrs. Gold," Tommy began. "Please tell us what you were doing the evening of the raid."

"It was a quiet evening at home, and I had just finished serving dinner and was helping my nine-year-old daughter with her homework. My husband had a visitor earlier in the evening. I said hello to him, and the two of them headed off into the den. Relatively soon after that, the two of them left, and my husband said he would be back in a couple of hours. I came back into the kitchen, and about an hour or so later, there was a loud knock at the door. I was startled and jumped up and answered the door. There were a bunch of men at the door, and one flashed a badge. I let them in, and at the same time, another group entered from the back door."

"What was your reaction to this?"

"I was extremely frightened."

"Had anything like this happened before?"

"If you are asking whether there had ever been a raid on my house, the answer is no."

"What did you do?"

"I followed what the cops told me to do, which was to move into the kitchen and out of the way of their search."

"Did anyone say anything to you?"

"One cop said: 'Sit down and keep your hands on the table.'"

"Where was your daughter?"

"She was with me. I asked my sister Kate to take her upstairs, which she did."

"Did your daughter say anything to you after the raid was over?"

"Yes. She told me she had seen what her aunt had seen: a cop taking money from behind the shadowbox."

"So, there were two witnesses to this crime, correct?" Tommy asked.

"Yes."

"But you, yourself, did not witness the police do this?"

"No, sir."

"That's all, Your Honor. Thank you, Mrs. Gold."

Boone stood and approached the witness box, launching his first question. "How could you really not know what was going on in your own house?"

"Objection, Your Honor."

"Overruled. You may answer the question."

"I don't know what you're talking about," Eileen said.

"You cannot tell me or this court with a straight face that you didn't know your husband was a drug dealer and your house was being used to store the drugs."

"I don't know what you're talking about. I was unaware of any drugs in our house. I believe the guy that came in here put them there."

"You mean Detective Cross?"

"Yes."

"Really? What was he carrying when he came in?"

"I don't remember."

"How convenient. Finally, would you please tell the court who the father of your daughter is."

"Objection!" Tommy jumped to his feet. "Relevance."

"I will allow it," said Judge Summers. "Continue, Mr. Boone."

"My boyfriend—my daughter's father—was shot and killed in South Boston five years ago." Eileen started crying.

Boone didn't show any sympathy but, instead, continued on. "Did you know there was money behind the shadowbox?"

"No."

Boone kept going, trying hard to discredit Eileen Gold's testimony. On the stand, Eileen seemed believable to Carly, but she, too, found it hard to believe that Eileen had no idea what was going on in her own home. Carly had that thought in the back of her head from the beginning.

CHAPTER THIRTY-FIVE

Next up was, perhaps, the most potentially important witness—the nine-year-old daughter, Jill. She was a sweet looking girl with light brown, shoulder-length hair, wearing a light blue dress with a bow in the back and a black cardigan sweater. It almost looked like Jill was dressed for a show.

A hush descended on the courtroom as Jill walked up to the witness stand.

Tommy knew he had to be careful and just let her tell her story. They'd rehearsed it in his office, and Tommy expected that Jill would make a remarkably strong witness.

"Jill, good morning. I am going to ask you a few questions. Are you ready?"

"Yes, sir, I am," she said while clasping her hands.

"Do you remember what happened the night that the police raided your house?"

"Yes, I do."

"Where were you?"

"I was with my mom, doing homework in the kitchen."

"Were you scared when the police came in?"

"Yes. I was very scared, and I went to hug my mom."

"What did she say or do?"

"She told me that everything would be okay; no one would get hurt. Then she asked my Aunt Kate to take me up to my bedroom. She took my hand, and we went up to my bedroom together."

"And did you see anything before you went up to the bedroom?"

"Yes. I saw a man reaching from behind this picture frame thing that was hanging in the living room and take out money."

"You could tell it was money?"

"Yes. I saw what looked like a roll of money."

"Do you see that man sitting here today?"

"Yes."

"Can you point him out?"

Jill extended her hand and pointed at Dalton Cross.

"Are you sure that's the man you saw?"

"Yes. I am sure."

"Thank you very much for your testimony."

Carly was blown away by the girl's confidence; there was no question that Jill would be the lede for that night's story.

"Mr. Boone," the judge called out. "Do you have any questions for the witness?"

"No, Your Honor."

Boone had—wisely, Carly figured—declined to cross-examine pretty little Jill Gold; there was no way he could win that exchange.

"Thank you, dear; you may step down," said Judge Summers.

Looking continuously at her mother, Jill left the witness stand and returned to her seat.

Next, Tommy called Gold's friend Brian to the stand. His testimony established that there was, indeed, $5,000 and that he had lent it to Gold for taxes that were owed.

Lieutenant James was next. Carly was nervous for him.

"The Commonwealth calls Lieutenant Henry James to the stand."

It was hard for her to watch this interrogation: Tommy did not go easy on Hank. Tommy had been waiting for this day, and Carly knew he'd practiced painting this picture of a drug raid gone wrong.

Hank was dressed in civilian clothes: a navy-blue blazer; an open-collar, white dress shirt; and grey pants. Hank refused to wear a tie because, as he put it: "You can dress up a duck, but he's still a duck." Just remembering the line brought a smile to Carly's face.

At Tommy's prompting, Hank went through his professional background and said that his prior position was in the Internal Affairs unit.

"Can you please tell the court why this raid was set up?" asked Tommy.

"Yes. As is true in many of these drug dealing situations, we had arranged for an informant to go to Gold's house and buy some cocaine. When he had done that, he called us to let us know the cocaine and some hot jewelry was in the home."

"Had you successfully used information from this informant on similar raids?"

"No. Not since I have been head of the Drug Control Unit, anyway. There may have been cases before I got there."

"Then what made you think this was a solid lead and worth all the manpower and time and energy to plan for and carry out this raid?"

"As the head of the Drug Control Unit, I put my faith in my men. These guys are on the street every day, collecting intelligence about criminals and drug dealers in the city of Boston. They know what they hear and see and who to believe or disbelieve. They were convinced that Gold's home was a good target, and the informant knew him; they had done business before."

"How did you assemble the team of detectives assigned to the raid?"

"I have a dozen guys in the unit, and I figured that I would need a good number of them to carry out the raid without getting people hurt. If we could create a kind of total surprise raid that caught the Gold family unaware, we'd have our best shot."

"How did you get Gold out of the house?"

"I can't really tell you the details, as it was an undercover operation, but I can say that the informant let us know when Gold left the house."

"And had you had previous experience with this particular informant?"

"Again, I had not. But others in the unit vouched for his reliability." Hank looked straight ahead, clasped his hands, and rested them on the edge of the witness stand.

Tommy was methodical in his questioning. "Where were you during the raid?"

Hank cleared his throat and began the story of how the raid unfolded, as well as the arrest of Gold and his friend. "I was outside in an unmarked car with my deputy, Sergeant Hawley. I had decided that the men in the unit were best suited to actually carry out the raid and that I would enter the house once I got the okay from the guys inside."

"And when you did get the okay and entered the house, what did you find?"

"I found my men finishing up the raid and assembling all that they had seized—including bags of cocaine and jewelry."

"Was there any cash among the items seized?"

"No. I did not see any cash."

"Where were Gold's wife and her sister? Did you see them?"

"Yes. They were in the kitchen. One of the members of the unit was watching them."

"Did they say anything to you?"

"Kate Maloney told me that one of the members of my unit had taken money from a shadowbox in the living room."

"What did you say to her once she told you that?"

"I asked her if she could identify the detective who allegedly took the money."

"And could she? Did she?"

"Yes. She pointed to Detective Cross, who was standing in the living room."

"And then what did you do or say?"

"I went over to Cross, asked him whether he had taken any money. He assured me he had not. His word was good enough for me."

Tommy looked skeptical. "Lieutenant James, as a former member of Internal Affairs, I am surprised you were so willing to believe Detective Cross."

"Objection, Your Honor," said Boone. "That is Mr. Blake's opinion."

"Overruled. You may continue, Mr. Blake."

"Did anyone else tell you they had seen Detective Cross take money?"

"Yes. One of the other detectives in the unit later said that he had witnessed him take the money."

"And what did you tell that detective?"

"I thanked him for coming forward and told him I would further investigate the situation."

"And is it true that, since the raid, that detective has since left the police department and started work at the fire department?"

"Yes, sir. That's true."

"Why did that happen, do you think?"

Boone jumped up again. "Objection, Your Honor. Mr. Blake is asking the witness to make a supposition about the thought process of another individual."

"Sustained. Mr. Blake, please confine yourself to the witness at hand."

Tommy continued his questioning of Lieutenant James for about another half hour. From Carly's perspective, no major revelations came out of this probe. Hank clearly believed there was enough evidence to conduct the raid, and once he entered the house and had spoken with Cross, he took his word for what happened.

But Boone had a different idea, which became clear as soon as he started his cross-examination of Hank.

"Lieutenant, I've got a pretty easy question to begin. Were you in the room when this so-called theft is alleged to have happened?"

"No, sir; I was not."

"So, you didn't see anything, is that correct?"

"Yes. That is correct."

"Where were you during the raid?"

"As I said, I was outside in an unmarked car with my deputy."

"And when did you go into the house?"

"I got a call on my walkie-talkie that the raid was over that and it was okay to come in."

"Who was the detective who called to tell you that?"

"Detective Cross called me. It was his raid. He was in charge."

"And why Detective Cross?"

"It was his informant. He had developed the information that led to the raid. It was his idea and plan."

"So, just to be absolutely clear for the court: you saw nothing, you heard nothing. You came in after the raid was completed and the drugs had already been confiscated. Correct?"

"Yes. That's what happened."

"Thank you, Lieutenant. I have no further questions."

Hank stepped down and took his seat with his men. The trial was adjourned for the day.

Carly waited for most of the courtroom to clear out, and she grabbed Tommy as he walked by.

"Let's take this outside," Tommy said, and they walked together, without another word, to the hallway. Carly and Tommy were in clear sight of everybody, but that didn't matter at that point.

"You were great," Carly told Tommy.

Tommy smiled. "Thanks. It went pretty damn well, if I do say so myself."

"Jill Gold was amazing."

"Yup. That sweet girl was my secret weapon, for sure."

"What do you think Boone will do?"

"He'll have a tough time disputing the testimony from Kate. It will just look bad, though I don't put it past him."

Carly spotted Hank leaving, but she didn't get a chance to talk to him or to even catch his eye. Tomorrow would come soon enough.

Larry and Carly headed back to the station. Carly wrote her lede on the way so that, when they got back, she was ready to edit the piece and get it on the six o'clock news. The trial was the leading story, which made Carly proud.

CHAPTER THIRTY-SIX

The next day, it was the defense's turn to try to paint a different portrait of Dalton Cross and what had transpired at Gold's house. Carly assumed there was no way in hell that Boone would call Cross to the stand and expose him to Tommy's interrogation.

The first witness called by Boone was Rob Gold, who was wearing a grey suit with a light blue shirt and blue and red patterned tie. On Rob's wrist was a gold watch, and he had rings on several of his fingers. It was the first time Carly had seen Gold dressed up in a suit and tie, and she thought he cleaned up well and looked good and put together.

"Mr. Gold, please tell the court your name and your occupation."

Gold played it straight. "My name is Rob Gold, and I own a sandwich shop called 'The Hen' in the Financial District."

Boone raised his eyebrows. "Mr. Gold, please tell this court what else you do for a living. Do you have anything at all to do with dealing drugs like cocaine?"

"I don't know what you're referring to," Gold answered with a straight face.

"Really? You don't? Please, don't make a mockery of this court. We know who you are and what you do. Now, please tell the court."

"Objection, Your Honor," Tommy said. "Mr. Boone is being

overly aggressive in his questioning."

"Overruled. You may continue."

"So, tell us: have you ever dealt cocaine?"

"Yes, I have."

"And have you ever been arrested for that?"

"Yes, I have."

"Now we're getting somewhere," Boone said. "So, you're a drug dealer, and your so-called restaurant is a front for your real livelihood," Boone said with utter disdain.

"Objection, leading the witness!" Tommy shouted out again, and again, he was overruled.

The questioning of Gold continued, and Carly thought it was brutal. Rob came off looking like the ultimate drug dealer; a criminal who had every reason to be on the police radar.

Once Boone was finished, Tommy stood up to ask a few questions. He picked up the shadowbox, which had been set on a table in front of Judge Summers.

"Mr. Gold, please tell us about this shadowbox and why it was in the living room and what you had tucked away in it?"

"It was a decoration in the living room that had fake flowers in the front drawer. In the back is a kind of pocket, and I found it was a good place to stash cash."

"Did your wife know that you hid money there"

"No. She did not."

"Did anyone else know about that money?"

"No."

"And what did you have in there?"

"I had $5,000 in cash."

"That's a lot of money. Why did you have that much cash?"

"Because that way I always knew where it was and didn't have to worry about going to a bank to take money out."

"How long had it been there?"

"I have no idea. A while. It was there for emergencies."

Boone shook his head. "Thank you, Mr. Gold. No further questions."

Gold left the stand and returned to his seat next to his wife and daughter.

The glares from the cops on the other side of the room were palpable; members of the Drug Control Unit regarded Gold with equal measures of anger and disdain.

Boone then called three members of the Drug Control Unit, who testified to Cross's strong work ethic, his loyalty to the unit, and his commitment to root out drug dealers. The officers painted a picture of a guy who was a model detective. Carly was impressed, but not surprised, that the other members of the unit were coming to Cross's defense.

As expected, the defense wrapped up without calling Dalton Cross to testify. Then came closing statements.

Tommy drew a compelling picture of an innocent girl seeing Cross take the money and emphasized the testimony of Kate Maloney. There were witnesses who watched what Cross was doing. Carly thought Tommy did a good job.

Boone, on the other hand, used his closing statement to lay out the stakes, the cocaine dealing and crime record of Gold and the outstanding and honorable record of Cross, and drew the contrast of the two. Who would you believe?

In the end, Carly believed Judge Summers would make his decision based not on Gold's testimony, but more likely on that of his daughter and sister-in-law. The judge called a recess but told everyone to stay nearby, as he was likely to come to a decision sooner rather than later.

The courtroom emptied out, and each side gathered in the hall. As Gold left, one of the uniformed cops pushed up against him, throwing him off balance.

"You're scum," the officer said. "You'll get yours, sooner or later. Don't worry about that." With the courtroom's high ceilings, stone floors, and wooden benches, the words echoed.

Carly didn't want to appear to take sides, though it was pretty obvious which side she was on. She waited down the hallway and started going through her notes. She suspected that this trial was the biggest story of her career, and she felt the pressure bearing down on her to get it right and to make a splash.

CHAPTER THIRTY-SEVEN

After less than an hour, a court officer came out into the hallway, looked to the right and to the left, and announced that court was back in session. Carly watched the crowd eagerly file back in. She noticed that Gold seemed to wait until everyone was seated, maybe to avoid any confrontation.

As Judge Summers entered the courtroom, the clerk yelled: "All Rise!" and everyone stood up until the judge said: "You may be seated." He looked out at the packed courtroom, then said: "Will the defendant please rise?"

Dalton Cross and Boone both rose from their seats.

"We, the public, believe in our justice system," said the judge. "And while mistakes may be made, it is difficult to hear a story like we have over the last several days that implicates a Boston police detective in theft...but that's what we have here. The testimonies of Kate Maloney and, particularly, of Jill Gold were compelling. Thus, I am left with no choice but to find the defendant, Dalton Cross, guilty of robbery in the first degree.

Boos and hisses came from the cops.

"Please, please, order in the court." It took a few moments for everyone to settle down, and Cross looked crestfallen at the verdict. Attorney Boone held Cross in a bear hug.

"I am releasing Mr. Cross under house arrest and fully expect you to live by these restrictions. A sentencing hearing will be scheduled for a month from now."

As both sides started exiting the courtroom, Carly stayed back, waiting until the room cleared so she could talk directly to Tommy. Though she figured Tommy would hold a press conference, Carly wanted to be the first to get him on camera. "Great job, Tommy. Really well done. I would love to get a quick interview with you outside the courtroom. Meet you in the hallway?"

"Deal," Tommy said.

Carly went out to the hallway and grabbed her cameraman, Larry, who was sitting and waiting for direction from her. There were other reporters who gathered around to watch the interview.

"What would you like to tell the public about today's verdict?" Carly asked Tommy.

"I want them to know that it doesn't feel good to know that a Boston police detective thought nothing of breaking the law himself. It was an act of greed and arrogance, and he deserves to be found guilty. We can't abide this kind of behavior in the Boston Police Department."

"Thank you," Carly said, then the reporters gathered around Tommy to get their own quotes.

In the meantime, Carly looked around to see if she could find Boone and get him on camera. He stood across the hall, surrounded by police officers. She was a little nervous to walk over to Boone, but she knew she had to do it. She took a deep breath and a few steps, with Larry close behind.

"Mr. Boone, can I get your comment on the guilty verdict of your client?"

Boone moved close to the microphone and, in a loud voice, said: "This is outrageous! A gross miscarriage of justice! An innocent man was railroaded by a drug dealer's family. We will appeal this verdict and we will have a trial before a jury. Outrageous!"

While Carly had known this was a likely outcome, she now had it on the record. It was now time to wrap the story up and head back to the station. There was no question that the story would lead the news, and Carly would have to write several versions of the story both for the six o'clock and eleven o'clock broadcasts.

Carly spotted Chris and Rob on their way out the door. She did not, however, see Eileen, Jill, or Kate; they must have made a quick exit.

Chris gave Carly a thumbs up and a big smile.

Carly smiled, knowing full well they would be celebrating back at Chris's office. There was a pretty good chance she would swing by later.

When Carly got back to the station, Jim was waiting for her, eager to get the run down. Carly was so pumped from the verdict, and she just needed to take a minute to come back down to earth.

"It was better than I thought it would be. The star of the trial was Gold's daughter Jill. She wasn't intimidated at all, and she told a story that was hard to counter—most likely because it was the truth."

"What was the reaction to the verdict?"

"As you can imagine, the cops were so pissed, they hurled verbal threats at Gold, Tommy, and even me in the hallway after the case. I don't know what they thought would happen, but Cross gets another trial anyway. They've already indicated they will appeal, and the second time around, it will be before a jury. I can't wait to see what the DA or the Mayor have to say about this. It's starting to look like there's a pattern of corruption here."

Carly headed to her desk and typed out the story that began: "After two days of testimony and cross-examination, a Boston police detective was found guilty of robbery during a drug raid . . ."

As soon as she had the script, Carly headed downstairs to the segment's producers, who'd made a few minor changes and assigned the story to one of the editors to put it together.

Larry poked his head into the editing suite just to make sure that the shots he wanted were featured in the story. It went without a hitch, and the story led the news with the anchor introducing it. *"Tonight, we have a story about police corruption that was uncovered by our very own Carly Howell . . ."*

It was a great feeling. After the news was over, Carly got her share of high fives from the producers and other reporters in the newsroom. It felt great.

Carly wanted to celebrate. She figured she should stop by Chris Kelly's office to thank them for coming to her with the story. By the time she got there, the two of them were already flying high. Since the front office lights were off, Carly rang the doorbell. Chris came out to let her in, then gave her a bear hug.

"Carly, this is big. You may not realize it, but it's been more than twenty years since anything like this has happened in the police department, and you deserve credit for staying with the story."

"Thanks. I owe both of you. I wouldn't have known about the story without Rob bringing it to me."

Together, Chris and Carly walked back to Chris's office, where Gold was neatly arranging lines of coke.

"Help yourself, Carly."

"I'll pass."

"You're missing out," Rob said with a wide grin on his face.

"I know, I know." Carly turned to Chris. "What do you think happens next, Chris?"

"No question they will appeal the verdict, and next time, they will get a jury trial. That will change the dynamic, and it will take a slightly different approach by Tommy to make a case that doesn't just focus on what a bad guy Cross is, but digs deeper into the corruption of the Drug Control Unit."

"And what do you think happens to Lieutenant James?"

"That's a good question. He's in a tough position. He doesn't want to perjure himself, but he also wants to maintain respect among his men. That will be hard to do."

Carly stayed for an hour, then decided that what she really wanted was to be in a crowd and leave the case behind. She headed back down to Lansdowne Street with hopes that Frank was there; she was anxious to see him again.

It was a moonlit night. Carly parked her car at her apartment and decided to walk down the few blocks to Fenway. As she started walking, she carefully looked on both sides of the street to see if she could spot the car that she had seen a few weeks ago. She didn't and felt a sense of relief. She looked up at the sky and saw a full moon and a starlit sky. The stars were with her, she thought to herself.

As soon as she walked up to the bar, Carly noticed Frank standing there. He was wearing a long-sleeved blue sweater with a zipper in the front that highlighted his fit physique. Carly liked what she saw. It could be a good night; the stars were right!

The dance floor was crowded, and the music was perfect: songs from The Jackson 5, Donna Summer, and Earth, Wind & Fire. It was just what Carly loved, and she did a little hip swinging as she headed over to the bar.

Frank smiled when he saw Carly, and that sent a shiver down her spine.

"Hey, babe, fancy meeting you here," Frank said, reaching over to guide Carly in closer. "It's been a couple of weeks. I take it your work has you pretty well occupied."

"For sure. The trial I was covering just ended today, in fact."

"So, what now?"

"Before we dive into that, I would love a drink. You buying?" Carly winked at Frank.

"Of course, darlin'. Ask and you shall receive." Two can play the charm game.

"I'd love a vodka and tonic."

Frank ordered the drink, and the bartender mixed the drink, then set it in front of Carly. Carly moved to clink glasses with Frank.

"To a night of dancing, drinking and a little romance."

"Salud," Frank said, and Carly reached over and planted a quick kiss on his cheek.

Frank extended a hand, and he and Carly walked together onto the dance floor, where there was a slow song playing and an opportunity for Frank to get a little closer. He pulled Carly in close to him, and they did a little grinding to James Taylor's smooth singing.

"This feels so good," Carly said. "Just what the doctor ordered."

The dancing went on for a few more songs, then Carly took Frank's hand and led him to an empty table. While the din of the music was loud and quiet conversation was out of the question, they looked each other in the eyes, and Carly knew there was chemistry between them.

"Let's get out of here." Frank extended his hand.

"Shall we go to my place—it's nearby," Carly said.

"If that's okay with you, it certainly is with me," Frank answered. In the back of her mind, Carly heard a voice telling her to take it slow, but she ignored that voice.

CHAPTER THIRTY-EIGHT

"Did you drive here, because I walked?" Carly asked.

"Yeah, my car's just down the street," said Frank. Frank and Carly walked together about half a block and, under a streetlight, Frank pointed to a black Honda Accord. He opened the passenger door, and Carly slid in. The interior was black leather and smelled almost new.

"I take it this is a pretty recent purchase?"

"Yes, indeed."

"I have a Honda, too. Small world. I hope we can find a parking spot on Comm. Ave.

"I've got good parking karma. I'm sure we will." And sure enough, they did, almost right in front of Carly's building.

"Guess you weren't kidding about the karma."

Carly opened the door and got out and searched for her keys. She waited for Frank, then led him by the hand to her front door. "Just one short flight up."

Carly realized there was almost nothing in her refrigerator to serve. Oh, well, what was there would have to do. In any case, there was a bottle of vodka in the freezer—a small reminder of Hank. Carly's mind momentarily wandered, and she wondered what Hank must be doing or thinking at this moment; the guilty verdict had to be doing a number on him. Was he at Richard's with other cops, or was he at home with his wife and kids? Carly quickly returned to the present and Frank.

No sooner were they in her apartment than Frank helped Carly out of her coat, then pulled her close to him and gave her a kiss. It was a polite kind of kiss, and she appreciated that; Frank was a gentleman.

"Let's get to know each other a little better before we dive into anything," Carly said.

"Sure. There is no rush. I think it makes sense to take it a little slowly. Okay at least if we kiss?"

Carly moved even closer. They each took a deep breath and started to kiss. Carly took Frank's hand and headed over to the couch. "Do you have any favorites when it comes to music? I favor Motown."

"Well, ain't it a small world after all? Me too. I'm assuming you've got some Temptations?"

Without another word, Carly walked over to the record player and put on *Cloud Nine* that featured the songs "I Heard it Through the Grapevine," "Runaway Child, Running Wild," and "Hey Girl."

Frank stood up and moved toward Carly. He grabbed her from the back, turned her around, and started dancing.

Perfect, Carly thought. This is how it should be, yet so rarely is.

They danced for a while, then Carly took Frank's hand and brought him back to the couch. They talked until midnight about Frank living in Boston as a Black man, about City Hall and his job, about the news business and the special view it gave Carly of the city. Carly was thoroughly enjoying her time with Frank, but it was a weekday, and she did have to go to work in the morning, as she assumed Frank did too.

"I hate to be the spoiler," Carly said. "But I think we should call it a night."

"Really? I thought you would invite me to stay over," Frank smiled as if he knew that wasn't going to happen.

"Not tonight. Maybe soon."

"No harm in trying, right?"

Carly reached up and gave Frank a peck on the cheek. "Nope. None!"

Carly went and got Frank's coat out of the closet and helped him on with it.

"This was great, and I would love to get together soon," Carly said, her eyes focused on Frank's smooth skin and copper-colored eyes.

"As would I. I will be in touch." Frank kissed Carly and turned toward the door. "Sleep well."

"I will, thanks to you."

No sooner had Carly fallen into a deep sleep than the telephone rang. Carly glanced at her clock; it was three a.m. Her heart raced. She took a few deep breaths before answering the phone.

"Watch yourself, bitch!"

That was it! The guy hung up. The phone call was enough to rattle Carly, and she jumped out of bed and walked around the apartment. The apartment was dark with the curtains drawn, and she felt eerily alone. At the window, she pulled aside the shades and looked into the alley, but she didn't see anyone. She turned the television on for a bit but at three in the morning; there wasn't a lot on TV.

Eventually, Carly calmed herself down enough to go back to sleep.

A few hours later, when she woke up, Carly decided she had to tell someone about the call. Jim, for sure. Tommy? Why not? What about Hank? He should, at least, know what his guys were up to, since there was no doubt in Carly's mind about who made the call. There might not be much that could be done, but folks should be aware of what these corrupt cops were doing.

CHAPTER THIRTY-NINE

Jim was already at his desk when Carly walked in. She sat down in the only other chair that was there, leaned in, and focused on Jim's face so she could see and sense his reaction. Carly was still unnerved by the call.

"You're not going to believe what happened last night, or should I say early this morning? It was three a.m., and the phone rang, and a man's voice yelled—'watch yourself bitch.' It scared the shit out of me."

"If it's a cop, I am a little surprised they would do that to you, a reporter," Jim said. "It just goes to further demonstrate that these are bad guys, and you just helped convict one of their 'band of brothers.'"

"I am going to call Tommy just so he knows. I'm not sure what can be done, but I'll feel better," Carly said. She didn't mention that she was going to call Hank, too; some things were better left unsaid.

"Thanks for listening," Carly said and got up, then she headed next door to her office and dialed Tommy. He answered his office phone on the first ring. "Top of the mornin' to you," Tommy said after Carly's greeting.

"You're in a good mood. Guess you deserve it. Might as well savor it while you can."

"You got that right. What can I do for you, Carly?"

"Would it surprise you if I told you that I got a threatening phone call last night—or should I say this morning? Woke me out of a deep sleep and scared the shit out of me."

"Hell no! I'm actually surprised I didn't get a call. These are bad actors, and they'll likely stop at nothing to get their revenge. You'd better watch your back. Do you want a security detail out front of your building? I can probably arrange that."

"Hmm . . ." Carly thought for a minute. "Why not, right? What do I have to lose?" No sooner did she utter the words than she realized either Hank or Rob could show up unannounced at her apartment—day or night. "Let's wait a day or two and see if there's anything else that happens before we do that."

"Okay. Just let me know."

The next call would be tougher. Carly was hesitant to phone Hank but knew she had to let him know what his men were doing. She went ahead and dialed Hank's number. The phone rang a couple of times before he picked it up.

"Uh, hello. Lieutenant James here. How can I help you?"

"Well, actually, there are a couple of ways, but that's a story for a different day."

Hank laughed. That was a good sign; at least Carly could still tickle his fancy.

"I just wanted you to know that, early this morning, about three a.m., I got a threatening call on my phone. I figured it was one of your guys, and I'm not sure you can do anything about it, but I wanted you to know."

"Sorry about that. If, indeed, it was one of my guys, it was pretty stupid on their part. Not sure I can say anything, but I can certainly make clear that they should be careful with any retaliatory steps they are thinking about. By the way, do you have a listed phone number?"

"Yes, I do. I guess it would make sense for me to have it unlisted. Good point. So, how are you? How have things been since the verdict?"

"I've been better. I figure it's only a matter of time 'til I get reassigned. I've been keeping my head down."

"Not much I can say. I'd say I'm sorry, but these are your guys, and I guess you should have had a better idea of what they were up to."

"I've thought a lot about what I could have done differently and, yes, keeping a better handle on what they were doing is on the top of that list. Not easy to do, given the independence with which they operate." Hank paused. "I'm not sure when we can see each other again. It's a little awkward at the moment . . ."

"Maybe once things quiet down a bit—assuming that will happen," Carly offered.

"Not for a while, I'm afraid," Hank said. "There is no way that Cross won't appeal the verdict. He has a chance to have a trial before a jury, which is much more likely to believe him over Rob Gold."

Carly had the same thought. However, it might be a while before that happened. In the meantime, either she was going to have to find another story to work on or try to keep the drip of this one going.

It had gotten to be a reflex action at this point: Carly dialed Chris Kelly's number. The phone rang a couple of times, but Chris didn't pick up; she'd try again in an hour or two. Carly spent the rest of the day appearing to be working on reviewing her notes from the trial and deciding what her next step would be with the story. The work made Carly reflect on what had been going on, the story, the characters involved, Hank and Frank, and it all felt a bit overwhelming.

Carly got up and knocked on Jim's door: "You know, I am really not feeling great. May have something to do with getting awakened in the middle of the night with that nasty phone call. If it's okay with you, I am going to go back to my apartment and take it easy for the rest of the day."

"I understand," Jim said. "Get some rest. See you in the morning."

It was a beautiful early spring day. After Carly got to her apartment in the Back Bay, she decided to take a long walk down the Esplanade along the Charles River. The birds were chirping their little hearts out. Carly felt like, outside in the fresh air, she could relax a bit, but there was the nagging feeling that the drug cops could be out there watching her, waiting to do something to her.

CHAPTER FORTY

Dalton Cross knew that his friends on the Drug Control Unit were as pissed as pissed could be about the verdict. It was part of the one-for-all and all-for-one tradition among the cops.

Somehow, they'd forgotten that they were on the side of law enforcement and, instead, it was all about getting as much as they could from their dealers and seeking their own form or revenge before the whole game was up. The clock was ticking.

Cross was grateful that his buddies wanted to show their support for him, so he invited them over to his house, where he was now under arrest. Cross lived in the Hyde Park neighborhood in a modest triple-decker on the first floor. The house looked like every other triple-decker in the neighborhood: it was yellow with white trim, and there was nothing to make it stand out from the crowd. The night they gathered, the street was lined with unmarked cars, back-to-back-to-back. You'd think there was a funeral actually…this meeting kind of was.

There were eight guys seated on the brown leather couch and the two reclining chairs in the living room. Cross put down a platter of store-bought appetizers and plastic plates and glasses and three six-packs of Budweiser.

One of the detectives lifted a can to make a toast to Cross: "We're with you. Don't ever forget that. We are a team, and we need to stick together."

The beers were flowing freely, and the men consoled Cross

and vowed to get even. Paul O'Malley, one of the most corrupt of them all, huddled around Cross and a few of the other guys and offered up a plan: "I've got an idea. We've got to make our money while we still can. I think we should hit up as many of our informants as we can and as soon as we can."

"Give me a fucking break, Paul," said Cross.

"You can't be serious," said another of the cops. "We've got a giant bullseye on our backs. The department can't let this go unanswered. We'd be hard-pressed to pull this off."

"It's now or never. The more time we let go by, the less of a chance we have. We can make a few raids and grab our share of the haul."

"I like it," another guy chimed in. "It'll be our revenge."

"Look, I have it from one of my informants that there is going to be a pretty big deal happening tomorrow night—in Roxbury, of all places. I suggest we drop in on the deal, get our cut, and let the dealers go. They may be a little annoyed, but they aren't about to say a word," O'Malley said.

"What are we talking about in terms of amount?" asked Cross. "Do you have any idea?"

"My guy tells me there could be a good half kilo," the detective said.

"Damn! Do you think anyone else in the department knows about this and might possibly show up there?"

"I highly doubt it. These dealers are good and careful. The location in Roxbury is not easy to find, and without an informant, there wouldn't really be a way to find out."

By the time the officers took a vote, they were all pretty plastered, and they were all in. "Hey, Cross, we don't think it's a smart move for you to go. We'll bring you home some of the loot.

Don't worry!"

Cross hugged his brothers. "Thanks, guys!"

The officers stayed for a little while longer, drinking and telling story after story about the money they'd been able to take from dealers in the past. Cross felt much better when they left. He felt like he would not be alone as he went through this court process, and deep down, he was confident, as Boone had assured him that, with a jury, there was a very high likelihood he would be found innocent.

It was true, Cross had to stay put in his house, and that wouldn't be easy, given how small it was. But he chose to look to a future free of this trial thing hanging over his head.

CHAPTER FORTY-ONE

O'Malley had a plan. The next night, he called his "brothers-in-arms" to meet at his house in Dorchester around midnight. Ten of them, all the guys who were in on the raid at Gold's, gathered at his house. With O'Malley taking charge, they decided that five of them would pile into one car, and the other five would drive the second car to the location in Roxbury. The deal was supposed to go down at about two a.m.

It was tight quarters in the car, so it got pretty steamy. The cops rolled down the windows to let out their cigarette smoke.

While they'd never pulled off a heist all together, O'Malley felt like this was their way of getting some justice for Cross and what they felt was an unjust verdict, even though several of them knew that Cross did take the money. It was also, he thought, maybe the last time they would be able to pull this kind of caper, given that the unit was under increased scrutiny from the police department. This raid was about unity and the "brotherhood," O'Malley kept telling himself.

Roxbury had a predominantly minority population that was overwhelmingly poor. Throughout the neighborhood, there were swaths of unoccupied buildings, boarded up and abandoned. That made what was about to go down that much easier. No one was out here, not even the police—unless they were called.

Roxbury had also just been the scene of a horrific incident, labeled "The Roxbury murders," when twelve Black women were murdered in a series of crimes in the neighborhood. It was also just five years after the highly-charged desegregation of the Boston public schools, during which students from Roxbury and Dorchester were bused to South Boston and Charlestown, causing riots and violent demonstrations.

O'Malley yelled out the address: "212 Westminster." There were no working streetlights on this block, but he didn't see anything out of the ordinary. The officers parked their cars, turned off their headlights, and sat quietly, waiting.

Within a half hour, a dark Ford sedan and what looked like an old Lincoln town car inched their way down the street, making crunching sounds as loose gravel was crushed under the tires. The two vehicles took a right into an alleyway and parked.

O'Malley realized that they didn't have a great view from where they were parked, and he called the second car on the walkie-talkie and told them to move the car just a bit closer. Again, O'Malley led the way. When he got to a spot that gave them a better sight line, he stopped; the second car followed suit. O'Malley turned off the engine, got out of the car, signaled to everyone to move forward with guns drawn, and together, they walked toward the alley.

As they walked toward the alley, O'Malley could see that there were two or three guys standing around the cars, and he could hear the Spanish swear words going back and forth. The trunk of the Ford was open, and he could see piles of cocaine stacked up inside, just as he expected. O'Malley took a deep breath and gave the signal to move forward. Everyone followed him, quietly, with guns pointed straight ahead.

Suddenly, as the cops got closer, they were spotted by the drug dealers. A few *pop, pops* were heard as one of them fired his gun.

"Fuck!" Officer Frank Flynn fell to the ground, clutching his leg; he had been hit in the calf. Two of the guys quickly wrapped his leg to stem the bleeding.

The other guys, led by O'Malley, pointed their guns and yelled: "Put your weapons down!"

The dealers obeyed, and O'Malley and the others approached the Ford, pointing their guns directly at the dealers, who put their hands in the air.

"Give us the money, and you can keep the drugs!" O'Malley yelled. His heart was beating out of his chest. This wasn't an everyday situation. O'Malley knew and kept his hand on the trigger and his eyes on the guys in the car; there were four of them. It took a minute, but one of the guys reached into the glove compartment and handed O'Malley an envelope.

"That's it. Believe me."

O'Malley reached in and started to count. When he saw the stack of hundreds, he was confident they had gotten it all.

"Now get the fuck out of here!" O'Malley yelled to the dealers. After the dealers piled into their cars and sped away, he ran over to Flynn. The officers helped Flynn to the car and decided they would take him to the hospital rather than calling an ambulance; there would be fewer questions that way. But the officers did call in the incident to the Police Department and to Lieutenant James. On the way to Carney Hospital in the car, the officers talked about the story they would tell to make sure that every one of them was on the same page. They decided to leave it to O'Malley to be the spokesman for the group. As they pulled up to the ER entrance, the emergency staff rolled out a gurney and put Flynn on it.

By now, Flynn was pretty groggy and out of it. O'Malley worried that they might have waited too long and prayed he would make it. The cops were left to sit in the waiting room, which was surprisingly empty on this night.

One of the nurses came over to the cops and asked the obvious: "What happened?"

O'Malley spoke up: "We were in Roxbury, looking to bust a certain drug dealer we know, and we were standing outside our unmarked car when—the next thing we know—a car drives by, and two shots are fired, one hitting our buddy."

"Okay. Thanks. We will have to make a complete report, and you should as well," the nurse said.

"Of course," O'Malley said. "We will have to file a report with the department as soon as we are done here. We wanted to make sure Flynn was going to be okay first."

The nurse asked another obvious question: "Why didn't you dial 911?"

"We figured we were all together, and since we had a siren in our unmarked car, we could get here just as quickly on our own," O'Malley said.

"Okay. We will keep you updated. Are you all going to wait here?"

"We'd like to, if that's okay," O'Malley said.

"Of course. There is coffee over there." The nurse pointed to the far corner of the room. " You guys are welcome to help yourselves."

The officers paced nervously, getting up, sitting down, stepping outside for a cigarette, and even drinking what can only be described as rotgut coffee. After an hour or two, they were getting nervous, and O'Malley walked up to the nurses' desk and asked one of the nurses if she could find out what was happening with their buddy.

The nurse was writing and looking down. When she heard the

question, she turned her head to look at O'Malley, then said: "Here's what I know: they're in surgery. We will let you know as soon as there is an update. I promise."

Suddenly, O'Malley turned around and saw Lieutenant James and his deputy walk through the emergency entrance. There was a serious, concerned look on Hank's face. As soon he saw the lieutenant, O'Malley had an almost visceral response to look away. There was clearly no love lost between Hank and O'Malley, that was for sure.

"What the fuck happened?" Hank asked. He took a stance of authority with his hands on his hips, like he was ready for a showdown at the O.K. Corral.

"A drug bust that went just a bit off script," O'Malley said.

"Okay. That's obvious. I need a little more than that."

O'Malley repeated the story he told the nurse: "We were in Roxbury, looking for a drug dealer we know because we had gotten a tip that there was a drug deal that was going to go down. We were parked in an alleyway, standing outside the car. But before we could make the bust, one of the dealers shot at us, hitting Frankie in the leg. We were all pretty lucky, really, that it wasn't worse than it was."

"It must have been a pretty big bust if all of you were there. And if it was that big, you should have let me know it was going down. Just curious: why the fuck didn't you let me know?" Lieutenant James asked.

Eyes darted back and forth between the guys as they looked to make sure everyone was still on the same page.

"We just got word of it yesterday and didn't really have a lot of planning time. We wanted to make sure we were there," O'Malley said.

"Really . . . and how much coke did you get? And how much money?"

"They fled the scene before we could grab anything. It was pretty disappointing, especially since they shot Frankie. Once that happened, we were focused on him and making sure we got him to the hospital," O'Malley said.

Lieutenant James did not look convinced. "Well, here you are. How is Flynn?"

"He's still in surgery," O'Malley said.

CHAPTER FORTY-TWO

Hank already had a problem with loyalty among the ranks, so he didn't push his men too hard—at least not right now. But he couldn't escape the gnawing feeling in his gut. At this point, there was nobody he could trust. Hank went back and forth in his head about whether he should sit and wait to see how Frank was after surgery, and he eventually decided to stay. Hank didn't announce his decision. He just walked over to get a cup of coffee, came back, and sat down, feeling felt the awkward tension in the room.

Another hour went by before a doctor in scrubs approached the officers from down the hall. The guys gathered around. "I'm Dr. Edwards. I just operated on your buddy. Let me tell you, he's a very lucky guy, and it's a good thing he got here when he did. He lost quite a lot of blood, but he's going to be fine. Have you let his family know?"

"His wife is on her way," O'Malley volunteered.

"He's pretty groggy," said Dr. Edwards. "But follow me and you can go in and see him briefly."

After a collective sigh of relief, the officers quietly followed the doctor into an intensive care room. Flynn was tangled up, wires and tubes seemingly coming out of every orifice. He couldn't talk, but he was awake, and when he saw his brothers, he gave them a thumbs-up.

"Damn! We're so glad you're going to be okay," O'Malley said. "Sorry, man, that you had to take that bullet. You're our hero.

Your wife is on her way down here. We'll hang around 'til she gets here, don't worry."

Flynn gave his buddies another thumbs-up. The guys crowded around the bed, some with hands on Flynn. After fifteen minutes, a nurse peeked in and told them it was time to leave. The officers waved goodbye and headed back to the waiting room.

Hank went back with the officers and waited with them for Flynn's wife to show up. He had been given a story to tell his superiors, but he was unsure how much of it was true.

It hit Hank as he sat in the waiting room that what he had in his unit was pretty much an "us versus them" situation: it was him against his men. That wasn't good, and it certainly was not sustainable. The unit could not function properly or effectively without everyone working together.

Hank started to catalog the members of the unit: those he had a good relationship, with and those who might not be on his side. As he went through the checklist, Hank realized the majority were more rogue than team players. Maybe that was just part of what attracted these men to this work. They had the opportunity to develop their own leads, cultivate sources, create their own schedule, and—apparently—to take what they could get on the side.

While Hank sat in one corner of the waiting room, his men were huddled in another corner, almost ignoring him.

Fifteen minutes had gone by when the sliding waiting room's glass doors opened, and Flynn's wife Julie dashed through, with another woman by her side. Julie was clearly upset, even as she had pulled herself together. Hank had never met Julie before. She was a beautiful woman in her thirties. She was a slight woman, five two at most, and wore black pants and a light blue V-neck sweater, her blond hair tied back in a ponytail. Looking vulnerable, Julie was trying to hold herself together and not break down into tears.

Hank walked toward Julie, extending a hand as he said: "I'm Lieutenant Hank James, and I head up the Drug Control Unit. I'm sorry your husband got hurt. The good news is that he should be fine. I'm sure you want to go see him."

"Yes, please."

"Julie, we've got your back and Frank's," O'Malley said as he put his arm around Julie's shoulder. Suddenly, Hank was on the outside again as O'Malley led Julie to the ICU. Hank walked behind them, and the rest of the guys followed.

The door to the ICU slid open, and the officers let Julie go into her husband's room. As soon as she saw him all tangled in wires and tubes, Julie put her hand by her mouth and let out a gasp: "Oh, no!" Julie leaned down to kiss Frank and could see that he was sleeping. As soon as Julie kissed him, though, Frank opened his eyes and reached out his hand. Julie grabbed hold of it and started stroking Frank's arm, and Hank brought over a chair so Julie could sit down next to the bed.

"I love you," Julie said softly.

Hank watched as Frank squeezed Julie's hand, letting her know that he heard her. The room was quiet, with everyone's attention focused on the husband and wife. A nurse came in and asked everyone but Flynn's wife and her friend to leave the room.

"It's only right that we give them some privacy," the nurse told the others. "Okay?

As a group, the officers turned toward the door and headed out. Before leaving, Hank put a hand on Julie's shoulder and said: "Whatever you need, we're here for you. Please call me if you need anything."

"Thank you," Julie said, almost whispering.

The guys huddled outside the door together. "I think we can call it a night," O'Malley said to the group.

Hank knew full well he'd be thought of as the bad guy when he said: "Don't forget, we need a full report done."

"Yes, sir," the officers said, almost in unison, as the sound of their feet on the tiles could be heard down the hall.

"Okay with you if that happens in the morning?" asked O'Malley.

"Not really," replied Hank. "Given the nature of what happened, it's important that the report be written when the situation is fresh in your minds. Who's writing it?"

"I will," O'Malley said. Hank thought to himself, *of course it would be O'Malley*. This whole fiasco was probably his idea in the first place.

"Great. Please have it on my desk in the morning." Hank turned and headed down the hall to the exit.

"Fuck him," O'Malley said under his breath, then he said to himself: "It's okay. We've got this. We can certainly write a report that will be above board and explain what happened. No problem. Time to go. Quite a night, that's for damn sure."

CHAPTER FORTY-THREE

Carly heard reference to the shooting on the police scanner, and as soon as she could, she called the communications office at the police department the next day. She was told that there would be a statement released later that day. She alerted the newsroom to the story, and said she would let them know when there was a statement. Carly then told the news director that she would volunteer to do a stand-up with the story in front of police headquarters, and she kept her word.

"Late last night, a Boston Police detective was shot in the leg during a drug bust in Roxbury. The name of the officer is Detective Frank Flynn. He is recovering at Carney Hospital and is listed in good condition. The police department issued a statement saying it was launching a full investigation into the shooting."

Carly was at her desk, doing her due diligence in trying to find out whatever she could about Frank Flynn, but he didn't stand out, and she couldn't really find out much. She was feeling frustrated because, deep down, she knew this situation all had to be tied to the culture of cops gone wrong that seemed to permeate the department. Just then, the phone rang.

"Carly—it's Tommy here—I have news. Cross filed his appeal and will automatically be granted a new trial, this time before a jury."

"Well, you said all along that if he were found guilty before a judge, he'd get a second bite at the apple."

"Yes. Just giving you a heads-up since, I would imagine, you would want to report that."

"Thanks." Carly appreciated Tommy reaching out. While this update would likely only be a short "reader"—where the anchor reads the headline, and it doesn't become a full-fledged story—that was okay because the update would keep the story alive.

Carly asked Tommy: "Will a jury trial change your approach?"

"The truth is our case doesn't change. I'll still call the same witnesses and put forth the same story. But we do have to be aware that it's one thing for a judge to overlook the fact that it's a drug dealer making the charge and quite another for a jury to do that."

"Bummer," Carly said. "Though good for me. I get to do another story."

Tommy changed the subject. "I know you did a story about the cop who got shot last night. You know he's a member of the Drug Control Unit, right?"

"I suspected as much," Carly said. "But I hadn't yet confirmed it. Thanks."

Tommy laughed. "Ooh, you sound a little skeptical. I can't understand why."

"Hard not to. Supposedly, six drug cops were ready to bust a drug dealer in an alley in Roxbury when one of the dealer's guys fired shots, and one struck cop Frank Flynn in the thigh."

"Have they opened an investigation?"

"If they haven't yet, they will."

"Thanks very much. And thanks for letting me know about Cross. Talk soon."

As soon as she hung up the phone with Tommy, Carly put in a

call to Hank.

"Hello. Lieutenant James here."

"I won't bother asking how you're doing," Carly said. "It only seems to get worse for you, doesn't it?"

"I was just thinking the same thing. This is not at all what I envisioned when I joined the force almost thirty years ago."

"I heard Frank Flynn was shot last night. What happened?"

"There is not much I can tell you other than what you probably already know. And, of course, whatever I tell you is off-the-record. Flynn got shot in the leg and lost a lot of blood. He's going to be alright, but it was dicey there for a while."

"You may not be able to answer this question, but I have to ask: why the hell did they bring him in rather than calling an ambulance?"

"Damn good question."

Carly had the ability to get to the heart of a story and dig in.

"I can't really say anything about that," Hank commented. "It will obviously be part of any report that is written. They said they had a blue light in the car and were close to the hospital anyway."

"What were they all doing at this one deal? Isn't that a lot of guys for one bust—not that I know anything about policing."

"I'm beginning to think I don't know that much anymore either.

"Will there by an investigation?"

"Oh yes. You can count on that. Especially given everything else that's going on."

"You understand I will have to report that an investigation is underway. There's no way you're going to look good in this, either." Carly let herself get a little personal. "How are you holding up?"

"It's been rough. Last night in the waiting room, there was a clear divide between the men in the unit and me. That's just something I will have to live with for as long as I'm head of the Drug Control Unit."

Carly wondered to herself what the likelihood was that Hank would remain head of the DCU; she figured it was highly unlikely.

Carly wished she could somehow help. "Look, I'll be honest with you. I'm happy to be friends, whatever that means, but I've decided that, given you're married and not about to leave your wife, there is really very little point in continuing our fling—or whatever you want to call it. So, if we agree and restrain whatever feelings we have, I would invite you over just to talk."

"That's really considerate of you. I could use a shoulder to lean on. Not sure where we could meet. Not Richard's, that's for sure."

"What about Charlie's near me?" Carly offered. "It's big enough and anonymous enough that we could be able to find a spot away from the crowd."

"Good. Shall we say seven o'clock at Charlie's?"

"Sounds like a plan. See you then."

Carly walked into Jim's office to update him on what had happened; he wasn't surprised. "You know, I spent a lot of time researching the mob and the men who are part of the Angiulo gang, and the Bulger gang and these guys are really no different. You would think they would be but in the world of drugs and money; it's all there, and everyone wants a piece of the action. It's disappointing, but it's pretty obvious that being a drug cop is dangerous—not just because of what can happen during a raid, but because of the temptation that's right in front of your nose day in and day out." And then, Jim got right to the heart of Carly's dilemma: "You need to be careful that you keep your distance. You're covering this story. Make sure you aren't part of the story. That line is sometimes hard to discern. I know; I've been there."

As Jim was speaking, Carly cringed. She had already stepped way over the line. Tonight, she would be extra vigilant around Hank. Carly's better half knew that failing to hold the line would be the end of the story and, likely, the end of her career.

CHAPTER FORTY-FOUR

At home, Carly quickly changed into more casual attire: a pair of lightweight, black bell-bottoms and a pink, jersey, long-sleeve shirt with puffy sleeves and a bow at the neckline—nothing too fancy, but enough to turn a couple of heads. It was good enough for the Charlie's crowd. Carly donned a modest pair of gold hoop earrings, as well as rings on each hand, and got there early, as usual.

It was six-thirty, and the bar was not yet crowded. It was dark and smoky in the bar from cigarette smoke hanging overhead like a cloud. The after-work crowd was just starting to get there. Carly stepped up to a long, wooden bar with a mirror running its length and bottle after neatly stacked bottle of liquors. There was music blaring—*Lady Marmalade* by LaBelle, *Time in a Bottle* by Jim Croce, and *All the Young Dudes* sung by Mott The Hoople. Four bartenders, dressed in black pants and white shirts, were filling orders and shaking cocktails, which almost made a dance rhythm all its own. Carly took an empty seat and looked around to see if there was anyone there that she knew. She didn't recognize anyone, which, on this night, was a good thing.

Carly knew the head bartender, Joe. He looked her way and winked, putting up a finger to signal he'd be there in a minute. And when he finished pouring several drinks, Joe came down to Carly's end of the bar and said: "Good evening, darlin'! What can I get you? Oh, let me guess: a vodka and tonic?"

"Good guess, Joe."

Truth was that, ever since meeting Hank, Carly had adopted the drink as her favorite, too.

No sooner did she have her drink in hand than she spotted Hank at the front entrance. He saw her, walked over, gave her a kiss on her cheek, and turned to Joe.

"I'll have what she's having."

After his drink arrived, Hank took Carly's hand and led her to an empty booth. They slid in and looked at each other. It had been weeks since they'd seen each other.

"You look tired," Carly remarked.

"Yeah. Pretty hard to sleep with everything that's going on."

"I can only imagine," Carly said.

"I never thought I would get into a situation like this. I have, truly, always tried to be aboveboard and operate by the book. Maybe that's how I got put in the Internal Affairs Unit. Whatever. I am having a harder time than I thought I would be processing everything that's happened with this case."

"What are the higher-ups saying?"

"Not too many folks inside know what's really going on— another secret I've got to keep. And there is something fishy with the circumstances of Flynn's shooting. It doesn't add up. It's been referred to Internal Affairs. —I have faith in them to do a fair and thorough investigation, and, hopefully, the truth will come out."

Carly was more than a little shocked by Hank's willingness to admit his mistakes. She followed his eyes closely, then noticed his shoulders sagging as he put his elbows on the table. Hank cradled his head in his hands. "After what's happened with Cross and O'Rourke and the aftermath of Flynn, I wouldn't be surprised if I get reassigned. It's not at all how I imagined my career in law enforcement would go. But I can at least take some solace in knowing I played it straight. I told the truth. And, ultimately, that's what got me into trouble with my men. They couldn't trust me because they were playing loose with the rules behind my back. My trust was betrayed."

Hank took a deep breath and let it out; he had bared his soul to Carly, and it was a lot for her to absorb. It was Carly nature to want to fix things, but this was a situation she couldn't fix.

Carly reached out her hand and Hank took it. "This has been a weird situation all the way around," she said. "I'm sorry for your situation and what you're going through, but I don't regret playing a part in exposing what is clearly a broad culture of corruption that's been going on for way too long."

"Before this happened, I would have argued with you...but now it's pretty hard to argue with what's in plain sight. I'm just glad I'm one of the soldiers in this fight and not a general."

Once they finished their drinks, Hank and Carly got up and walked out of the bar together, and once they were on Newbury Street, Hank gave Carly a quick kiss and headed outside to Hereford Street, where his car was parked.

Carly waited for Hank to leave, then walked the block to her apartment, feeling good about her ability to restrain herself. It did seem likely that Hank would get reassigned, but the superiors in the department were unlikely to do that before Dalton Cross's second trial ended; the optics just wouldn't be good.

CHAPTER FORTY-FIVE

That summer, for two glorious weeks, Carly rented a lovely cottage in Truro on Cape Cod with several friends. She loved nothing more than being at the beach; it was a great getaway from the day-to-day.

The smell of sea air, the feel of sand between her toes, the fun of going into Provincetown and barhopping and shopping . . . Carly and her friends watched the sunset as it settled beneath the Provincetown skyline. The rainbow of reds and yellows made the water glow and sparkle. And this was one of those glorious summers so special on the Cape. Carly let down her guard and let herself have a good time without worrying about drug dealers or cops or trials. She was more focused on her tan and reading crime novel after crime novel.

The weeks flew by. Why was it that vacations always went by so fast? It wasn't long after Carly got back to the TV station before Dalton Cross's second trial was scheduled to begin in September.

The best way Carly could get an update on the case and trial was to call Tommy. On the phone, after some pleasantries and Carly rhapsodizing about wonderful Cape Cod, she got down to business: "How different will this trial be from the first, and how will your approach change?"

"Given all the nonsense that's gone on, some of Cross's troublemaking colleagues are going to get called to testify this time around. They'll likely lie to save themselves and their buddies, but it's worth a shot. At the least the jury will be presented a picture different than what Boone will provide them with."

"Any more stings in the works?"

"The DA wasn't exactly happy about the last one. I'd be pushing my luck to try another, even though I'm pretty sure we could nab another cop."

"But if they are called to the stand, don't you think these guys will lie and do whatever it takes to spin the storyline the way they want it?" Carly asked.

"But now I have more info from my informants about what these guys routinely do—so I may be able to paint a wider picture than just one bad cop like Cross," Tommy said.

Then Carly volunteered: "Anything you want to get out to the public before the trial, you know where I am and how to get in touch, so feel free. I thank you for all you've done for me. I wouldn't have been able to do the reporting I've been doing without you. But you know that, don't you?"

"Truth is, we are each serving our own purposes, and that's okay. As long as we both want justice to prevail."

Carly was dying to know what Gold and Chris were thinking about the second trial and what tricks they had up their sleeves this time. She called Chris, who was in the office, and he invited her to come down for a little "pick-me-up" and to talk about the case.

When she got down to Commercial Street and parked her car at about three in the afternoon, Carly took a few minutes, as she always did, to inhale the smell of the ocean, bringing back visions of Truro. It was a beautiful late summer's day, and the water glimmered with the sun's reflection. Carly looked out to see a combination of sailboats and a tanker ship; it was a working harbor as well as a recreational one.

Looking out, Carly could also see planes coming and going from Logan Airport. She walked into Chris's office, which, for the first time she could remember, resembled a somewhat normal workplace. Chris was at his desk, and his assistant Marie was in the office, as was his partner Robert Heilman, whom Carly had never previously met.

"Carly, meet my partner, Robert. We've been working together for about fifteen years."

Robert rolled his chair out to the edge of his office to peek out to say hello. Then, just as quickly, he went back to his work.

Chris and Carly went into Chris's office, and Chris sat down and put his legs up on his desk; that seemed to be his favorite position.

"Let me call Gold and see what he's up to. He might be at the Hen."

"Go ahead, but it might be good for the two of us to have a conversation without him for a change and, frankly, without you being high on coke. It will give you a chance to be as honest as you can be about where the case is and where you think it's headed."

"Fair enough."

"So, let's start with your assessment. What do you think are the chances that Cross will be found guilty by a jury when Tommy has to call Rob to testify?"

"It depends on the jury Tommy helps select. If they get a bunch of law-and-order folks who look at any drug dealer with skepticism, it'll be tough. It's one thing for a judge to use his wisdom and experience and figure out the truth, but it's totally different when it's a jury."

"That's kind of what I figured, too. And that puts pressure both on Tommy and Rob. Does Rob get that?"

"For better or for worse—and, mostly, for worse—he is who he is. He's a drug dealer who has managed to get caught a couple of times but also to evade the cops and get away with a lot of shit almost as many times. He knows how to play all sides of any situation. I don't worry that much about how he'll do on the stand, but that doesn't change the fact that he's a convicted felon. Time to call him up, whaddaya say?"

"Go ahead."

Chris took his feet off the desk, reached across the desk for his phone, and dialed Gold's deli. He put the phone on speaker so Carly could hear.

"Hey there, it's Chris. Your favorite reporter is sitting here with me. Have time to come over? We could use a pick-me-up."

"I'm on my way." With the deli nearby, it was only fifteen minutes before Rob walkedthrough the door. He looked like he fit perfectly into the North End, with gold jewelry, crisply pressed pants, and a matching shirt.

"My favorite folks. Everybody feelin' good? I am. I've actually never felt better. To have the cops chasing their tails...I love it! They deserve everything they get."

Rob moved closer to Chris's desk, pulled out his vial, and proceeded to lay out lines ofcocaine. Chris went first, and then he passed the straw to Carly, who, again, declined. She really wanted to partake but just knew she couldn't.

"You're not joining us?" Rob asked.

"I would truly love to, but I just can't. Sorry. Go ahead, though. Don't let me stop you."

"Trust me. You won't." Rob took the straw and quickly inhaled a line.

"Carly was just asking me what I thought about the chances of repeating the conviction in a jury trial," Chris said. "I told her it depends on who's on the jury." Carly was a little pissed that Chris immediately told Gold about their conversation; guess nothing was sacred in this world.

"Yeah, it's kind of a crapshoot. At least my sister-in-law and daughter are very believable, don't you think? If they do as well the second time as they did the first, that should help establish credibility, don't you agree?"

Carly turned to Rob. "Have you noticed the cops paying closer attention to you? Or are you just doing what you always do and continuing to deal?"

"Who says I deal drugs?" Rob laughed and winked at Carly. "But no, I haven't noticed anything out of the ordinary. In fact, maybe just the opposite. Of course, I try to be as careful as I can." As if to show off, Rob took out a roll of bills from his pocket and put it in front of Chris.

"There you go. For your work so far. Do you want to count it?"

Chris grabbed the and put it in his pants pocket.

"Nope. I trust you."

CHAPTER FORTY-SIX

Carly walked into the Superior Court building in downtown Boston, the site of Detective Dalton Cross's second trial. The building's massive front doors made anyone entering feel the building's gravitas. Carly took a deep breath and entered. After passing through a security checkpoint, she took the elevator up to Room 303 and was struck by the difference between the two courthouses. Superior Court was a dignified and wood-crusted building that reflected the grandeur of the criminal justice system. When she walked in, the voir dire process of choosing a jury was already underway. Carly quietly took a seat and listened intently. She was without a cameraman.

"Have you ever been on a jury before?" Tommy Blake asked a middle-aged woman who was sitting in the witness seat.

"No sir. This would be the first time."

"Do you believe that police are above the law?"

"No. I do not," the woman said with a certain force and definitiveness.

"If you heard evidence that proved a police officer had broken the law, would you be willing to find that person guilty?"

"Yes, I believe I would."

"And have you ever been involved in any situation with a police officer?"

"Well, if you mean have I ever been given a speeding ticket by one? The answer is yes."

"Has anyone you know been arrested?"

"No."

"Have you read or seen anything about this case?"

"Yes, I have seen a story on television—Channel 8, I believe." Carly smiled to herself.

"And will that influence your view of this trial?"

"No, sir. It wouldn't."

Then it was Boone's turn. He stood up, in his three-piece suit, and asked: "Do you have any sense of what a police detective does?"

"Well, in truth, only from television."

"Are you willing to believe a drug dealer?"

"I don't know how to answer that," the woman said. "I would have to hear their testimony."

"Thank you, ma'am. You may step down."

On both sides of the aisle, Tommy and Boone were taking notes. Next up was a white-haired man of about sixty in a plaid shirt and black pants.

"Have you ever been on a jury?" asked Tommy.

"Yes. Actually, I have served on two previous juries."

"Can you tell me what they were?"

"One was a DUI case, and the other was an assault case."

"And did you find the defendants innocent or guilty?"

"In the case of the DUI, we found the woman innocent. In the assault case, we found the defendant guilty."

"Did you have a problem making a decision in either case?"

"No. I did not."

"Do you know any police officers or anyone in law enforcement?"

"Yes. My son is a police officer in Cambridge."

"I move to have this potential juror dismissed," Tommy said.

"Objection, Your Honor!" Boone yelled out.

"Mr. Boone, please restrain yourself," the judge said.

"Thank you, sir. You are dismissed," the judge said, addressing the potential juror.

A group of about twenty-five people in the jury box waited to be questioned, which ended up taking almost three hours. Carly found the whole process fascinating. She had never been on a jury, but the very thought of it was intriguing. When the process was done, the jury was made up of seven men and five women, with two people of color. It looked to Carly like the jurors were mostly middle-aged folks. She didn't know what that might mean for the verdict but would ask Tommy when next they talked.

The trial was scheduled to begin in two weeks before Judge Arthur Beck, who, in his twenty-five years as a judge, had developed a reputation as a straight arrow. Carly waited for the judge to leave and went over to talk to Tommy.

"Well, how do you think it went?" Carly asked. "Are you happy with the jury?"

"In truth, I would have liked to have a few more men. I think women might be more likely to dislike Gold and believe Cross. But one never knows what will happen when they hear the evidence. The pressure is on, I know that much."

CHAPTER FORTY-SEVEN

It was two weeks after the jury was chosen that the trial was scheduled to begin. The courtroom was packed. Even the hallway leading to the courtroom was buzzing with conversations, and small groups huddled in the corners. When Carly walked onto the floor, she looked to see if there was anyone she should say hello to before opening the courtroom door. The brass knobs and tall wooden doors had a certain patina to them.

When Carly opened the door and entered the courtroom, it struck her that the layout of the seating was like a wedding. The wooden benches in the gallery were somewhat like church pews without the bibles. The cops were on one side, and Gold's family and everyone else were on the other side. Glares and dirty looks were exchanged across the aisles. Luckily, the court had anticipated this hostility, and there were court officers stationed throughout the courtroom to ensure the trial remained orderly.

There was a row reserved for press, so Carly took a seat and glanced over at Chris Kelly, who was on the Gold side of the room. He smiled. The press section was packed with media, print and broadcast. One after one, the reporters acknowledged Carly's presence; they knew this was her story.

Just then, Tommy turned around and saw Carly. She walked over to the bar, which was as far as she could go.

"Ready?" Carly asked.

"I'm as ready as I can be. It feels a little like a 'Take two' on a movie set, but this is real. The big unknown is how having a jury hearing the case will change the defense or even my presentation of the case. It's going to be much harder to prove Cross's wrongdoing when his accuser is a bad guy like Gold. Just imagine if you had to put your faith and belief of what happened in a guy who will be presented as the criminal he is. Wish me luck."

"You got it! Break a leg. Actually, maybe in this situation, I shouldn't even say that."

Tommy smiled.

Carly saw Boone, who was seated at the defense table in a grey suit with a vest and a flashy, red, striped tie, turn around and catch the eye of a blonde-haired woman in the gallery. She was seated among several policemen and was dressed in a striking red dress that was low-cut and more suited for a nightclub than a courtroom. Boone winked at the woman, and she winked back.

Carly was intrigued. Who was this woman, and why the winks between the two of them?

The judge entered the courtroom, and the bailiff shouted out: "All Rise. This court will now be in session." Everyone waited for the judge to be seated.

The judge took one look at the gallery, noticed the woman in the red dress, and immediately called both lawyers to the bench. After the lawyers returned to their seats, the judge said: "Bailiff, please remove the woman in the red dress."

Carly knew she would have to get to the bottom of this at the next recess. Carly had no idea what had just happened, but she turned around and saw Chris Kelly smile as he watched the scene unfold.

When it was time for recess, Carly practically ran over to Chris and asked: "What the hell was that all about?" When she heard the answer, she almost couldn't believe it...but with this case it seemed, almost anything was possible.

The gossip, according to Chris, was that the judge had a proclivity for prostitutes, and he figured this woman was exactly that—someone who has or had some kind of connection with the judge.

Boone wanted to embarrass the judge, and he was just getting started. Once he had pulled that stunt, Boone had license to do whatever else he wanted because he had put the judge in his place and sent a clear message that he could hurt him if he wasn't careful.

CHAPTER FORTY-EIGHT

After the distraction, the trial began. Assistant DA Tommy Blake rose from his seat and addressed the court: "Your Honor, the people of the Commonwealth are here to prove that one of Boston's so-called 'Finest'—a police officer sworn to uphold the law—brazenly used a drug raid at the home of Rob Gold to line his own pockets." Tommy turned and pointed to Rob in the audience.

"We will prove that Detective Dalton Cross—" Tommy looked in Cross's direction. "Used a drug raid at the home of Rob Gold to line his own pockets. There are those who might excuse such behavior as part of the job. It's not, and it can never be overlooked or excused. Law enforcement is just that. Those who choose to serve the public as police officers take a solemn oath to honor and obey the law. To steal and treat their targets as prey does a disservice to that oath. It cannot and should not be excused. On the contrary, the public must be able to have confidence in law enforcement to do the right thing. And any police officer who betrays his oath should be punished. We intend to prove that Dalton Cross is one of these officers who has used his position to line his own pockets at the expense of the law. He must be found guilty and serve as an example to the police department and to the community at large."

Carly was impressed with Tommy's forceful and emotional opening. The opening statement was an opportunity to position the case as the prosecution wanted it to be seen by the jury. She looked over at the jury box and noticed that all eyes were focused intently on Tommy.

The rest of the prosecution went pretty much as the first trial had. Gold's daughter Jill testified as powerfully as she had the first time; she was clearly the star witness.

When it was the defense's turn, Boone was ready to turn the courtroom into a theater. Whether you were on his side or not, Carly thought it was hard not to find his style entertaining.

There was also none of the polite "Your Honor." When Boone addressed the judge and the jury, he pointed to Gold and said: "Didn't you shoot Mr. Hamilton in the head? You murdered him, didn't you?"

Carly knew from her research of Gold that he had been implicated in a murder in Newton, where two other men went to prison but he was not charged. Word was, she knew, that he had turned state's evidence for the prosecution.

"Objection!" Tommy yelled, which elicited a warning by the judge, whom Boone had already neutered with the prostitute drama.

"Mr. Boone, I am warning you," said Judge Beck. "Stick to the case at hand."

Boone just smiled in response; the cat devouring the canary.

Carly had to restrain herself and not laugh out loud in the courtroom; that would be bad form. She knew that she had her story for tonight. Carly decided to leave out the prostitute stunt since it was nothing more than a stunt and did not pertain to the trial.

Defense lawyer Boone called to the stand several members of the Drug Control Unit who had not been implicated in any wrongdoing to vouch for Cross's character and what had happened on the night of the raid.

"Detective Knight, please describe, if you would, your opinion of Detective Cross. Is he a good cop? Is he responsible and honest?"

"Without a doubt," Knight said. "He has been a great colleague and good friend, and everything I know about him reinforces that view. I know I can count on him, no matter what."

"Thank you, Detective."

One by one, each officer said Dalton Cross was a great guy, a good friend, and very honest. They also said Cross would never do what he was accused of.

Tommy Blake did his best to throw doubt into the mix. When one of the cops testified that he was at the scene at Rob Gold's house, it gave Tommy a chance to rehash what Jill Gold had said.

"Detective, did you see Dalton Cross the night of the raid?"

"Yes sir, I did."

"Where did you see him?"

"I saw him in the living room."

"Where were you at the time?"

"I was in the kitchen, watching Gold's wife and sister-in-law."

"Then you had a good view of the living room, didn't you?"

"I guess so."

"And did you see Detective Cross go near the shadowbox?"

"No, sir, I did not."

Four cops testified, and they all said the same thing. Meanwhile, Carly watched the jury to see what their reaction was. They were all listening carefully but not giving much away.

Carly assumed, and Chris had said this, too, that there was no way Boone would put Cross on the stand to withstand whatever cross-examination would likely come his way.

"I call Rob Gold to the stand," said Boone.

Now, Carly thought, it will get interesting.

Rob had dressed for the occasion. He had what looked like a very expensive dark grey suit, with a light blue shirt and a patterned tie. He looked like he was ready to go and almost had a slight smile on his face.

"Please tell the court your name."

"Robert Gold."

"And what do you do for a living?"

"I have a deli, The Hen, in the Financial District."

"But that's not all that you do, is it?"

"Objection!" Tommy yelled out.

"Objection denied. Please continue."

"You deal drugs, don't you? Specifically, cocaine?"

"Objection. Leading the witness."

"Objection denied."

"I have, on occasion, sold cocaine."

"Exactly," Boone said. "We know that. We know that you are a crook and a thief and a criminal."

"Objection!" Tommy yelled again.

"Please, Mr. Boone, stick to the questions and don't insert your opinion," the judge admonished him.

Boone didn't let up.

"How many times have you been convicted and served time?"

"Objection! Irrelevant to this case," Tommy said.

"You may answer the question," the judge said to Gold.

"I have been in jail three times for minor offenses," Gold said.

"Minor? Mr. Gold, please. Don't try to fool this court. Armed robbery is not a minor offense."

When Rob's questioning was over, Carly looked at Chris, who put up his hands as if in surrender.

Tommy's closing remarks focused on Gold's daughter. "Jill Gold gives us an honest view of what happened. There's no guile there. No one has put her up to this. She is telling you, the jury, what she witnessed that night. She is telling you the truth: she saw Detective Cross take something from the shadowbox and put it in his pocket. Plain and simple. End of story. She led you to the only verdict you can reasonably decide: Detective Cross is guilty."

Then it was Boone's turn. Carly was kind of looking forward to this since she had heard so much about his courtroom antics and seen what he had done with the woman in the red dress.

"Judge, it should be clear to everyone in this courtroom and the jury, in particular, that this charge by a convicted felon against an upstanding and duty-bound police detective is built on a lie. Are you going to take the word of a drug dealer over that of a Boston police detective? Are you willing, for an instant, to believe that guy?" Boone pointed over to Gold and stared for a long moment before continuing. "Of course, you're not. You have heard from friends and people who know Detective Cross well. He's an honest man, a devoted public servant, and a loving family man. The Boston Police Department has been his life for more than twenty years. He's a Boston cop to his core. The facts presented leave you only one choice—to find Detective Cross innocent. Thank you."

With that, Boone turned back around to face his client and smiled.

The judge then gave the jury its instructions and sent them off to deliberate. Carly had to file her story. She'd be doing a live shot at six, so she went out to the video truck to write her opening:

"Today, the second trial of Boston Police Detective Dalton Cross for larceny wrapped up with closing arguments from both the prosecution and defense. (The tape of excerpts of the closing arguments are inserted here). The judge gave the jury its instructions and dismissed them to begin their deliberations; we will bring it to you when they have reached their verdict. This is Carly Howell, outside the Suffolk County Courthouse."

Carly got the okay from the control room, and she was done for the day, then she headed over to the North End, which had become a habit. She decided to walk, giving her the chance to unwind and to take in the history-laden streets that are part of the Freedom Trail: past the Parker House and past old City Hall, which was like an old grey mare with its grand steps, grey stone exterior and an outside area that had been turned into a restaurant. Then, Carly passed Faneuil Hall Market, with its bustling stores and restaurants and its cobblestone streets—they were always a bit of a hazard with anything but flats on. Carly finished her walk down along the harbor, where she could pause and take in the ocean view and listen to the cry of the seagulls. It took Carly a good hour to make the trek.

Carly was not at all surprised to find Chris and Gold squirreled away in Chris's office, with the lines laid out.

"So, Chris?" Carly asked. "The trial went as everyone expected...except for the lady in the red dress?"

"Carly, Boone was his flamboyant self, and I have to say he's an entertaining character. Bringing in the prostitute to face the judge and embarrass him was classic Boone. Tommy did the best he could under the circumstances. It's pretty tough to have a convicted drug dealer as your accuser against a cop," Chris pointed to Rob as he spoke.

Rob looked over at Chris and Carly and laughed. "You know my daughter is still a convincing witness. Her story hasn't changed, no matter what Boone says."

"Of course," said Chris. "But I'm just reacting to the courtroom dynamics. And Rob, you saw those as well as anyone. There's a reason Boone is a respected criminal defense attorney. He's brilliant at directing his witnesses and questions to tell the story he wants to be told. And having a convicted drug dealer as your main accuser is a tough hurdle to overcome. So, it becomes your word against his, and in this case, truth hardly matters."

"Any bets on how long the jury will deliberate?"

"I think it will be at least a day, though it could be longer before we get a verdict. It will be interesting to see if they come back with any questions for the judge."

"I kept watching the jury's reactions to both closing arguments, and several were vigorously taking notes," Carly said. "I don't envy them. This is an important case, and they clearly know that."

Chris then looked beyond the verdict. "You know, if Cross is found not guilty, the cops will take that as a license to continue doing what they've been doing all along."

CHAPTER FORTY-NINE

It took the jury just one day to reach its verdict. Both sides were notified by the court officers that court would reconvene at two p.m. Carly got a call from Tommy to let her know. She ran downstairs to the newsroom, frantic to find her favorite cameraman, Larry; luckily, he was available. Carly alerted the desk to what was happening and got the okay, and she and Larry quickly drove over to the courthouse, arriving with a little time to spare.

Within minutes, it seemed, Larry was set up in the courtroom, rear center, on a stand that had been set up for the cameras, and they were ready to go. Carly counted four cameras and about half a dozen reporters. The courtroom was packed—mostly Boston police, some in uniform. They were all clean-shaven white guys jammed into the wooden benches, leaving barely room for anyone else; a clear show of force and support for one of their comrades in arms. Carly noticed that there were more court officers than normal lined up on either side of the room to maintain order.

Tommy Blake was pacing in front of the prosecution table, where another lawyer from the DA's office nervously sat, drumming his fingers. When Tommy turned around, Carly caught his eye and gave him a hopeful smile and a prayer posture with her hands.

Chris Kelly was seated in the front row next to Rob and Eileen

Gold. Chris looked straight at Carly and winked. Rob stayed rigidly facing forward. At the defense table, Carly saw Boone with his arm resting on Dalton Cross's shoulders.

Carly looked at the jury, which was already seated. She couldn't conclude anything from their faces. They looked serious—as they should—and were all looking straight ahead.

With the tension in the room building, Carly took her place next to her cameraman. She was wearing a blue and white dress with a navy blazer over it. Carly was ready for this part of the trial and knew, deep down, that this was her big chance. The story had already been picked up by ABC News. Though she had never voiced this to anyone, Carly hoped that this story would lead to her dream job: a network offer.

The bailiff declared: "All Rise. Court is in session. Judge Rudolph Beck presiding."

The judge faced the jury. "Have you reached a verdict?"

"Yes, Your Honor, we have," said the foreman, a tall, thin white guy with an open-collar shirt, khaki pants, and blue blazer. The bailiff came over and picked up the paper with the verdict on it. He brought it to the judge and handed it to him.

Judge Beck took a look at the paper and read the verdict:

"We, the jury, find the defendant, Dalton Cross, not guilty."

The courtroom erupted in raucous cheers and jumping up and down from the police. "Hallelujah! Yes!" they yelled

Judge Beck banged down his gavel. "Order in the courtroom. Bailiff, please make sure that everyone remains seated."

The bailiff motioned to the assembled crowd to sit down. And then the judge declared: "Mr. Cross, you are free to go. This court is now adjourned."

Cross and Boone were hugging each other, and on the other

side of the courtroom, Tommy was shuffling papers and looking down at the floor.

The celebration was on. It was hard to keep the cops from rushing the defense table. They gathered around Cross and gave him a group hug.

On the other side of the room, Chris walked over to Tommy and patted him on the back. Somehow, no matter what, Chris kept his cool. "It was always going to be a tough sell to the jury. You knew that."

"It sucks all the same," said Tommy. "Gold was telling the truth, and corrupt cops are bad for Boston."

"Yep. But when you have a judge compromised by a hooker and you have Boone free to put on a show like only he can do, you have a tough job with a drug dealer as your best witness whom you can't call to testify. You did your best."

"For all that's worth."

CHAPTER FIFTY

Carly was not totally surprised by the verdict either, though, just like Chris and Tommy, she felt that justice had not been served in this case. She looked around the courtroom and noticed Hank James out of the corner of her eye among his cop colleagues. He didn't join the scrum of cops surrounding Cross. Instead, he calmly walked out of the courtroom.

Carly followed after him and caught up with him in the hallway. "Hey, whaddayah think?"

"What do I think? That's a story for another day. But I am glad that the jury came down with the verdict they did. I know you don't agree, but I think they arrived at the only decision they could have, given the testimony."

That statement set Carly off; she needed to vent. "But you know as I do that it's bullshit. A guilty man is going free. The only good news here is that at least he retired so he won't be stealing from other drug dealers."

Carly looked Hank straight in his baby blue eyes. "And what will this mean for you? Will you be back in the good graces of the department, or will you still be in the doghouse with your superiors?"

"I don't know. I tend to think it's not going to lift much pressure off me. They've still got to be pretty pissed that this even happened and the spotlight it placed on the department. I'm happy to talk to you about this further in a more private place. Any thoughts?" Hank gave Carly a wink that lifted her spirits. *Funny how that happens*, she thought.

"Well, I am sure that can be arranged. Let's give it a few days," Carly said.

"You just let me know, babe."

Hank turned and walked down the long hallway—alone, which, to Carly, was a symbol of where he stood with his men and with his superiors.

Carly returned to the courtroom to find Larry and discuss the footage he'd shot and how to assemble the story.

"I've got some great shots of the cops after the verdict is read," Larry told her.

"Yes. No question we'll use that. Before we head back, I should do a stand-up. Can you give me a half hour to write the script?"

"Of course. I'm yours for this story. I'll hang here."

Carly wrote her story and did her stand-up so that it could be assembled back at the station for the six o'clock news.

While Tommy was not immediately available for comment, Carly knew Tommy would talk to her and, probably, do an on camera interview. It wasn't clear that he would do an all-out press conference.

Just as Carly was helping Larry pick up his gear and head to the car, Boone came out into the hallway to let reporters know that he was about to do an impromptu "presser." Carly and Larry most certainly had to stay for this.

There were about a half-dozen reporters there, and they all set up their microphones and tape recorders.

Boone came out into the hallway with a big grin on his face.

What a circus, Carly thought to herself.

With numerous microphones pointing in his face, Boone looked straight at Carly and said: "From the beginning of this case, it has been apparent that the district attorney's office would do whatever they could to convict my client, Dalton Cross. But they failed, and we are thrilled that the jury saw through the case and, despite the prosecution's best try, justice has ruled, and Dalton Cross has been found innocent. Now he can go on with his life and that scumbag of a man, Rob Gold, has been proven the liar we all know he is."

That was it. No questions.

Carly felt vaguely nauseous. "Let's head back, Larry. I can call Tommy when we get to the station." She helped Larry carry his gear to the car, and they drove back out to Needham, about a half hour drive.

At the station, the producer on the desk told Carly that her story would lead the six o'clock news and they would want her on the set; that was a big deal! Larry went downstairs to an editing suite. Carly quickly went up to her office to phone Tommy.

"Can I get a quote from you that we can put up on a chyron?"

"Yes, here it is: Are we disappointed in the verdict? Of course, we are. We know what Detective Cross did, and we are deeply disheartened that a jury did not see that he committed a crime. At least a previous judge understood the crime and convicted him."

"Thanks. I know how frustrated you must be, and I will call you later. You did what you could, Tommy."

Carly quickly wrote the story and, together, she and Larry chose the best video. The howls and screams of the cops when the verdict was read were especially impactful; she knew she had to lead with that.

Later, Carly stopped in the bathroom to freshen her makeup for her "cameo" on set. Jim came down to the set to join her and support her. After the story aired, there was a round of high fives that Carly got from the newsroom. She felt as if she was floating on air, even though she was obviously dissatisfied with the verdict itself.

Jim was also proud. "This is definitely award-winning material, and we should enter every contest we can think of—certainly, the regional Emmy's."

CHAPTER FIFTY-ONE

It didn't take long for Carly to find out about Hank's professional future. It had been a month since the trial, and Carly was already looking at other stories about corrupt cops through the documents she had gotten access to through the Freedom of Information request. Clearly, there were other cases beyond the Drug Control Unit.

The phone rang at Carly's desk. "Carly Howell speaking . . ."

"Well, well, if it isn't the famous reporter who covered that drug dealer cop story," Hank said.

Carly laughed. "Yes, this is she. How can I help you?"

"Well, since you asked, how would you like to go for a ride in Boston Harbor? You are now speaking to the new Boston Harbor Master. Ain't that a surprise?"

"That's an understatement. Wow! So, they moved you to Boston Harbor. Guess it could have been a lot worse."

"I've been here on the job about two weeks. Have to say it's a blast. What could be bad about getting to sail around Boston Harbor looking for bad guys?"

"Who replaced you at DCU?"

"Lieutenant Reed. Good guy. I wish him the best, but with the guys still in the unit, he's going to have a tough time."

"Well, how can I pass up an offer like yours? Name the time and place."

"Let's say tomorrow morning around ten o'clock. I'll meet you at the Harbor Towers entrance and take you out. Wear sneakers and bring a warm jacket because it can get pretty cold and windy."

"Just curious, are you steering the boat?"

"Hell no! I've got a crew of four guys who handle all that. Makes it even better. I get to look at the big picture."

"You're right. You've died and gone to Heaven."

Carly was intrigued by the invitation and the notion that, somehow, Hank managed to come out of this situation with what, on the surface, seemed like a pretty cushy job.

Carly did a little research before going out to meet Hank. The Harbor Unit: "patrols both the commercial and recreational use of the harbor and its islands to ensure they are safe." Part of the unit was a dive team, and they patrolled forty-two square miles of the Harbor. And, just like with any crime scene on land, a lot of what gets tossed into the ocean can be recovered, including jewelry, cars, guns, and drugs.

Activities in the harbor are monitored by other law enforcement agencies as well, including the Coast Guard, the Massachusetts Port Authority, and the U.S. Customs and Border Patrol. But for emergencies, the Boston Police Harbor Patrol serves as the first responders.

It was a beautiful October day, which can get cool on the Harbor, so Carly donned a sweater and headed down to the waterfront. The Harbor Towers was one of the first tall buildings to be built on the waterfront. While not exactly a beautiful architectural masterpiece, it did give its residents a spectacular view of everything from Logan Airport to the comings and goings of the ships.

Hank was there, waiting for Carly, and as he said hello, he grabbed her hand, and they walked over to the dock. There were two other guys manning the boat, and Hank made the introductions. "Welcome to my new home away from home."

"Nice digs for sure." The boat was a fifty-seven foot Sea Ark that had state-of-the art navigation and communications equipment.

Hank handed Carly a life vest to put on, which she did, though she hated them and always felt like it was hard to look good in one. But everyone on board was wearing one, so she went along with the request.

"Let's take a short cruise of the harbor," Hank directed his men. And in that short directive, the stark difference between what he was doing just days ago and now came into focus for Carly. Though clearly a demotion of sorts, it could have been a lot worse. Hank could have been demoted or assigned somewhere onerous. This job got him out of command central and out of sight of his superiors.

Carly thought to herself that there was definitely a story here for the newsroom on the Harbor Patrol and what it does.

"It's hard to imagine that you can actually see anything out of the ordinary happening in real time," Carly said.

"Well, as you can imagine, I'm just learning the ropes out here on the water. I really depend on the crew, most of whom have been doing this for a long while. You'd be surprised at what you can see on the sea."

The reporter in Carly took over. "What's the biggest crime they've found out here?"

"No surprise, it was a drug trafficking deal with some hundred kilos of coke being smuggled into Boston. These guys got three Dominicans cold. They tried to turn around and speed out of the harbor, but they weren't quick enough!"

"Maybe we could do a 'Day in the Life' kind of story where we spend the day and night filming what goes on. Of course, there's no guarantee we'd see anything like that."

"Hmmm . . . Given all that's gone on, I kind of doubt that the folks at headquarters would give the okay for that. Let's table that for a while until things quiet down for me."

"Got it." Carly smiled and winked at Hank, who returned the smile.

Carly thought to herself that, given the drug smuggling that happened out here in the harbor, it wasn't so far-fetched for Hank to have gotten the job. He obviously knew a lot about drug crimes.

They docked after a couple of hours touring the harbor. Carly got dropped off, and Hank walked her to the parking garage. Standing there, he looked her straight in the eyes.

"You know I appreciate how you've treated me in your stories. It could've been a lot worse, and I know that."

"You got mixed up in something that really wasn't you're doing. Yes, you oversaw the Drug Control Unit, but I believe deep in my heart that you didn't have any idea just how corrupt the guys were. But you gotta admit, you know now," Carly said.

"It was a rude awakening. I know corrupt cops are everywhere, but I guess I wanted to believe deep down that my guys were different. The truth is, the lure of money corrupts almost everyone."

"You know you're going to have to testify at Bobby O'Rourke's trial?"

"Yup. But I really didn't know what he was up to either,

though, between you and me, I never fully trusted the little weasel."

Carly was taken aback. She'd never heard Hank use such language to describe his guys.

Hank gave Carly a kiss on the cheek and squeezed her hand, then Carly turned and started to walk away. There was no talk of when they might meet again. She had a feeling in her gut that this might be it for her and Hank, and she was okay with that. It had been fun and somewhat exciting. But ultimately, Hank was a married guy with a lot on his plate, and Carly didn't really fit into his life.

Carly turned around one more time and waved at Hank as she headed to her car, and he waved back.

CHAPTER FIFTY-TWO

O'Malley and his comrades in arms were feeling pretty emboldened. And why not? The court had cleared their friend of larceny, so they were confident that they could continue business as usual and get away with it.

O'Malley decided to wait awhile after the trial for things to settle down before organizing a get together with other some of the members of the DCU at Cross's house in Dorchester, a modest three-family home on a quiet street in the Readville section of Hyde Park, to celebrate and talk about what was next. Hyde Park was a neighborhood of Boston that was a combination of the Irish, Polish, and Italians, along with a sizeable African American population. Hyde Park had been home to the 54th Army Regiment, the all-Black regiment that fought in the Civil War.

There was one guy who wasn't invited for an obvious reason—and that was Bobby O'Rourke. O'Malley knew that, even though they were sympathetic to where O'Rourke found himself, but he knew they needed to keep their distance from O'Rourke.

Truth is, O'Malley had always been skeptical of O'Rourke and thought that he was a little too willing to push the boundaries. So, he wasn't too surprised that he was the one who'd gotten caught in the sting.

When they met at Cross's, O'Malley brought the beer and a platter of sandwiches. He had appointed himself the leader of the gang, and the other members were willing to follow his lead.

"The bullseye is on each of us," O'Malley said. "We have to be careful, but we also still have a chance to get what we can from the drug dealers that are out there. Agreed?"

"I'll drink to that," said Reilly, another one of the cops who had been at the raid at Gold's house. They all raised their glasses and drank.

"I, frankly, think we should be watching Gold even more than we were before. He shouldn't be allowed to get away with dealing anything. He's a complete criminal shit, and he doesn't deserve to be on the streets. Fuck him," O'Malley said.

There was a new guy who was heading the DCU: Gil Reed. He'd been a detective for more than twenty years and was well respected by his superiors. The guys in the unit didn't know him, and given their relationship with Hank, they were skeptical, to say the least. So, whatever they did on the side, they knew they had to watch what they said and did when they were at headquarters.

The officers decided to take turns watching what went on at Rob Gold's deli in the Financial District. If that was where the coke was coming in and out, they would see it happening. Batterymarch Street was a pretty quiet patch of the city, particularly at night. The narrow streets felt almost haunted, with few people walking or driving through the neighborhood. It was a dead zone—perfect for dealing coke.

O'Malley and Reilly volunteered to take the first night shift. Together, the guys had decided they didn't need to worry much about the daylight hours. Gold was less likely to do anything illicit during regular business hours. The officers set up close by the deli on Batterymarch Street, about four or five buildings away, with a good view of who was going in and out.

The first few nights passed without any suspicious activity.

O'Malley was beginning to suspect Gold operated out of another location. Then, on night three, at about midnight, a black Cadillac pulled up in front of the deli, and three guys got out. They knocked on the back door and were let in.

The detectives brought a camera and started taking shots of the car and the license plate. They wanted to nail Gold, and they knew that, if there were photos, it would be harder for Gold to deny what he'd done. O'Malley ran a check of the license and found out that the car was registered to a Luis Gonzalez; no tickets or fines showed up.

CHAPTER FIFTY-THREE

After an hour, the back door opened, and the three guys walked out, carrying what looked like plastic garbage bags. O'Malley motioned to Reilly, and the cops' camera went into overdrive. The detectives stayed in the car and agreed that it made sense to follow the Caddy.

O'Malley was driving, and he kept a safe distance as the car wound its way through downtown Boston. The cars drove through Commercial Street, with the elevated subway tracks above it. Then they got onto the Expressway headed south, and when they got off the highway onto Columbia Avenue, they couldn't help but notice the many churches greeting them, a tribute to the Catholic heritage of so much of Boston. But many of these streets looked grim.

The distinctive Boston triple-deckers lined the streets, standing side by side like soldiers at attention. Many of the buildings were boarded up or burned out, with graffiti marking the damaged houses and broken glass strewn along the sidewalks. Even the grand, Queen Anne style houses looked less than their formerly noble selves. O'Malley and Reilly watched as the Cadillac turned off onto a small side street.

The detectives stayed a safe distance behind the Caddy, but O'Malley knew it would be difficult to photograph the scene in the dark. There weren't the streetlights here like in downtown Boston.

The two cops watched the three men in the Caddy jump out of

the car and go around to the back of a single-story brick building with no signage, but with plenty of graffiti and a garage door resting near the edge of the sidewalk. Pretty quickly, the detectives saw someone inside the building open the door. The three guys entered, carrying the bags. O'Malley figured they'd, at least, located a central distribution point for Gold's drug business.

"How long do we want to wait? What's the plan?" Reilly asked.

"Let's hang out here for a while and see what happens—if anything," O'Malley said. "Now we know where Gold is storing his stuff and can always come back. We don't have to pounce tonight. Besides, it would be a hell of a lot better if Gold was inside." The detctives waited for a couple of hours, listening to the radio and carefully watching.

Nothing...no one coming in or going out.

At one a.m., O'Malley decided it was not worth going in for the kill and decided to leave the scene, knowing full well they'd be back—likely sooner rather than later; he and Reilly had discovered valuable information. O'Malley also decided that someone should be watching the building more often, maybe even nightly, to get a better sense of how often anyone came to the building and what the delivery pattern looked like.

O'Malley volunteered to mount the watch detail for the next week, maybe even longer.

The next night, O'Malley started his watch at midnight. He'd brought everything he needed: binoculars, camera, and coffee. O'Malley turned on WXKS to listen to some disco music; he preferred country, but it was nearly impossible to find in Boston. Disco would help him stay awake, he figured. O'Malley slumped down in his seat a little so that he wouldn'tbe so obvious to anyone passing by, though he figured at this late hour that was highly unlikely, and with the absence of streetlights, it was hard to see anything anyway.

This stakeout became O'Malley's new routine. He didn't mind the many nights when there was nothing to see. He was hopeful that, one night, he would "strike Gold"—as he told his buddies.

After a week of waiting and watching, O'Malley observed the same guys bringing more cocaine to the building. After they finished depositing it in the garage, he decided to follow them and see where they went afterwards. They didn't go far. About a quarter of a mile down the road, the car stopped on an undistinguished street in front of a yellow triple-decker. The two guys got out of the car and went into the house. There was nothing particularly distinctive about either of these men, who were dressed in black and hard to make out in the dark. They both had dark hair cut short and were of average height and weight. They wore gloves so there was no jewelry that gave them away.

Okay, now O'Malley knew where at least one of these crooks lived or hung out.

CHAPTER FIFTY-FOUR

O'Malley took the new results of the monitoring back to Reilly.

"I think our best bet is to try to turn one of these guys. If we had an informant, we would have a far better chance of grabbing Gold in the act, don't you agree," O'Malley said to Reilly. Reilly agreed. These delivery dudes were just pawns in this effort.

O'Malley and Reilly spent the next several nights in view of the yellow triple-decker, noting the comings and goings of these two Gold operatives.

A couple of nights went by with no sightings. Then, on the third night of their vigil, the detectives saw a guy who looked like he was one of the guys they had seen the first night get in the Caddy, which had been parked on the street, and take off. This time, the gloves were off, and the detectives noticed a big, gold ring on the pinky finger of one of the guys. The men were both wearing black leather jackets, with heavy, gold chains dangling from their necks.

Detectives followed the car, which parked in front of Cuchi-Coo, a well-known Latino nightclub in Dorchester. The club's neon sign was flickering a bit, but it was there for all to see with an arrow pointing down to the door. The men got out of the car and went into the club.

Reilly stayed in the car, and O'Malley went into the bar after the men. He knew he might stand out in the crowd but didn't care.

The venue was dark, and the Latin music was blaring. There was a big dance floor, with folks having a great time movin' to the beat. O'Malley went up to the bar and got the bartender's attention and ordered a Dos Equis—looking around to see if he could spot Gold's men, and he did; the ring and gold jewelry helped.

O'Malley watched for a while, and one of the men hit the dance floor with a woman who was dressed to kill in a tight-knit black dress that hugged her body.

Tonight was a reconnaissance mission to gather as much information as possible on the habits of these two guys. Ultimately, O'Malley was going to have to undertake the impossible task of getting one of Gold's men alone without blowing his cover.

After surveiling Gold's men for a while, O'Malley felt like he had a good mental picture of these guys: their height and weight—one of them was fairly thin, the other a bit stocky; their hair styles, which were short cropped; and their black, leather jackets. O'Malley paid the bill and headed out to the parking lot, where Reilly had been napping.

"Well … What'd you see?"

"A typical crowded and noisy bar. Let's wait here 'til they come out and we'll follow them home," O'Malley said.

"Okay." They each lit up a cigarette and waited in the dark.

Two long hours went by before detectives finally spotted the guys walking out of the bar to their car. One was wrapped around the woman in the tight dress, and she looked pretty drunk, as if she'd fall down were she not being held up by the guy. The other guy was walking with them to their car. They opened the Caddy's doors and helped the woman in by almost lifting her into the back seat, where she proceeded to flop over and lie down.

As soon as the Caddy moved out of the parking space, the detecttives followed, leaving enough space to escape notice. The car headed back to the Dorchester neighborhood they'd come from, parking outside the triple-decker from which they had started.

One of the men—the stocky guy—entered the triple-decker, and the other stayed in the Caddy. O'Malley and Reilly looked at each other and nodded. Without even saying anything, they both knew they had to follow the car. This was perfect because they could get this guy alone and try to turn him.

The Caddy drove about a mile toward the intersection of Summer and Annapolis Streets, with a housing project on one side and modest triple-deckers on the other. The car pulled up by the curb in front of 2 Annapolis Street. O'Malley and O'Reilly got there just as the man was getting out of the car. It was dark despite a couple of streetlights. Lucky for the detectives, it was quiet; there was no one on the street.

Before the guy could get too far, O'Malley and Reilly split up, approaching him from both his back and front. The man was cornered with no place to go. When the detectives showed their guns, the guy put his hands up in the air.

"Lie down on the ground with your hands behind you!" O'Malley yelled. The guy complied and lay down on the sidewalk. There was no one around. And in this neighborhood, even if there were, they would probably keep walking or driving to avoid being implicated in any way.

O'Malley walked over slowly and took the handcuffs from his pocket and put them on the guy's hands, then helped him to his feet. When he had a chance to look into his eyes, O'Malley saw dark round circles and a deep scar from his scalp down to his ear on one side.

"Let's walk over to that car," O'Malley told the guy, pushing him forward to the Crown Vic. He opened the back door and pushed the guy into the back seat.

O'Malley did most of the talking. "We've watched you take and deliver drugs from Rob Gold. We can arrest you and make sure you are found guilty and end up in jail for a long time, or we can do things a little differently. But first, what's your name?"

"Juan Rivera," the guy said nervously. He looked to be in his thirties.

"Where are you from?"

"I live here in Dorchester."

"No. I mean where are you really from?"

"I came from Guatemala . . . to make a better life for my family."

"How did you get mixed up in the drug trade then? Do you have a real job?"

"I work construction when there is work, but it's not regular, and it's not enough."

"Would you like a cigarette?"

"*Si*. I mean, yes. Thanks."

O'Malley took a Camel out of his pack and handed it to Juan; he even lit it for him.

"Look. Let's be straight. We want to get Gold for the dealing he continues to do. We've watched you these last few days, so we know that you're working for him and helping to move the blow around. We've got photos and enough evidence to put you away, but we've got bigger fish we're after. So, we're willing to make you a deal. You help us, and we'll let you go free. But if we get any hint or whiff that you're not being straight with us, we'll take you down with him."

Juan stayed quiet for a few minutes. O'Malley imagined he was reviewing his options in his head, then he heard Juan say: "Yes. Okay."

O'Malley was pretty pleased. They had Gold in their sights and planned to get him if it was the last thing they ever did. O'Malley looked at Reilly, then they gave each other a high five and said: "This one's for Cross."

"By the way, we also want you to wear a tape recorder," O'Malley told Juan. In Massachusetts, you need consent by both the person being recorded and the person doing the recording..but law enforcement breaks those rules all the time.

"You will leave the other guy I work with alone, okay," Juan said.

"No worries, man," O'Malley assured him. "We're not interested in you guys. You're just the way to get to Gold. Here's what we are going to do—we are going to have you show us where the cocaine is being stored. Okay?"

CHAPTER FIFTY-FIVE

It was seven-thirty on a Tuesday night, the air was cool, and there was a serious breeze blowing in from the water. Carly had not been to Chris's office since the not guilty verdict, but she felt she needed to get caught up on where things stood

Chris's office looked dark from the outside as Carly stared into the windows to see if she could see anyone at all. She had spotted Rob Gold's car on the street, so she figured he and Chris were in there, probably holed up in Chris's office and, as usual, snorting the coke.

With no doorbell, Carly knocked hard on the glass door. After a few minutes, Chris's office door opened, and Chris let her in.

"I thought you were finished with us and had moved on to some other bigger story."

"I could never be finished with you two. You should know better than that." Carly knew, though, that, sooner or later—probably sooner—she would, indeed, move on to the next story and leave them behind...but not just yet.

"Come in. What can we do for you?"

"Well, I just wanted to get a sense of what, if anything, was happening with Rob. Is he here too, or is that a stupid question?"

Chris led Carly through his tiny front room to his office, and there, sitting in front of the desk, was Rob Gold, the usual lines laid out.

"Carly, how the heck are you? We haven't seen you for a while. What's up?"

"Well, Rob, I have the same question for you. What have you been up to? How's the deli?"

"All good from my end. Business is good." There was never any discussion of the cocaine business, but the unspoken topic hung over everything.

"Have you noticed any more surveillance of you since the Cross verdict? I would imagine that they've got their sights on you."

"I haven't noticed anything out of the ordinary."

Chris dropped into his chair. "You know, Carly, I keep getting anonymous tips from people about the corrupt practices of the drug cops."

"Really? People just randomly call you?"

"Yup. They let me know that they've had stuff stolen from them as well, whether it was cash or other valuables."

"I've gotten a few of those calls as well," Carly said. "But what, exactly, do you plan to do with that information?"

"Not much other than to listen and take notes. Can't exactly report it to the police, can I?" Chris laughed out loud.

"You could call Tommy Blake and let him know, though I'm pretty sure he's gotten similar calls."

"Actually, I haven't spoken to Tommy since the verdict, have you?"

"No, but I'm going to 'cause he's obviously gearing up for the Bobby O'Rourke trial. And this one's bound to be a little different, given that the FBI was in on the sting."

Carly hung around for a while and had to admit that Rob and Chris were entertaining. But after a glance at her watch, Carly said: "Thanks for everything, guys. I couldn't have done this story without you."

"Ain't that the truth," Gold laughed.

On her way home, Carly committed to herself to call Tommy the next day to get an update on the O'Rourke trial and find out the timing of the upcoming trial. She just couldn't let go of the story until it was all wrapped up in a neat little bow. Carly had already invested so much of her journalistic prowess, as well as personal capital.

Given how she was feeling now, Carly wanted more stimulation and headed over to Lansdowne Street to the bar she frequented. She wanted to see whether Frank was there. Unfortunately, this time, she didn't see him. Carly stepped up to the bar and ordered a drink. It was baseball season, so even on a weeknight, the bar was busy. The music was pounding amid the black lights and disco ball hanging from the center of the room.

Carly decided to hang around a little while to see if Frank showed up.

Being extremely outgoing and willing to talk to almost anyone, Carly chatted up some guys and gals at the bar and enjoyed the distraction of talking about the Red Sox and topics that had nothing to do with corrupt cops or drug dealers. She enjoyed the distraction.

Carly was at the bar around an hour or so and was just about ready to leave when she felt someone brush up against her from the back. She quickly turned around and saw it was none other than Frank.

"I was really hoping I would see you tonight. And I was just ready to walk out the door when I didn't," Carly said.

"Your lucky night, I guess." Frank smiled and put his arm around Carly's shoulders. "You've been on my mind lately. I apologize for not being in touch, but it's just been busy at work."

"I get it. I feel the same way. Want to come over to my place for a little nightcap, so to speak?"

"I was hoping you would ask. Yes! We can jump in my car."

Frank and Carly had a drink together and did a little dancing, then headed to Carly's apartment.

While Carly had been careful and taken it slowly with Frank, tonight, somehow, felt like she was ready to take it to the next level, and she hoped Frank would be ready too.

As they walked into the apartment, Frank pulled Carly close and gave her a big, juicy kiss. She felt tingly and gave into the urge to let him go on with his desire.

Carly took his Frank's and led him to her record player and put on the Temptations. They did a little slow dancing/grinding before she guided him into her bedroom.

"Follow me," Carly said, and Frank did. She pulled down the green and red floral covers, then pulled Frank down onto the bed.

"You turn me on. You really do," Frank said as he lifted off Carly's sweater and unhooked her bra. She flashed her smile back at him and took Frank's well-pressed shirt off and unhooked his belt. The undressing took just a minute or two, and then they were lying naked together on the bed. Frank turned toward Carly and started to touch her breasts, then moved his hand down toward her crotch. Carly took her hand and wrapped it around Frank's dick and worked up and down until he was hard. With his fingers in her vagina, she was moist, and Carly encouraged Frank to go further, culminating in her repeated cries of: "Yes, yes, yes!"

The sex was good; they both enjoyed it. When they were done,

Frank moved off Carly and, together, they lay side by side, smiling.

How different this was from Hank, Carly thought to herself. This felt real, like there was a relationship possible and that that sentiment went both ways.

"You're a rare find in today's world," Carly said. "You're good looking, fun to be with, smart, and thoughtful. You actually seem to care about how I feel, and that is pretty rare or, at least, has been for me," Carly said.

Frank reached over and looked Carly straight in the eyes, then said: "And you are a special lady." Frank gave her a long kiss.

"Do you want to spend the night?" Carly was almost surprised at herself as she asked the question.

"Yes. I would."

Frank didn't know just how rare that offer was. Carly hadn't had a guy stay over in a long time, but this felt good and right.

"Great." Frank and Carly engaged in another round of sex, and then, when they were both exhausted, they decided it was time for bed. Carly felt better than she had in a long time. Finally, a guy who wasn't married! Carly let herself relax and watched Frank as he slept.

When Carly woke up, she looked over at Frank, who was still sound asleep. Given that it was Saturday, she decided to let him sleep in. She climbed out of bed and headed for the shower. By the time she was done drying her hair, she opened the door and saw Frank splayed out naked on the couch. Carly walked over and sat in Frank's lap, and they hugged and kissed each other.

Carly waited to see what Frank's next move would be.

"Let's go find breakfast somewhere. You game?" Frank asked.

"Sure."

They got dressed and walked hand in hand to the South End Deli, which was a local favorite, and because it was in the South End, it was one of the few neighborhoods where a white woman walking with a Black man wouldn't set off alarms or get a lot of looks from passersby—though they couldn't avoid that altogether, given it was Boston, which was not exactly known for its liberal leanings when it came to race.

Carly was feeling good about Frank and their budding romance. She wondered whether this would last or would be just another fling...but that was a topic for another day. Today, Carly just wanted to hold onto the here and now and let the feeling wash over her.

CHAPTER FIFTY- SIX

It had been a particularly long day at the office for Frank. He worked on the third floor of City Hall, and as he got up from his desk to leave, he looked around and noticed that there was no one else anywhere in sight. That wasn't that unusual, really. Frank was often the first one in and the last to leave; it's just how he was. Frank turned off the lights in his office, grabbed his briefcase, and took the stairs down to the garage.

Driving on the Southeast Expressway, Frank headed toward his apartment in Dorchester. The dashboard clock said it was already eight o'clock, and it was dark. It usually took Frank about twenty minutes to get home if there was no traffic, and tonight, it was quiet on the highway.

Just as he got ready to turn off onto Columbus Avenue, Frank noticed a cop car with its lights flashing behind him. He had no idea what was going on, but as he focused on it, Frank realized the cop was following him.

Frank pulled over, then waited as the cop got out of his vehicle and walked over to the driver side of the car.

"What's the matter, Officer," Frank said politely.

"Really? You don't know what you did?"

"No sir, I don't."

"You were turning without turning on your turn signal. That's a violation. And I also noticed going through your records that you have several unpaid tickets. Please get out of the car."

"Seriously? Why do I have to get out of the car?"

"Because I said so."

As a Black man in Boston, Frank was in a vulnerable position, and he didn't want to escalate the situation, so he did what the officer asked and got out of the car. As soon as he did, the cop told Frank to put his hands over his head and walk to the back of the car.

"Keep your hands on the trunk of the car so I can see them."

And then, Frank saw a second cop car pull up and another cop get out. Now he was getting nervous. The two cops spoke out of hearing distance of Frank, so he kept his position as instructed, though it was getting uncomfortable, to say the least. He watched car after car slow down to see what was going on. After a few minutes, the two cops came back to where Frank was standing and told him to put his hands behind him, then they placed handcuffs on his wrists.

"What are you doing?" Frank asked.

"We're taking you down to the police station," said one of the officers.

"Down to the police station for unpaid parking tickets?" Frank asked incredulously.

"Yes. Exactly."

"And what about my car?"

"Your car will get towed to a lot where you will be able to retrieve it when we are done at the police station."

"Isn't this a bit extreme?" Frank asked.

"You can ask all you want, but we're the cops, and we are

here to make sure that the law is followed, something you clearly don't care about."

Frank thought to himself that here was a situation that would, likely, never happen to a white driver. But this was Boston, and racial tensions were high.

The officers took Frank to one of the cop cars and put him in the back seat, then drove about two miles to the nearest police station. When they got there, the officers took off Frank's cuffs and made him sit down and wait...and wait. Eventually, another officer came over and brought Frank to the front desk, where he was booked for failure to pay the parking tickets and then let go. Frank looked at his watch. It was ten o'clock, and now, he had to find his car.

"Can you please tell me where I can find my car?"

The cop at the desk gave Frank the name and phone number of the lot and gave him a phone to use. He had to call a cab to get down to the lot, and by the time he got there and had to pay a $150 fee to get his car, it was eleven o'clock. Frank quickly got in his car and took off to his apartment. When he got home, Frank dialed Carly.

"Sorry to bother you, sweetheart, but you are never going to believe what just happened to me."

"Do tell."

Frank went through the last few hours, and he could tell Carly was appalled, as he hoped she would be.

"That is unbelievable. You hear stories like this, and you think that can't happen to anyone I know. Welcome to Boston, huh? So sorry you had to go through this."

"Thanks. I knew you would understand. The police department clearly has other issues beyond corruption. How about racism?"

"Definitely. Hope you can get some sleep. Let's talk in the morning."

"Sounds like a plan," Frank said. "I am glad I have you in my corner."

Carly vowed to look into this issue more closely to see how often Black drivers were arrested by police for issues that white drivers were not.

CHAPTER FIFTY-SEVEN

Carly was feeling wiped out, and she had the urge to just get out of town for the weekend. She debated with herself about whether she should just pick up and go alone or whether she should try and see if Frank was up for the idea.

Carly called Frank at work—a first for their relationship. He picked up right away.

"Hello, this is Frank Upton; how can I help you?"

"Well, the truth is, there are numerous ways you can help me."

"Cute. How you doin', sweetheart? I've been thinking about you."

Carly didn't even question whether Frank was just saying that; she believed him and felt good about him and their new adventure.

"I have an idea. I need a break and thought about taking a quick weekend trip to Ogunquit. Would you be up for that?"

"Great idea! Love it. Absolutely. I'll even offer to drive, if you'll let me."

How great is that, Carly thought. Frank got that Carly was a bit of a control freak, but he didn't let it bother him at all. Now there's someone she could really like!

"Sure. Do you feel safe doing that given what just happened to you with the cops?" Carly asked.

"Yeah. I will roll the dice for you. And I can't let that incident make me crawl up into a ball and not live my life. It's a reality that Black men, in particular, live with throughout their whole lives. And being in Boston, I wear it on my sleeve every day. So, yeah, it's time to blow this pop stand."

"Let's plan on leaving around five Friday night," Carly said. "If you trust me, I'll go ahead and make the reservations." They hung up.

Carly had been to Ogonquit once before with a friend and had stayed in a basic motel. This time, she wanted an upgrade. So, Carly called a travel agent and landed on the Cliff Hotel. The agent told her about the hotel and the hotel's history. Turns out, it had a long and storied history, dating all the way back to just after the Civil War, when the property was bought by Elsie Jane and built by her brother, Captain Charles Perkins, who used wood from family lots. The family paid carpenters one dollar a day in gold, so the history is told. In 1872, when the hotel opened, the rates for in-season were six dollars per week per person and included three meals. The hotel attracted the best of the best: the Cabots and Lodges, as well as guests from England and Europe. By 1960, the then owners razed the top two floors of the inn, and it was operated primarily as a motor hotel.

The weather forecast was for rain—obviously, not ideal. But Carly hoped there was a fireplace in the hotel that she and Frank could snuggle up in front of to read and lounge. Frank stopped by Carly's apartment around four, managing to find a parking spot on Comm. Ave. Carly buzzed Frank in, and he found her ready to go, suitcase packed and coat already on. Carly had dressed casually but wanted to be sexy at the same time, so she had on a pair of tight black pants and a pink top that hugged her chest. Carly hoped Frank notice.

"I know. I know. I'm always early. Chronically early. What can I say?"

"I'm good with early," Frank said.

Frank came over and gave Carly a hug. "You are looking hot, honey. Let's hit the road."

"Yay! A road trip! No work required!" There was part of Carly that couldn't quite believe her good fortune and where she was with both her career and her newfound love interest.

The two-hour drive in Frank's black Honda Accord went by quickly, and the two of them being alone in the car proved to be a lot of fun. Carly was eager to get to the hotel and be able to get into bed with Frank again. Somehow, sex was even more erotic away from home in a strange, beautifully made-up bed. Just thinking about it made Carly get a little turned on, and she reached over to grab Frank's hand. He, in turn, reached down to her crotch and rubbed it just hard enough to really get her excited.

"We could pull over at the next visitor parking area," Carly volunteered.

Frank laughed, gave Carly a quick kiss, and said: "There's part of me that would, obviously, love to, but let's just keep going, and once we're in our room, we can let it all hang out."

While, in truth, Carly would've rather not have waited, Frank was the driver, so she gave in, and they kept driving, up I-93, where they passed through New Hampshire before hitting Maine. Carly was captivated with watching Frank and didn't really spend much time looking out the window.

Radio reception got worse, but they could still get WBZ, an all-news station. By the time Frank and Carly got to Ogonquit, it was late afternoon. They didn't have that much stuff between them, so they took out the suitcases, and walked up to the reception desk. A casually dressed middle-aged woman greeted them.

"Welcome to the historic Cliff Hotel. And, just so I know, are you two together?"

"Well, yes, we are," Carly said. "Why do you ask? Isn't that kind of obvious?"

"Well, yes, you look like a couple, but, and I don't mean anything by the question, it's just not that often that we see a mixed-race couple in these parts."

Carly looked at Frank, and the two of them held hands and said: "Well here we are, and we are eager to be here and hope the hospitality is as advertised," Carly said with a hint of sarcasm in her voice. She had a weird feeling that someone would acknowledge that they were a mixed-race couple right out in the open.

CHAPTER FIFTY-EIGHT

Carly let Frank do the checking in, even though it went against her feeling that it shouldn't always have to be the guy who was in charge. Carly would settle up with Frank for the room tab when they checked out.

"We have a small dining room here, if you would like to have dinner at the hotel,"said the woman at the front desk.

"That might work," Frank said.

"Is there room service?" Carly wanted to know.

"We're sorry, but there isn't." The woman pointed down the hall. "I hope you like your room. It does have a lovely view of the ocean."

"Thank you," said Frank, taking the offered key.

Entering the room, they saw a lovely, old-fashioned room with blue and white décor. The dark curtains were open, allowing for what was, indeed, a beautiful ocean view. The room looked right over the cliff—a stone cliff—Carly felt surrounded by blue: the blue of the room, the sky, and the ocean.

Carly and Frank went in and quickly unpacked their suitcases, and with the sun starting to set, they went out on the patio, gazing at the water crashing onto the shore. It was just as wonderful as Carly had hoped. She breathed in deeply and let herself relax.

Frank took Carly's hand and squeezed it tightly. "You are just what I need right now."

Frank bent down to kiss her hand. Gazing into her eyes, he gently held her face and kissed her. Frank's tongue made its way into Carly's mouth. She took his hand, led him back into the room, and lay down on the bed.

Frank unzipped his pants, removed his dick—which was already hard—and started to move Carly's mouth up and down on him. While breathing quickly, Frank reached down and unzipped Carly's pants and started to use his fingers to stimulate her vagina. Carly could hardly control herself, let out a groan, took her hand, reached Frank's dick, and brought it to her vagina. Frank mounted Carly and proceeded to penetrate her. Carly was moaning and ready to come, which she did, letting out a "yes" with the rhythm. Frank came at the same time. It was a quick session, which was okay with Carly since she'd been waiting since the car ride. Afterward, they lay next to each other and held hands.

Frank was a guy who really valued Carly for who she was, plus he was hot and turned her on. It was too soon to really know if Frank was "the one" or if this would prove to be a lasting relationship, but Carly was ready to let down her guard, and that wasn't something she did easily or often.

The rest of the weekend went even better than she Carly have imagined. Frank was not only a handsome guy and a great lay, but he also knew how to "handle" Carly: how to be able to manage her strong personality without pissing her off. Handling Carly was not an easy thing to do, but Frank had the right mix of humor and smarts. The other positive was, because Frank was not in the "business," Carly could leave the craziness of the story and focus on someone and something else.

When they went into town to shop and dine, Carly did notice that a Black and white couple did get a few looks by others on the street. She sluffed it off and didn't let it stop her from walking hand in hand with Frank. Frank noticed the stares as well. He even pointed to a cop car that seemed to always be nearby wherever they were. Could it be a total coincidence? Frank pointed the cops out to Carly, who hadn't noticed but, once alerted to it, said it was definitely a little weird.

"I'm used to it," Frank said. "And I refuse to let it get in our way or give in to paranoia."

"And I won't either," Carly said. But the couple did end up spending most of their time in the room, and that satisfied both of them.

CHAPTER FIFTY-NINE

It had been two months since the Cross retrial, and Tommy Blake had been keeping a low profile in the DA's office, keeping his eyes on the prize and focusing on Bobby O'Rourke's upcoming trial. He was feeling a lot more confident about this one; in part, because he had the FBI backing him up, and because they'd caught O'Rourke red-handed. The evidence seemed pretty black and white to Tommy. He was still hoping though that O'Rourke would avoid a trial by pleading guilty. Tommy had been going back and forth with O'Rourke's lawyer, who was adamant about going to trial, particularly given Cross's jury verdict. The trial date was still a month away, so there was still time for O'Rourke to change his mind. The loss in the Cross trial still stung. So, while Tommy was not after revenge, he was pouring his heart and soul into this new case to make sure that he'd nailed down every possible scenario.

Carly hadn't been in touch with Tommy since the second trial, and she gave him a buzz and asked where he was at with the O'Rourke case.

"I'm pretty confident. The FBI is as solid a witness as you can get, so I'm going to rely pretty heavily on Cole's testimony. You're also going to hear from another informant who came forward with a story of getting held up by O'Rourke. That should put an exclamation point on the case."

"Who's O'Rourke's defense attorney?"

"A notorious mob defense attorney, Richard Viale. Ever heard of him?"

Oh yeah, Carly thought to herself. What a small world Boston was. Wait till she tells Chris and Rob, though Carly suspected they might already know. Viale was the guy who'd approached Gold early on.

"Yeah. I've heard of him but never met him or really even seen him in court. What do you think? How does he compare to Boone?"

"He's nowhere near as flamboyant nor as clever. He's got his work cut out for him, that's for sure."

"When's the trial start?"

"Two weeks. I assume you're going to cover it. I even got a new suit so I can be even more handsome on camera this time." They shared a laugh. Carly took it as a good sign that Tommy was joking around.

"Are the powers that be over there okay with this trial?"

"They'd be happy for this all to just go away. It's given a black eye not just to the police department but to the mayor and my boss. They don't have a choice, but I think they're nervous about all the press this could get—not just in Boston, but nationally, too."

"Let's hope," Carly said, thinking the more attention the story got, the better for her next move.

CHAPTER SIXTY

Two weeks later, Carly was ready for the O'Rourke trial. She had reviewed the film of the sting and saw him again take the money. Carly also went through her notes and looked at the informants who had specifically called out O'Rourke as the one who had ripped them off. The day before the trial was scheduled to begin, Carly was at her TV station desk when Tommy called her.

"Carly, I just learned that O'Rourke is going to plead guilty to avoid a trial."

"Well, that's a good outcome. You get the guilty plea without the trial. Congrats. Of course, from a selfish perspective, I'm a little disappointed at the lack of potential drama, but I get it. Are you available for an interview?"

"Sure. Come on down. I'm here."

Carly updated Jim, who was in his office speaking with a source about a mobster from the Angiulo family. Jim was obsessed with the mob; Carly had learned this after working side by side with him day in and day out. Jim had great sources, too; both from the DA's office and other independent investigators. Carly had to admit that the Mob didn't have the same allure for her.

Downstairs, Carly found Larry in the newsroom. After getting the okay from the assignment editor, the two of them headed into town.

Tommy was at his desk, which he had obviously straightened up especially for the interview.

Larry and Carly arranged the chairs so that they could get some of the atmosphere of the office in the shots: the cramped space, the papers stacked high.

Tommy seemed to be in a pretty good mood. When Carly asked if he was ready, heanswered with an emphatic: "Let's do it!"

Carly asked the question: "Can you tell me what happened today with the trial of Bobby O'Rourke?"

"We were informed by his attorney that he pled guilty to the charge of larceny, thereby avoiding a trial."

"Why do you think he did that?"

"I think the evidence was pretty overwhelming, and I don't think anyone on his team really wanted to hear from the FBI on this case. He was also very likely to not go down alone and to take some other cops down with him and allege that there were police leadership who were in on these deals."

"Really?" Carly asked. Tommy had piqued her interest in what might be a whole new avenue of investigation.

"Do you think that's true?" Carly asked Tommy.

"Likely, though I don't have any names, so it might be tough to track down," Tommy said.

"It's not Hank James, is it? I would find that very hard to believe," Carly said.

"No. I think he is, truly, one of the good guys. It could be even higher up, though. I just don't know," Tommy said.

"Well, well," Carly said. "The story keeps turning."

"What's the sentence he's likely to get?"

"Hard to know, exactly. We will recommend five to ten years."

"How do you feel?"

"It's hard not to feel that justice has been served in this case and another bad cop has been stopped in his tracks."

"What does it say about the Boston Police Department?"

"I am not going to make blanket statements about the department, but it's clear there are some bad cops, and I would hope the department leadership would take a close look at that."

"Anything else you want to add?"

"Nope. I think you got it."

"That's a wrap." Carly motioned to Larry. The interview was short and sweet, and Carly had gotten what she needed.

"Thanks, Tommy. It's been great working with you on this story, and I appreciate your willingness to trust me."

"Carly, you're actually the first reporter I have let get this close to a story, but you knew almost as much as I did about it."

They broke down the lighting and the equipment and left Tommy in his office, then headed out to the WBRN van.

"Larry let's head back to the station. There's one call I need to make."

"Sure, Carly; I'm yours."

Before she could write the story, Carly needed to call the Boston Police Department to try to get a comment from someone high up—preferably the Commissioner. When they got back to the station, Carly dialed the PR office and got the department's Communications Director, Ronald Abrams, who was not exactly friendly or helpful. His answer came pretty quickly.

"I doubt there will be anyone willing to talk to you, but I will ask the question and get back to you. What's the deadline for this?"

"I'm running the story tonight, so I need to do the interview before four o'clock."

"I will call you back as soon as I get an answer."

Abrams called Carly right back to say that he would provide a statement, but no one was willing to do an on-camera interview. She wasn't surprised; it was the easy way out. The police department wouldn't let it go without a comment, but they also would not subject the Commissioner or his lackeys to any potentially embarrassing questions.

No surprise.

The six p.m. producer came down to the editing suite to ask if Carly would be on set with the anchors to talk about the guilty plea.

"Sure." As soon as she agreed, Carly realized she had about two hours to get the story together. Larry was quick, so the editing wouldn't be a problem. Carly headed upstairs to let Jim know where things stood, and she banged out the script on her typewriter.

"I'm not at all surprised that O'Rourke chose to plead," said Jim. "He was going down anyway. Saved everyone the drama."

"Yeah, but I was looking forward to the trial."

The on-set interview gave Carly another chance to distinguish herself as a thorough and knowledgeable reporter. It was her second live, on-set interview, and though she had butterflies, it went smoothly. Carly got help with her makeup from folks in the newsroom and looked pretty darn good, if she did say so herself.

"Carly, can you give us a sense of what this guilty plea means to the Boston PoliceDepartment more broadly?"

"I think that that the leadership of the department understands they have a problem with rogue cops who have been allowed to act freely until now and that they will have to take some strong corrective measures moving forward."

Jim had come down to the set to watch and gave Carly a thumbs-up when she finished.

"You nailed it," Jim said.

"Thanks, Jim. I couldn't have done this without your help and guidance, that's for damn sure."

Once the interview was over, Carly let it sink in that this might be the end of the story, and she had to admit that she felt a little let down. Carly had been so all in for so long that it seemed odd to leave it behind. But the story also put Carly in a more prominent position for what she really wanted: a spot as a national reporter.

Carly felt like this occasion called for a celebration and Carly got a few folks at the station to go to a neighborhood bar.

"Here's to Carly and to a great job for all of us at the station and for the city of Boston," one of the other reporters said. "Let's raise a glass!" Everyone downed their drinks, and the merriment continued until, slowly but surely, folks trickled out of the bar.

Carly was feeling as "high" as she ever had about her job. She knew, deep down, that she had given this story her all, and the success of her reporting was even more than she could have hoped for. She was proud of herself.

So, when she got home, Carly called her father to let him know how the story had ended.

"I am so very proud of you," Carly's father said. "I know that it was not easy to take on the police and root out the bad apples, but you did, and you will always have my love and admiration."

"Dad, you don't know how much it means to have you in my corner."

"I'm here for you, always."

CHAPTER SIXTY-ONE

During a couple of weeks of surveillance and with the help of Juan Rivera, their newly recruited informant, O'Malley and Reilly had gotten a sense of the rhythm of Rob Gold's coke business.

Still, they had tested Rivera as their informant to see if he was comfortable giving them information about Gold's comings and goings. He had proven to be a compliant and useful source of information. Just watching when and where Juan went gave the detectives a good idea of what the flow of Gold's business was and how often they were moving coke around and where.

In addition to Gold's house, where, for all they know, he still might be hiding his cocaine, the detectives had also discovered the building in the heart of Dorchester where most of Gold's drug supply was being stored.

O'Malley wanted to make sure that they caught Gold at the optimal time when there was enough coke to both arrest him and grab some cash for themselves. O'Malley knew Gold was a tricky guy, and they had to be careful. If he could, Gold, obviously, wouldn't hesitate to go public and press embarrassing charges against them once more. But this time, the police were not going to get him anywhere where there might be witnesses like his sister-in-law or daughter; that lesson was learned.

It was time for a meeting with their informant. They knew where Rivera lived: in an unremarkable, dark grey triple-decker in

Dorchester, on a busy street. O'Malley invited Reilly over to his house to make the call at about seven p.m., when O'Malley figured that Juan might be home. They had Rivera's home number, which he had volunteered to give them, and left a message for him to get in touch. It took about a half hour for Rivera to call O'Malley's beeper. They called him back right away. O'Malley held the phone out from his ear so that Reilly could hear the conversation, too.

"Hola—what's up?"

"That's what we're hoping you can tell us," said O'Malley. "We haven't heard from you in about a week. Everything going according to plan?"

"It's all *bueno.* We're expecting a big delivery. I was just about to call you to let you know when it gets here."

"Guess we saved you that call," O'Malley said with a glance to his partner. "So, what's the deal: when and where?"

"Saturday night, at the abandoned warehouse in Dorchester, the one you already know about."

"What time exactly? And how much is supposed to be delivered?"

"It's supposed to be delivered around one a.m. And should be about a kilo."

"Is Gold going to be there?" asked Reilly. "It only works if he is. So far, whenever we've seen you at that warehouse, it's been without him."

"He will be there. When there's a new delivery, he comes there to check it out."

"Altogether, how many people will be there?"

It took Rivera a long moment to answer: "I think there will be about four of us."

"Excuse us for a minute."

Reilly covered the phone so Rivera couldn't hear. "You think we might need another guy for this job," he asked O'Malley. "I hate to let anyone else in on this bust, but four folks is a lot."

"I think we're good," said O'Malley, exuding his macho side. "We have to figure they will be armed, but we will be too. And we have the element of surprise. If we absolutely need to, we can always call for backup."

While appearing a little uneasy about the bust, Reilly agreed. "Okay, we'll be nearby, parked on the street in the dark blue Crown Vic, and you'll give us a thumbs-up as you leave the building and walk by the car. You don't want to give any indication that you know anything. It's important you act like nothing is different this time, okay?"

"*Si, Si.* Got it," Rivera said.

The two cops felt confident that, this time, they would get Gold and put him behind bars for good. It would be different if he were caught red-handed with the cocaine. Gold would not be able to deny it, and they'd have him by the balls.

"I know it's a little early to celebrate," said Reilly. "But let's go grab a beer."

"You're on. We are finally going to get this asshole."

Neither O'Malley nor Reilly really wanted to go to Richard's, their usual hangout. Too many of their buddies might be there, and they'd rather keep their plans to themselves. Instead, O'Malley suggested they go over to J.J. Foley's, the oldest continuously-operated family bar in the city, in the South End. This was a hangout for pols and cops and hangers-on—perfect for these guys.

Reilly and O'Malley got to J.J. Foley around seven-thirty, and the place was relatively quiet. Decorated in wood from the almost endless bar to its columns and tables, the bar's ceiling was old tin, and the bartenders—all men—wore a standard uniform of a white shirt, white apron--tied at the waist--and ties tucked into their shirts. Classic! The only customers were at the bar. The detectives sidled up to the bar and ordered—a scotch and soda for Reilly and a cold Bud for O'Malley.

O'Malley picked up his glass, and Reilly followed suit. They turned to each other and clinked:

"To a successful grab," O'Malley said, smiling. "We got this." They knew they couldn't get too cocky. Gold had slipped through their fingers too many times before. But each of them was committed to doing whatever it took to catch him this time.

Even so, the detectives were distracted by a couple of gorgeous young women walking through the door.

"Wow. There's something you don't see every day," O'Malley said.

"Be careful, buddy. You're a married man, and your wife would not be happy." Reilly laughed.

"Don't worry. I'm a 'look-don't-touch' kind of guy. But that doesn't mean I don't appreciate a beautiful woman when I see one."

"Here's to beautiful women. The more, the merrier," Reilly said.

Together, the detectives grabbed a table in the back of the room where they could see who was coming and going without drawing attention to themselves. They each had another round and wasted some time yakking about the job and their families. Then, Reilly finally got down to business:

"How will we move in on Gold? Let's map out our plan minute by minute."

"Okay, first thing we should do is some more detailed reconnaissance," said O'Malley. "We need to go down to the building and take photos of the street, the building, its entrances and exits, and anything else we can think of, so we can cement it all in our minds."

"That's good, but when it comes time to act, basically, we sit in the car and wait 'til we see action—and in particular, we wait 'til we see Gold. Ideally, we photograph him entering the building so we can prove he was inside. Then, Juan will give us the thumbs-up, and when Gold drives out, we block the car and make the arrest. Make sense?"

"Yeah, I guess so," Reilly said.

O'Malley could sense Reilly's hesitation. He had been more cautious all along, O'Malley thought to himself. He knew he had to be the cheerleader here and make sure that Reilly stayed onboard.

"Why don't we just grab him while he's inside?" Reilly asked

"Then we risk having more folks in a confined space and a greater likelihood that a gunshot could meet its mark," O'Malley said. "I don't like the odds."

"Good point," Reilly said. "Should we hang together or each take a different part of the street?"

"I think we stay together," O'Malley said. "Given that there are only two of us, we need to know that we have each other's backs at all times."

"Got it."

"And what about Rivera?" Reilly asked

"He knows to get out of there as soon as possible. We'll let him go and make sure he doesn't get hurt in the process."

"Do you think Gold has any idea of what's coming his way?"

Reilly asked.

"I don't know why he should. He risks arrest every time he goes over to that building."

O'Malley pushed his chair away from the table, then said: "Let's head on over now. What the fuck. Why wait? We know what we need, and it's dark, so we're less likely to attract attention, though my sense of that neighborhood is that it's pretty deserted, anyway."

As the detectives walked toward the door, they gave the bartender a nod.

"Thanks, Pete. See ya soon," O'Malley said.

Pete shouted out over the din as he dried glasses: "Be careful out there."

All three men gave a little laugh.

CHAPTER SIXTY-TWO

The two men left the bar and got into the blue Ford Crown Victoria, a cop's favorite car. The vehicle was in good shape, with no major dents, and in the dark of the night, the car was unlikely to draw much attention, which was the whole point.

The detectives headed to the Dorchester address that Rivera had given them. They'd driven by the building a few times since he let them know about it. It was an abandoned, one-story, tan-colored, aluminum-sided building with a 'For Lease' sign above it. The building had three double garage doors in front and an unremarkable front door entrance. It was set back from the street, with a parking lot in front of it and a vacant lot on one side.

Streetlights lined the street, but none of them worked. It was nearly impossible to see anything unless right on top of it. *Perfect*, O'Malley thought. The darker, the better.

After parking just up the street, the officers stayed in the car at first and checked out the area. They didn't see anyone anywhere near the building. Before the drug deal went down—and while no one was around—they studied the building as well as they could from the outside.

The detectives got out and, together, walked around the building. They saw another door on the side of the building; each had a double-lock. There was a field on one side of the building, which was strewn with trash but looked like it wasn't used for anything else.

O'Malley snapped photos.

"They'll probably use one of these garage doors to get in the building," Reilly said, pointing to the front of the building."

O'Malley agreed. He knew that would make it a lot easier to spot the dealers going in the building.

"Yup. Just thinking the same thing. We've got our walkie-talkies so we can communicate with each other. I think we should leave the car on the street, though; it will draw less attention," O'Malley said.

After walking around the building, searching for anything distinctive or unusual that could make their job harder, O'Malley called it a night. The detectives felt confident that they knew what they had to do when the time came.

The offiers didn't have to wait long. Two days later, O'Malley got the call from Juan.

"*Hola*, it's going down tonight around one a.m. I'll be there, and so will Gold."

"What car will you be driving?"

"A new, black '79 Cadillac; Gold's car," Rivera said.

O'Malley drove to meet Reilly at his house in Dorchester, which was closer to the building. They each downed a black coffee and headed on over. Reilly's heart was beating so fast that he imagined O'Malley could practically hear it. While they were used to making drug arrests, this one came with a whole lot more risk, and Reilly knew that.

A block from the building, O'Malley parked and turned off the lights, but kept the engine going for a few minutes. Eventually, O'Mally turned it off. It was really, really quiet. There was no car or foot traffic.

There was a full moon—lucky for them, as it was the only light they had.

CHAPTER SIXTY-THREE

Gold was ready for this deal, the first big deal since he had driven down to New York that harrowing night almost a year ago. He was pleased but also surprised by how well his business had been doing since Cross's trial. It was almost as if the publicity of the trial had given him even more customers than he had before. Maybe it was true what they say—there's no such thing as "bad" publicity. But after that night in Queens, when he felt like he and Manny had escaped by the skin of their teeth, there was fear in Rob's gut every time he actually had to meet with his connections. He knew that, on some level, he was taking a chance with his life. Rob was good, very good, actually, at playing the macho guy who was afraid of nothing and no one, but deep down, he always had a fear. It followed him wherever he went. The fear did help keep him alive when he was in prison and probably helped him survive his "business," but it was there, nevertheless.

Rob could feel that fear stir as he headed over to the building where the deal was going to go down. His friend Manny Salvato was with him, as was Juan Rivera.

It was just after one a.m. when they turned into the driveway and parked. Manny got out, went to the side door, and unlocked and opened it. Gold entered, flipped on the lights, and walked to the back of the building. They opened the garage door and drove the car inside.

O'Malley and Reilly saw the car and knew it was not the delivery car; that was yet to come.

They waited. Within the hour, the Lincoln Town Car came down the other end of the street and into the driveway. Almost automatically, the garage door opened, and the car drove in.

The detectives waited. It took all of about a half hour, and then they saw the garage door open and the Lincoln Town Car drove out. They let that car go; they were focused on Gold. O'Malley started up the engine; he knew it was only a matter of minutes.

It was another fifteen minutes before the detetcives saw the garage door open. O'Malley put the car in gear and drove to the entrance of the building and was there to block Gold. They heard the car engine start up, and they both got out of the car with guns aimed straight ahead.

"Don't move. Stay where you are!" O'Malley and Reilly yelled.

"Go fuck yourselves!" Gold yelled back. "If you think you're going to bust this deal, you're crazy."

"Don't do anything stupid, Gold!" O'Malley yelled out. "Drop the weapons, and we can end this peacefully," O'Malley said as he and Reilly moved slowly through the dark toward the car.

A gunshot rang out. The officers ducked as the bullet flew by their heads, and O'Malley fired back, hitting the front tire of the car, making it impossible for Gold and his men to drive off.

Then a bullet flew past O'Malley's head.

"Don't do anything stupid!" O'Malley yelled at Gold.

Two more shots were fired.

O'Malley looked at Reilly and signaled that he should call for backup. They knew it was inevitable that the two of them might not be able to do this bust alone. Once it was over, there would be a lot of questions to answer. But right now, the detectives had to make their move, given the firepower aimed at them.

Reilly talked into his walkie-talkie, quietly ordering an emergency response with no sirens or lights.

"Code two. Code two. Come to the front of the building." Reilly gave the officers the address.

O'Malley and Reilly walked toward the Caddy. They yelled again: "Drop your weapons so no one gets hurt. You are surrounded."

O'Malley heard a gunshot, and a bullet raced past him, closer this time.

"Put your weapons down!" O'Malley screamed.

"Okay. Okay," Gold shouted and dropped his gun, and he signaled to Juan and Manny to do the same.

"Put your hands in the air and keep them there!" O'Malley yelled as he and Reilly walked toward the Caddy.

When they got to the car, O'Malley looked Gold in the eyes.

"You motherfucker. You're a no-good motherfucker who has ruined the life of our buddy. You're not going to get away with it this time, though. Time's up! Put your hands behind your back."

Gold turned his back to the officers, and they grabbed his wrists and handcuffed him.

"Move."

O'Malley thought Gold was surprisingly quiet. Maybe, he thought, after all the arrests and jail time, Gold knew that it was far better to just stay quiet then to put up a fight or possibly say something that could be used against him.

O'Malley pushed Gold forward and led him to their car and put him in the back seat.

Just then, a squad car arrived with two cops in vests and helmets and guns drawn. They moved toward the car together.

"We could get questions about why we did this alone. We have to be ready for that," O'Malley said. "Our answer has to be that we figured we could handle this by ourselves."

"Got it," Reilly said.

"Thanks for getting here so quickly," Reilly said to the two cops.

"Why were the two of you here alone?" one of the cops asked. "Wasn't that kind of unusual? You realize we will have to include that in our report."

"It was our bust, and we thought we could handle it." O'Malley knew it was an innocuous answer that, clearly, wouldn't put an end to the story.

"You were damned lucky this worked out the way it did," the cop said. "Pretty dumb move on your part," he added. "We will have to include it in our report, just so you know."

The other cops took Juan and Manny in their car, and Gold went in the second car, leaving O'Malley and Reilly to comb through the Caddy. There was over five pounds of cocaine in the trunk. O'Malley and Reilly looked at each other after everyone had left, and O'Malley decided their best move was to head back to headquarters to file their report before anyone else had a chance to weigh in.

"Let's get the fuck out of here," said O'Malley. "We've got to decide the story we're going to tell, and we have to stick to it, no matter what. You're good with that, right?" O'Malley looked at Reilly.

"Yeah. We're in this together. And let's, at least, celebrate the fact that we got the bastard. He's going away for a long time, and we can tell Dalton that we got revenge." The detectives high-fived each other, got in the car, and headed to police headquarters.

While they were driving, O'Malley decided to present the bust as a situation that quickly developed and one they were confident they could handle alone. He included the flipping of Juan, who had provided them the info about where and when the delivery was happening. O'Malley also had to make sure that Juan wasn't charged and was let go.

CHAPTER SIXTY-FOUR

Carly was already working on another story that had come from her request for the files from the BPD about other potential corrupt cops or, at least, accusations to that effect. She had the hope that this story would build on her reputation for digging out the truth about the police.

The phone rang, and it was Chris Kelly.

"Carly, you might be interested to know that Gold is in jail. He was arrested during a drug raid in Dorchester two nights ago. I'm going to arrange to meet with him at the Suffolk County Jail. It doesn't look good. I'm afraid they're not about to let him go."

"To tell you the truth, Chris, I've been amazed that he's been dealing all this time. It's kind of inevitable that this would happen, isn't it?"

"Yeah. I'm not sure I'll be the one representing him, either. But we'll see what happens. I'll let you know what I find out."

Carly couldn't resist saying: "You may have to go cold turkey."

"Ha! Very funny."

Carly knew that Gold had gotten Chris pretty hooked on the white powder, given that each and every time she saw the two of them together, they were doing coke.

"I also may have to do this story." Actually, there was no doubt about it. After hanging up with Chris, Carly called police headquarters to get a statement from them. When she got it from the communications office, she wrote a short "reader" for the news: "Rob Gold, the man who accused Police Detective Dalton Cross of larceny, has been arrested during an alleged drug deal that was busted by the police. We will bring you additional information as we get it." Short and sweet! Carly brought the reader down to the newsroom for the noon show.

Carly's next call was to Tommy.

"Did you hear what happened to Gold?"

"Yep, I did. Can't say I'm surprised. He had a target on his back. There was no way the drug cops were going to let him get away with putting their buddy through two trials."

"Chris is going down to the jail," Carly said.

"This could be his last stunt. But he's a bad guy, so I don't feel sorry for him in the least," Tommy said. "Maybe he will finally get the justice he deserves."

Carly had mixed feelings. On the one hand, Gold really was a guy who had literally gotten away with murder. But he was also a charmer and an excellent source for her reporting on Dalton Cross. Carly decided to go over to Chris's office after he'd been to the jail to see what was going on and decide her next steps.

Carly went to Jim and updated him on the arrest.

"I guess he's lucky they didn't find a way to kill him."

Carly went back to her desk and called Frank. "Hi there. Remember me?"

"How could I forget? What's up?"

"Any interest in grabbing dinner tonight? I'll fill you in on the latest with the story. I don't care where we go, just someplace quiet. Around eight-ish?"

"Sure, sweetheart. I'll make a reservation somewhere and let you know."

Just talking to Frank, even for even a few minutes, made Carly feel better. He was the tonic she needed, and she was grateful that she'd found him and that he was still interested in her.

Carly figured she would just head home, change her clothes, and put on something a little sexier than what she was wearing.

Frank called as soon as Carly walked into her apartment and let her know they had a reservation at the Chart House, a steakhouse with a gorgeous view of the harbor. It worked out well because she could stop in to see Chris before, then go just a few blocks down Atlantic Ave. to the restaurant.

What to wear? Choosing an outfit was always a decision with implications. Carly decided on a black miniskirt that highlighted her figure, with a flowered blouse and a pearl necklace. *A little bit of Twiggy*, Carly thought.

Carly drove to Chris's office in the North End. She found him pacing his office. She'd never seen him like this. Usually, he was at his desk, his feet propped up, looking relaxed and assured...but not tonight. Clearly, the arrest or, maybe, the lack of coke was having an impact.

"Carly, I have to say I'm very glad to see you. I irrationally hoped he'd find a way to avoid this day."

"Okay. Back up, fella. Have you talked to Rob?"

"I talked to him briefly on the phone but haven't seen him up close and personal yet," Chris said. "I am going to go down to the jail, though, and talk to him in person."

Carly knew that—given the relationship they'd established during the Cross case—Chris would tell her whatever he knew, lawyer-client privilege be damned.

"Apparently, Rob and a couple of his men were meeting up with some big dealers to get a delivery of coke. They were using an abandoned building in Dorchester. At almost the exact moment of the deal, O'Malley and Reilly from the DCU busted it. Shots were fired from both sides, and the cops arrested everyone."

"Revenge?" Carly asked.

"Hard to think it could be anything else. And they must have had an informant, too, because how else would they know when and where the deal was going down."

"What are they holding him on?" Carly asked.

"$500,000 cash bail. He's in there. He's not getting out this time, and a defense will be tough, too."

"Can we go sit down?"

"Of course. Sorry. I would offer you a little blow, but my main source is a little tough to reach."

"Hope you can manage without it."

"Me too. It will be a test, for sure."

They walked together back into Chris's office. Carly took a seat across from him. "Are you going to represent him?" Carly was in reporter mode. "You said you might not. Why wouldn't you?"

"I think he's going to need a real criminal defense attorney, and I'm not sure that's me. Obviously, he is pretty used to being in prison, but it has been a long time, so I'll have to see how's he doing. He knows how to make friends."

"I wonder if they'd let me talk to him," said Carly.

"Not sure. The DA is clearly not a big fan of yours."

"I did write a brief reader to say he'd been arrested. How

much coke did they seize?"

"Five pounds."

"That's a lot of coke. Okay. Call me when you learn anything. And take care."

"Thanks, Carly."

Carly dashed out of the office and headed down to the Chart House, which was close by. She parked the car and walked down to the end of a pier to the restaurant. It was a starry night, and Carly looked up and took a deep breath.

The restaurant was red brick on the outside and inside. Inside were wood rafters and brick walls. Between the smell of the harbor outside and the wood fire, the restaurant had a cozy feel. The white, starched tablecloths made the restaurant a go-to place for the everyday, as well as the special occasion. When Carly walked in, the restaurant was kind of dark. She looked around and spotted Frank, waiting at the bar.

Frank didn't immediately see her, though, so Carly sidled up to the bar and bumped into him.

"Excuse me."

Frank turned around and saw Carly, then gave her a kiss and a hug. Then, Frank took Carly's hand and escorted her to the hostess desk.

"We'd love a quiet table," Carly said, and Frank nodded in agreement.

"Not a problem." The hostess took them into the dining room near a window."Okay?"

"Yes. Thanks very much."

"How's your day been?" Carly asked Frank.

"Nothing out of the ordinary. Good, I guess. And dare I even ask you the same question?"

"You know me all too well," Carly said. "Turns out the drug dealer was arrested during a bust. He's in jail, and it's not looking good for him getting out on bail. This might literally be the end of the line for Gold."

Frank took Carly's hand across the table and held it tight. "I think it's great what you're doing. I admire it and you, really. I feel lucky that a Boston bar brought us together." Frank brought Carly's hand to his lips and kissed it.

Carly couldn't help but notice that some of the other guests were looking at them.

"Don't look now, but there are folks staring at us."

"Let 'em stare. We're better than that. And if we ignore them, we'll be doing the best thing we can."

They enjoyed the meal, the view, and the chance to be out and about. They also had a few drinks, and Carly was feeling the buzz.

"You want to come over?" Carly asked.

"I thought you'd never ask. Yes. Of course."

Another good night lay ahead, and Carly was hoping that, this time, the relationship was for real.

CHAPTER SIXTY-FIVE

The Charles Street Jail was a solid brick structure that sat at the bottom of Beacon Hill, across the street from the Esplanade and the Charles River.

The jail was a hellhole, Chris knew. Every visitor got a locker where they could put their valuables, and each person had to get patted down and go through a metal detector. Chris did what was asked and winced when he heard the metal doors slam closed behind him. He'd been here before, but not often.

Chris was led to a small, cell-like room with two chairs and a table.

"Wait here," the guard said.

Chris tried to get comfortable in a very uncomfortable wooden chair.

After about ten minutes of looking at the ceiling and floor, the door opened, and Gold was led into the room with his hands cuffed to a chain around his waist. The guard unlocked the cuffs, and Gold, dressed in a basic orange jumpsuit, gave Chris an unexpected hug that took him by surprise.

"Do you miss me yet?" Gold smiled as he asked the question.

"You'd better believe I do," Chris said.

"Not surprised about that. You know that you can always go

visit my wife. She should be able to help you out."

Chris didn't really want to let on that he was in a kind of withdrawal, but that's exactly what it was.

"I just might pay Eileen a visit. How're you doing?"

"Well, I'm in here, ain't I? There isn't much I can do, actually. I've got some of my guys in here, so I don't feel totally alone. You know this is not exactly new to me, so I'm fine. I can manage. Any chance you can get me out on bail?"

Chris was afraid Gold would ask him this, and given his past history and the recent history, the chances of bail were slim to none. But Chris didn't totally want to quash any meager hopes the guy had.

"I can try. That's all I can do. But you know it's a long shot, right?"

"Yeah. I get it. Not exactly your model citizen."

"Listen . . . I think we should try to find you a real criminal defense attorney. I'd recommend Lawrence Boone—" They both chuckled "—But somehow, I don't think he'd take the gig. So, let me call around."

"Okay."

"Give me a day or two, and I'll be back."

"You know where to find me."

They both got up and gave each other a man-hug.

Chris left the jail feeling pretty down. He knew this was likely the beginning of the end for Gold, and whether it was the coke or just the excitement he'd added to Chris's life, Chris knew he'd miss Rob hanging around his office. He tried to imagine what a winning defense might look like given Gold's recent past, let alone his long rap sheet.

Chris headed back to his office and called Carly.

"Hi, I just paid a visit to our favorite client. I'm hoping I can find a defense attorney who might be able to spin this the right way. Tough assignment, for sure."

"Okay. Thanks for letting me know. Please keep me updated. It's definitely a story I'm still interested in."

Chris hung up and got a lightning flash: a great idea for a lawyer. There was a two-person firm in Boston that was well known for their defense of the toughest clients: murderers, rapists...the scum of the earth.

Chris called one of the partners, Bob Shactman. Shactman was a Yale Law School alum and a very smart guy with a self-deprecating sense of humor. He didn't care about the limelight—also a positive, in this case.

And like Chris, Schatman even answered his own phone.

"Shactman here. How can I help you?"

"Bob, my name is Chris Kelly. I don't know if we've ever met, though I know of your reputation, and I've got a client who needs a good criminal lawyer. You're right up there in this town and willing to take some pretty challenging clients. You may have heard of Rob Gold—he's the guy who accused a cop of stealing money from him during a drug raid."

"Oh yeah. I followed that case pretty closely. I was rooting for him," Shactman said.

"He came close. But now he's sitting in Charles Street, charged with drug dealing and assault on a police officer. It's going to be tough. The cops caught him in the act with some other guys during a drug deal in Dorchester. Could we talk?"

"Sure. You want to come over to my office? I'm just across from the Aquarium."

"Turns out I'm just down the street a little, at the end of the North End."

"I'm here. I don't have a trial tomorrow, so come over around ten o'clock."

"See you then."

Chris walked to Bob Shactman's office. Strolling the brick sidewalks along the way, he looked out at the harbor and smelled the ocean's briny water.

Shactman's office was on the third floor of a brick rowhouse right across from the Custom House, with its iconic clock tower.

Chris knocked on the door and walked into what could hardly be called an elegant office. The walls were a stark white mixed with brick arches. There was a paper-strewn space with several wooden desks and a couple of assistants typing away. Not exactly a white shoe firm—more like Chris's office.

Shactman sat at one of the desks and motioned Chris over. He had a kind of blonde 'fro hairdo and wore dark pants, a white shirt, and a tie hanging loosely from the collar.

They shook hands.

"Guess you found it with no problem. Tell me more about the case and what he's charged with. I give Gold credit for even pressing charges in the first place. That took balls," Shactman said. "Tell me about what happened: the raid and the charges, whatever you can."

Chris knew it was best to be honest and upfront with Shactman.

"Rob Gold is a lifelong criminal: he served time for some pretty bad crimes, got away with others, and just keeps it up. Even after pressing charges against a cop, pretty unprecedented in itself, he's still dealing drugs. It is obvious that Cross's buddies in the

Drug Control Unit targeted him. And while I don't know this for a fact, my hunch is that they turned one of his gang into an informant."

"So what happened, or how did it happen? Do you know?"

"I know what Gold told me, which is that there was a delivery set up for an abandoned building in Dorchester. I don't know how much cocaine was delivered. There were four guys in one car, and he came with two guys. The guys who brought the coke left after dropping it off and getting paid, and Gold and his guys pulled out of the building they were in, and a car with two guys—drug cops—blocked the driveway. A shootout ensued, and a bullet hit one of the tires of Gold's car, so he couldn't go anywhere. There were shots exchanged in both directions, and, eventually, the cops got them and arrested them. Gold was among those arrested."

"And the charges?"

"Possession of illegal drugs, and assault against a police officer."

"Pretty standard stuff."

"Something you might be interested in?"

"Sure. Why the heck not? Can your guy pay?"

"No problem there. He's got money, even if it's mostly illegally acquired."

"Don't ask, don't tell. We'll need to arrange a session in jail so I can talk to him and start to prepare a defense, once he agrees that he wants me as his lawyer."

"If I tell him you're the man, he'll be good with that. I should let you know that, early on, one of Whitey's guys, a numbers guy, came to Gold and asked him not to press charges against Dalton Cross. Obviously, Rob didn't agree, so he's not exactly on Whitey's good side."

"Definitely not a good place to be. Thanks for the heads-up on that," Shactman said.

Chris arranged for the two of them to visit Gold in jail together. Gold was surprisingly upbeat when they met, though Chris thought he looked like shit with bags under his eyes and a couple of days' worth of beard growing, which was very unlike the meticulous Gold he knew.

After Gold entered the small, dank, dark room with a table in the center, the guard unlocked him.

The introductions were made, then Chris let Shactman do the talking.

"The first thing you have to know is this is definitely a long shot. The fact that you were there when the bust was made and that the cocaine was there makes it a tough case to win."

"I get it. But you'd be surprised at other cases that looked like there was no way that I walked away from."

The Commonwealth doesn't want to discourage people from coming forward to call out wrongdoing by the police, as you did in the Cross case."

"Okay. Makes sense. And if it's dismissed, I walk out of here free and clear?" Gold asked

"Yup. But again, that's a long shot. If we can't get the charges dismissed, we'll have to defend the charges as they are," Shactman said.

"What am I looking at if I get convicted?"

"Well, there's a mandatory minimum in this state for as little as 200 grams of cocaine—that's a ten-year sentence. Yeah. It's crazy how little it takes for such a lengthy sentence. But it is what it is, and that's what we are looking at," Shactman said.

"Okay. Guess I don't have much choice. Let's go ahead,"

Gold said.

They agreed, and Chris said he would handle the money and then get reimbursed by Gold.

The trial got scheduled for three months out, which meant Gold was stuck at Charles Street. He made friends with other inmates, as well as some of the guards. It's what Rob did; he was a charmer, for sure.

CHAPTER SIXTY-SIX

It was shortly after the arrest of Gold that Carly kept finding things around her damaged. Like her car. She parked her car sometimes on the street in front of her building, but most often, she parked in the alleyway behind her building, where she had a rented space. One morning she walked out to her car and saw a flat tire. When she had it towed to her mechanic, he said the tire had been slashed.

"This wasn't an accident," the mechanic told Carly.

That triggered the fear that Carly had felt months ago to come back. She remembered the car with the tinted windows. She hesitated to call Tommy to ask for help, but she kept a close watch-out for any suspicious folks she saw. Carly had a great view of the alley from her living room window, and she would often find herself staring out there in anticipation of something happening.

It was summer, and the aboveground pool in the alley was a hub of activity and fun: beer on tap, stewardesses and cops enjoying it. Carly took full advantage of the pool when she could. She always felt like a bit of an outsider, since she was neither a stewardess nor a cop, but she also knew she looked pretty damned good in a bathing suit, so she took the opportunity to show off. Carly turned some heads; she knew it, and she liked it because it gave her ego a boost.

Carly even invited Frank over a number of times to take in the scene with her. She, of course, couldn't help noticing that Frank was the sole Black person at the pool, but he didn't seem bothered by it, so she wasn't, either.

And then one day, just as she was letting herself relax, Carly noticed a dent in the driver's side of the car, and she knew it hadn't happened when she was in the car.

Carly told Jim about both incidents, and he strongly suggested that she let Tommy know. She did, and he said he would make sure there was surveillance set up, which reassured her a bit.

Carly remained vigilant. Whenever she ran along the Esplanade, she couldn't help but notice what cars were parked where—both coming and going.

At work, Carly dug into the results of her information request to the Boston Police Department, and perhaps unsurprisingly, there were a number of detectives who had multiple complaints lodged against them. Carly decided to talk to several of the people who had filed the complaints, knowing full well it was a long shot that any of them would want to talk to her, but she wanted to do a broader story about the deep corruption within the Police Department and, specifically, the Drug Control Unit.

Rather than calling folks, Carly decided to pay them a visit. When you show up at someone's door, it's hard to pretend you are not there. She ended up talking to a half dozen people who said they were robbed by the cops. Carly knew if she could make it a broader story, it would give her the kind of stature she needed for the network to notice. It also gave her a way to put what was happening in Boston in a more national context. She worked with the FBI and the U.S. Attorney's office to compare Boston's police corruption with that of other cities. While Carly was pretty certain Boston was not an outlier, she did find that there were far more complaints against cops in Boston than in most other major cities, other than New York.

Carly did a series of stories about the corruption, and they were picked up by the network. Her reputation and profile were growing, and she was loving every minute of it.

She also started to rack up awards for her work, including the prestigious regional Emmy. She even started to be recognized walking down the street. People would occasionally stop her and stretch out their hands to congratulate her.

The powers that be in the city weren't happy, but that didn't really matter to Carly. She had her eye on the prize—a network job.

Within a few weeks, Carly was invited to come down to New York to interview with the network. She was elated and nervous at the same time. She didn't tell Jim in advance. She figured there was no reason until something concrete was offered. But she wanted to let Frank know and have an honest discussion about what would happen if she got a job in New York and whether their relationship could survive long-distance.

Carly really didn't want the relationship to end. She had felt so supported by Frank and didn't want to lose that. She decided to invite him over for dinner. She set the table with candles and flowers and the whole nine yards. Carly had the wine chilling and actually had cooked a meal of roasted chicken with a chocolate mousse dessert (that she had bought, if truth be told).

When Frank entered the apartment, they hugged for a long time, and Carly felt protected and cared for. Could she really give this up?

Carly took Frank's hand and walked over to her couch, where they sat looking in each other's eyes and holding hands.

"You are a very special lady and I am lucky to have found you," Frank said.

"And you are one of a kind," Carly said as she kissed Frank's hand.

Frank pulled Carly close and gave her a long, deep kiss that stirred her to the core.

"We make a good pair," Frank said.

"But I need to talk to you about something," Carly said.

"Sure, anything."

"I am going down to New York next week to interview with ABC News and, hopefully, to get offered a job as an investigative reporter."

"Wow! That's great and not at all surprising," Frank said.

"But if I do, will we be able to keep up our relationship? I don't want it to end, but long-distance is not the best way," Carly said.

"If we both want it to, we can make it work," Frank said.

How did he always manage to be so positive, Carly wondered to herself.

CHAPTER SIXTY-SEVEN

Gold's trial was scheduled for September. Chris called Carly to let her know. She decided to go down to the courthouse to cover it, and Jim gave her the go-ahead. She asked the newsroom if she could have Larry, and they sent him with her. When she walked into the courtroom, it was mostly empty. Carly saw Chris sitting on the defense side of the room, right behind Shactman and Gold. Gold was actually in civilian clothes. He turned around and saw Carly walk in and waved. Gold's wife was sitting next to Chris. There were a couple of the drug cops sitting behind the prosecution table.

The trial was a two-day affair, with the prosecution calling O'Malley and Reilly, who Carly thought did a good job of painting Gold as the drug dealer with testimony that they knew where and when the drug deal would happen and that Gold would be there.

Carly thought Shactman tried his best to paint the cops as dealing in revenge, attacking their lack of communication with the powers that be in the police department. But he had a hard time poking any holes in the fact that Gold was clearly at the scene.

After the concluding statements from both sides, the judge gave the jury instructions and sent them off to deliberate.

Carly caught up with Chris in the hallway.

"How long do you think they will deliberate?"

"Hard to say. But it could be a quick one."

"Just trying to decide whether to hang around or to head back," Carly said.

"I'll let you know as soon as they've reached a verdict. The judge will give everyone a little time to reconvene, so you should be okay," Chris said. "Not looking good for our guy," he added.

And after the judge gave his instructions, the jury deliberated for less than four hours.

Chris phoned Carly.

"Hey, they've arrived at a verdict in Gold's case."

Carly decided to go but didn't ask for a camera. She figured she would do a "live shot" or record a "stand-up" after the trial was over. She kind of doubted the producers would want more than a reader, anyway, so she headed downtown. Carly walked into the courtroom and saw Chris. He turned to her and said: "I can't imagine anything but a guilty verdict, which means he goes away for about ten years minimum."

Carly sat next to Chris and watched as Gold was brought in, dressed in black pants and a light blue shirt. Gold turned around and smiled at Chris and Carly; Chris smiled back, but Carly just nodded.

The judge called the court to order and looked at the jury foreman and asked: "Have you reached a verdict?"

"Yes, Your Honor."

"What is your verdict?"

"We, the jury, find the defendant guilty on all counts."

Boom! It was over.

Gold looked to Chris. He also saw his wife sitting in the chamber and tried to smile at her. Eileen was crying as she held her sister's hand.

CHAPTER SIXTY-EIGHT

Carly was at her desk, researching another story, when the phone rang."This is Carly Howell," she said.

"Carly, this is Bob Golden." Bob was the producer of the evening news at ABC in New York with whom she had interviewed a month before.

"Hi, Bob, good to hear from you."

"Carly, we want you to come and work for us. You are an impressive reporter, and all the work you've done on the investigative team at 'BRN is the kind of talent we are looking for. So, we would like you to join our investigative team. At first, it may be mostly behind the scenes, doing the research and interviewing folks on camera. Eventually, the idea would be that you'd go on camera. What do you think?"

Carly tried to maintain her cool. "That sounds wonderful. Thank you for your confidence in my abilities."

They went on to discuss salary, and Bob said he would refer her to the personnel department to hammer out the details of a contract.

"So, when can you start?"

"Well, I have to give 'BRN and my boss adequate notice. A month would make sense."

"That works for us. We can't wait to have you on the team. Congratulations!"

"Thanks. I'm excited to be joining you, and I look forward to being in New York."

As soon as she hung up, Carly went to Jim's office,

"You're not going to believe what just happened. ABC in New York just offered me a job, and I agreed. I'll be joining the investigative team."

"Whoa," Jim raised his fist to the air and yelled: "Congratulations!"

Carly was moved by Jim's reaction.

"I can't say I am all that surprised. You're a great catch for any network, and all the work you did here will serve you well. Obviously, I will miss you. When do they want you to start?"

"I told them a month. I want to give you time, and I need to find a place to live and then move down there. Does that seem fair?"

"Sure. It may take a little while for me to find someone to fill your shoes, but that shouldn't stop you. I held down the fort by myself before you came on board, so I am pretty sure I can keep the unit going until I find someone."

"Thanks, Jim. You've been a great mentor. You taught me so much about all that is involved in being an investigative reporter and gave me enough independence to pursue the Cross story."

"You've got a great future ahead. Look forward to seeing you on the evening news."

Carly couldn't contain her excitement. Her first call was to her folks. They were over the moon for her.

"You are our star," Carly's father said. "I knew that you were going to go places, and this is just so exciting. The Big Apple, huh? A far cry from little 'ole Indiana, that's for sure."

"But I will always have Midwest values, no matter where I live. And your faith and trust and love in me has really let me reach for the stars," Carly said.

Once she finished with the call, Carly picked up her briefcase and headed downstairs. She didn't want to tell folks in the newsroom quite yet, so she quietly left the building, got in her car, and yelled out loud: "Yes! Yes! Yes!"

When she got to her apartment building and opened the door to her apartment, Carly stopped, took it all in, looked around, and started figuring out what furniture would stay and what would get moved. She went to her refrigerator and took out the vodka, then poured herself a drink.

"Here's to you, Carly! You go, girl!"

It felt so good! Carly relished the moment.

And then, Carly thought about having to call Frank and worried about what to say and what his reaction would be. Could they continue a long-distance relationship, or was that just wishful thinking? Did they have to decide right away? Maybe it was better to tell Frank in person.

Frank was still at work when Carly called.

"Good afternoon. This is Frank. How can I help you?"

"Well, there are so many ways," Carly said, laughing.

"Hi there, babe. What's up?"

"Are you doing anything after work? Can we meet up somewhere for a drink?"

"Of course. Anywhere in particular?"

Carly could tell she had piqued Frank's curiosity.

"Let's meet in an hour at Charlie's. Okay?"

"I will be there," Frank said.

Carly put on black pants and a beautiful, pink, crepe blouse that highlighted her figure. She donned pearls and matching earrings, sprayed on her favorite cologne, gave herself a look in the mirror and a thumbs-up, and was out the door. Carly got to the bar first and spotted an empty booth, which she claimed. She watched the door carefully until she saw Frank enter. She got up and walked over to greet him.

"Hi, babe! You are looking lovely," Frank said as he landed a big kiss on Carly's cheek and pulled her closer so he could give her a hug. He followed her to the table.

"So, what's the big news?"

"Well, I just accepted a job at ABC in New York. I am excited, obviously, about the prospect of working for the network." Before Frank could ask a question, Carly continued:

"I know. I don't want you for one moment to think that I have been cavalier about our relationship. It's been wonderful. You are an amazing guy and maybe this doesn't have to end. Clearly being in two different cities won't make it easy. But New York is not that far away."

"As I told you, I'm not ready to give it up yet, and I will do what I can to keep it going. Obviously it will change our relationship. Maybe we can keep it going. I like New York as much as the next guy, so I am happy to come down occasionally."

Carly was grateful for Frank and for his willingness to give a long-distance relationship a try.

"Do you want to come over to my place for a nightcap—if you get my meaning?" Carly asked with a big smile.

"How could I not?" Frank smiled back. They held hands as

they walked back to her apartment, and as soon as they walked in, Frank grabbed Carly's waist and kissed her with an intensity she hadn't felt from him before. Maybe, she thought, deep down, he knew this might be the end. Carly took Frank's hand and led him to her bedroom.

"You are a very special and wonderful lady," Frank told Carly as he took off her sweater and bra and grasped her breasts. She, in turn, unzipped his pants and took hold of his dick and brought it to her mouth.

"And I enjoy this," Carly said as she continued to work her magic. It was a night of tenderness and emotion. She knew she would miss these nights. Frank stayed over, and the next morning, he got up and out of bed before Carly was even awake.

Before leaving, Frank sat on the edge of the bed and stroked Carly's back. She woke up and smiled.

"I will miss you," Frank said.

"I will miss you, too," Carly said. "But I'm not leaving for a little while, so let's not say goodbye quite yet."

Carly kissed Frank again before he turned and walked out the door.

Made in United States
North Haven, CT
04 September 2024

56934411R00202